Y0-BVO-051

NINETEENTH-CENTURY AMERICAN ROMANCE

GENRE AND THE CONSTRUCTION OF DEMOCRATIC CULTURE

STUDIES IN LITERARY THEMES AND GENRES

Ronald Gottesman, Editor

University of Southern California

NINETEENTH- CENTURY AMERICAN ROMANCE

GENRE AND THE CONSTRUCTION OF DEMOCRATIC CULTURE

Emily Miller Budick

Twayne Publishers
An Imprint of Simon & Schuster Macmillan
NEW YORK

Prentice Hall International
LONDON • MEXICO CITY • NEW DELHI • SINGAPORE • SYDNEY • TORONTO

Studies in Literary Themes and Genres No. 8

Nineteenth-Century American Romance: Genre and the Construction of Democratic Culture
Emily Miller Budick

Copyright © 1996 by Twayne Publishers

Twayne Publishers
An Imprint of Simon & Schuster Macmillan
1633 Broadway
New York, NY 10019

Library of Congress Cataloging-in-Publication Data

Budick, E. Miller.
    Nineteenth-century American romance : genre and the construction of democratic culture / Emily Miller Budick.
        p.   cm. — (Twayne's studies in literary themes and genres ; 8)
    Includes bibliographical references and index.
    ISBN 0-8057-0960-6 (cloth)
    1. American fiction—19th century—History and criticism.
2. Romanticism—United States. 3. National characteristics, American, in literature. 4. Democracy in literature. 5. Fiction—Technique. 6. Myth in literature. 7. Literary form. I. Title.
II. Series: Twayne's studies in literary themes and genres ; no. 8.
PS374.R6B83   1996
813'.308509—dc20   96-24265
                                                                    CIP

The paper used in this publication meets the minimum requirements of American National Standard for Information Sciences—Permanence of Paper for Printed Library Materials. ANSI Z39.48-1984. ∞ ™

10 9 8 7 6 5 4 3 2 1 (hc)

Printed in the United States of America.

General Editor's Statement

Genre studies have been a central concern of Anglo-American and European literary theory for at least the past quarter century, and the academic interest has been reflected, for example, in new college courses in slave narratives, autobiography, biography, nature writing, and the literature of travel as well as in the rapid expansion of genre theory itself. Genre has also become an indispensable term for trade publishers and the vast readership they serve. Indeed, few general bookstores do not have sections devoted to science fiction, romance, and mystery fiction. Still, genre is among the slipperiest of literary terms, as any examination of genre theories and their histories will suggest.

In conceiving this series we have tried, on the one hand, to avoid the comically pedantic spirit that informs Polonius's recitation of kinds of drama and, on the other hand, the equally unhelpful insistence that every literary production is a unique expression that must not be forced into any system of classification. We have instead developed our list of genres, which range from ancient comedy to the Western, with the conviction that by common consent kinds of literature do exist—not as fixed categories but as fluid ones that change over time as the result of complex interplay of authors, audiences, and literary and cultural institutions. As individual titles in the series demonstrate, the idea of genre offers us provocative ways to study both the continuities and adaptability of literature as a familiar and inexhaustible source of human imagination.

Recognition of the fluid boundaries both within and among genres will provide, we believe, a useful array of perspectives from which to study literature's complex development. Genres, as traditional but open ways of understanding the world, contribute to our capacity to respond to narrative and expressive forms and offer means to discern moral significances embodied in these forms. Genres, in short, serve ethical as well as aesthetic purposes, and the volumes in this series attempt to demonstrate how this double benefit has been achieved as these genres have been transformed over the years. Each title in the series should be measured against this large ambition.

Ron Gottesman

Contents

Chapter 6

Preface

In some ways the following study of 19th-century American romance is an old-fashioned book. It puts at the center of its investigation a set of texts that seemed to critics in the middle decades of this century the originating, perhaps quintessential, expression of America's self-conception, its exposition of its most fundamental beliefs and values. Like earlier critics, I read the longer and shorter fictions of James Fenimore Cooper, Edgar Allan Poe, Nathaniel Hawthorne, Herman Melville, and Henry James as mutually allusive works of art, which also constitute a part of a literary tradition both preceding and following them.

But if readings in the 1950s and 1960s proceeded by the then dominant assumptions of formalist criticism, which as much shaped as were determined by the literary tradition they undertook to analyze, my own theory of romance fiction is informed by its contemporary moment of composition. In fact, I attempt in this study to discover connections between earlier definitions of American romance and later challenges to those definitions and to the literary canon that they produced. For this reason, my investigation of the genre of romance is also an excursion into literary history. I set against each other new readings and older ones, and I try to recover the historical and ideological backgrounds not only of the literary texts themselves but of the critical interventions that produced the dominant interpretations of the genre. In this way I try to produce a definition of the genre of 19th-century romance that preserves the moment of the texts' composition and also reflects a tradition of response to those texts, in particular in the 20th century.

I begin my study with a general overview of the origins of American romance fiction in the 19th century, with particular emphasis on two sets of differences: the first, between American romance and the British novel, out of which the American romance evolves and which develops simultaneously with it; and the second, between American romance fiction and other 19th-century American literary traditions. Then I turn, in separate chapters, to the writings of the major romancers: Cooper, who is more a precursor of the tradition than a major practitioner; Poe, Hawthorne, and Melville, who define the genre proper; and finally James, who signals the demise of a certain embodiment of the tradition as he moves from romance to realism. In each of these chapters I provide close readings of paradigmatic texts, in which I self-consciously employ and challenge formalist, deconstructionist, new historicist, and feminist modes of interpretation. My hope is not only to provide fresh readings of texts and thereby produce a new definition of the genre, but also to demonstrate how textual interpretation is always a consequence of the theoretical perspective brought to bear upon the text, such theoretical perspective itself not standing outside the literary tradition but produced by it. My further claim about the romance tradition of American fiction is that, as itself a self-reflective, self-reflexive body of texts, it produces a heightening of this characteristic mutual interrogation and entanglement of text and theory. The romance theory I evolve, therefore tends to be less a theory about a particular tradition of American writing than an attempt to formulate the tradition's self-professed theory of itself.

I have dealt at length with the American romance tradition twice before, in *Fiction and Historical Consciousness: The American Romance Tradition* (1989) and *Engendering Romance: Women Writers and the Hawthorne Tradition, 1850–1990* (1994). In composing this book, I have occasionally adapted elements from those earlier studies. For the most part, however, I have tried to distill from these more thesis-bound investigations the basic principles that seemed to me to inform the genre and that, in any event, have guided my reading of it. I remain with my basic conviction as expressed in the earlier books that romance fiction is essentially a philosophical skepticist tradition. It dramatizes and explores the question, How do I know the world and other people in it? And it responds by demonstrating both the unanswerability of the question and the absolute necessity nonetheless for human beings to act in and take responsibility for a world they collectively manufacture. This is the major argument of an essay of mine entitled "Sacvan Bercovitch, Staney Cavell, and the Theory of American Romance" (*PMLA* 107 [1992], 78–91), much of which I have incorporated into my chapter on Hawthorne.

The research for this book was enabled by grants from the Faculty of the Humanities of the Hebrew University and the Kennedy Institute of the Free University of Berlin, which was kind enough to host me for a month's visit during the summer of 1991. Series editor Ronald Gottesman provided extremely helpful critiques of various versions of the manuscript, while my research assistant Janine Woolfson labored tirelessly, collecting materials, revising texts, and proofing final copy. As always, my family contributed materially and spiritually: I love you all.

Chronology

1837 *Twice-Told Tales*, Nathaniel Hawthorne.

1840 *The Pathfinder*, James Fenimore Cooper.

Tales of the Grotesque and Arabesque (2 vols.), Edgar Allan Poe.

1841 *The Deerslayer*, James Fenimore Cooper.

1843 Birth of Henry James (d. 1916).

1846 *Mosses from an Old Manse*, Nathaniel Hawthorne.

Typee, Herman Melville.

1847 *Omoo*, Herman Melville.

1848 *Eureka*, Edgar Allan Poe.

1849 *Mardi* and *Redburn*, Herman Melville.

1850 *The Scarlet Letter*, Nathaniel Hawthorne.

White-Jacket, Herman Melville.

1851 *The House of the Seven Gables*, Nathaniel Hawthorne.

Moby-Dick, Herman Melville.

The Snow-Image, Nathaniel Hawthorne.

1852 *The Blithedale Romance*, Nathaniel Hawthorne.

A Wonder Book, Nathaniel Hawthorne.

Pierre, or the Ambiguities, Herman Melville.

1853 *Tanglewood Tales*, Nathaniel Hawthorne.

1856 *Piazza Tales*, Herman Melville.

1866 *Battle-Pieces and Aspects of War*, Herman Melville.

1877 *The American*, Henry James.

1879 *Daisy Miller*, Henry James.

1881 *The Portrait of a Lady*, Henry James.

1886 *The Princess Casamassima*, Henry James.

1897 *What Maisie Knew*, Henry James.

1898 *The Turn of the Screw*, Henry James.

1924 *Billy Budd*, Herman Melville (posthumous publication).

Chapter 1

TOWARD A DEFINITION
OF AMERICAN ROMANCE

The subject of this book—19th-century American romance—seems, on the surface, straightforward enough; and one could easily, at this point, provide both a set of exemplary authors and titles as well as a basic definition. As the name of the genre already indicates, 19th-century American romance has as much to do with literary history as with form. Essentially, it designates a set of texts written in the United States in the mid-19th century. These texts, by most accounts, include the four romances of Nathaniel Hawthorne: *The Scarlet Letter* (1850), *The House of the Seven Gables* (1851), *The Blithedale Romance* (1852), and *The Marble Faun* (1860); Herman Melville's *Moby-Dick* (1851) and *Pierre* (1856) and some of his shorter fictions, including "Bartleby, the Scrivener," "Benito Cereno" (1856), and *Billy Budd* (published posthumously 1924), as well as many of the short stories of Hawthorne and of Edgar Allan Poe (among the latter "The Fall of the House of Usher," "Ligeia," and "The Purloined Letter"—all published in the 1940s). This group of writers who, until very recently, defined the genre—along with James Fenimore Cooper, Charles Brockden Brown, Washington

Irving, Ralph Waldo Emerson, Henry David Thoreau, and Henry James (especially the early and gothic James)—also dominated the American canon. This fact need not yet concern us, though it is the feature of the genre that has generated the most ground for controversy and revision.

Producing a definition of the genre is somewhat more difficult and will constitute the objective of this book. But it is nonetheless possible, even at this moment of setting out, to provide some of the basic lines of the genre's formal features. Most American romances manifest some affinity with the different British and European literary traditions from which they derive, namely, the classical epic (*The Iliad* and *The Odyssey* of Homer and the *Aeneid* of Virgil) as well as the epic romance, the quest romance, the medieval romance, and the Arthurian romance; and such texts as *Sir Gawain and the Green Knight* (1375–1400; author unknown), Sir Thomas Malory's *Morte D'arthur* (1485), Sir Philip Sidney's *Arcadia* (1590, 1593), and Edmund Spenser's *Fairie Queen* (1590). What all of these narratives share, which allows us to associate them, at least loosely, as a genre, is the dominance of a single hero-protagonist, who is involved in a plot that consists of various dramatic adventures and through which the hero proceeds toward a clearly designated, unambiguous goal or mission. Later evolutions of the form include Miguel de Cervantes' *Don Quixote* (1605) and such gothic fictions as Horace Walpole's *Castle of Otranto* (1764) and Ann Radcliffe's *Mysteries of Udolpho* (1794), as well as the historical romances of Sir Walter Scott. Since Scott is the most important predecessor for James Fenimore Cooper, he is also, insofar as the American tradition is concerned, the major progenitor of American romance as well.

Thus romance, as a genre, has its own internal history of development, moving from Europe and England to America. Nonetheless, the category *romance* also serves to distinguish one form of narrative fiction from another—*romance* fiction from what comes to be termed, in the 18th century, the *novel*. Thus the term *romance* constitutes, through its negation and displacement, an important element within the evolution of the novel as a literary genre. As George Dekker puts it in his study *The American Historical Romance,*

> Although the word "novel" did not come consistently to mean what we now mean by it until well into the nineteenth century, the

generic distinction between novel and romance has remained current and relatively stable in its starkly dichotomous terms for a little over two centuries, i.e., since the beginnings of a continuous tradition of novelistic fiction. . . . [T]he novel/romance opposition is a legacy of Renaissance Humanism's hostility to artistic expressions of what it denounced as medieval monkish ignorance and superstition, especially the chivalric romances beloved of Don Quixote and a host of the Don's spiritual and literary descendants. Whether or not *Don Quixote* was the first "novel," it manifestly was a paradigmatic masterwork of world literature which popularized while in many ways it transcended the humanistic critique of romance as shapeless in form, fantastic in matter, and corruptive in influence. . . . Of course romance had its eloquent friends—the greatest of them (Sidney, Spenser, Milton) at the heart of the Protestant humanist camp—but so powerful and diverse were its enemies that we cannot wonder that writers as different and in some respects incompatible as Fielding and Richardson both joined the cry against romance and felt obliged to distinguish their own fictions from it as sharply as possible.[1]

The term *romance,* in other words, although it begins as the simple designation of a genre, quickly becomes what another genre, namely the *novel,* defines itself against. And it is in the context of this opposition between *novel* and *romance* that the term enters the American literary vocabulary, where, in a kind of reversal of literary history, romance emerges as what opposes and attempts to displace novelistic fiction.

The attempt to celebrate romance fiction over the novel, and to claim it as a specifically American form, is the overriding feature of the definition of *romance* that comes to characterize American literary studies as the term is introduced into current usage, most famously and influentially, by Richard Chase in a 1957 book entitled *The American Novel and Its Tradition.* Building on earlier work in canon formation and literary theory by F. O. Matthiessen, Charles Feidelson Jr., R. W. B. Lewis, and Lionel Trilling and responding directly (and defensively) to F. R. Leavis's *Great Tradition* of British fiction, Chase insisted that 19th-century American fiction constituted a genre distinct from the novel. This genre, which (following Hawthorne and James) he calls romance, is distinguished for Chase by its antimimetic, allegorical, and symbolic structure, its explicit evasion of direct, realistic representation of the sociopolitical and economic world:

Doubtless the main difference between the novel and the romance is in the way in which they view reality. The novel renders reality closely and in comprehensive detail. It takes a group of people and sets them going about the business of life. We come to see these people in their real complexity of temperament and motive. They are in explicable relation to nature, to each other, to their social class, to their own past. Character is more important than action and plot, and probably the tragic or comic actions of the narrative will have the primary purpose of enhancing our knowledge of and feeling for an important character, a group of characters, or a way of life. . . .

By contrast the romance, following distantly the medieval example, feels free to render reality in less volume and detail. It tends to prefer action to character, and action will be freer in a romance than in a novel, encountering, as it were, less resistance from reality. . . . The romance can flourish without much intricacy of relation. The characters, probably rather two-dimensional types, will not be complexly related to each other or to society or to the past. Human beings will on the whole be shown in ideal relation—that is, they will share emotions only after these have become abstract or symbolic. . . . Character itself becomes . . . somewhat abstract and ideal, so much so in some romances that it seems to be merely a function of plot. The plot we may expect to be highly colored. Astonishing events may occur, and these are likely to have a symbolic or ideological, rather than a realistic, plausibility. Being less committed to the immediate rendition of reality than the novel, the romance will more freely veer toward mythic, allegorical, and symbolistic forms.[2]

Chase's definition follows fairly closely Hawthorne's, in the preface to his *House of the Seven Gables*:

When a writer calls his work a Romance, it need hardly be observed that he wishes to claim a certain latitude, both as to its fashion and material, which he would not have felt himself entitled to assume, had he professed to be writing a Novel. The latter form of composition is presumed to aim at a very minute fidelity not merely to the possible, but to the probable, and ordinary course of man's experience. The former—while, as a work of art, it must rigidly subject itself to laws, and while it sins unpardonably, so far as it may swerve aside from the truth of the human heart—has fairly a right to present that truth under circumstances, to a great extent, of the writer's own choosing or creation. If he think fit, also, he may so manage his atmospherical medium as to bring out or mellow the lights and deepen and enrich the shadows of the picture. He will be wise, no doubt, to make a very moderate use of the privileges here stated, and, especially, to mingle the Marvellous rather as a slight, delicate, and evanescent flavor, than as any portion of the actual substance of the dish offered to the Public. He can hardly be said, however, to commit a literary crime, even if he disregard this caution.[3]

The Chase definition recalls as well that of Henry James, who, at the end of the century, subtly shifts the direction of American romance fiction and introduces (or reintroduces) realism into the American literary canon. According to James, in the preface to *The American* (1877), romance is determined by "the kind of experience with which it deals":

experience liberated, so to speak; experience disengaged, disembroiled, disencumbered, exempt from the conditions that we usually know to attach to it and, if we wish so to put the matter, drag upon it, and operating in a medium which relieves it, in a particular interest, of the inconvenience of a *related,* a measurable state, a state subject to all our vulgar communities. The greatest intensity may so be arrived at evidently—when the sacrifice of community, of the "related" sides of situations, has not been too rash. It must to this end not flagrantly betray itself; we must even be kept if possible, for our illusion, from suspecting any sacrifice at all. The balloon of experience is in fact of course tied to the earth, and under that necessity we swing, thanks to a rope of remarkable length, in the more or less commodious car of the imagination; but it is by the rope we know where we are, and from the moment that cable is cut we are at large and unrelated: we only swing apart from the globe—though remaining as exhilarated, naturally, as we like, especially when all goes well. The art of the romancer, is 'for the fun of it,' insidiously to cut the cable, to cut it without our detecting him.[4]

Could any subject, then, be more straightforward than the genre known as 19th-century American romance?

Yet, no sooner do I venture this set of definitions and list of texts than I must acknowledge the passionate controversy that, in the last 20 years, has come to surround the romance theory of 19th-century American fiction. Although some critics have actually questioned whether such a genre as American romance even exists, most have been more concerned with challenging the definition of the genre, especially as it was developed by the critical line first established by Chase.[5] This challenge does not deal so much with the designation of the primary features of the romance text: its mythical, allegorical, and symbolical elements, as cited by Hawthorne, James, Chase, et al. Rather, it concerns the implications of what one critic (paraphrasing James) has labeled romance's "sacrifice of relation," its cutting the cable between earth and the imagination.[6] The question opened to the theorists of American romance by recent scholarship is, Does the form of romance fiction suggest a distancing of the text from the socioeconomic and political realm in which it is produced, as if romance fiction existed in what one critic has called a "world elsewhere," a world, in Poe's language, "out of time [and] out of space" or "between the Imaginary and the Real," in Hawthorne's phrase?[7] Or do the formal features of the text signify a particular form of "relation" between romance and the world it mediates? If so, what is this form, and how are we to understand the romancers' reasons for writing fiction this way?

I will explore the history of romance criticism in the bibliographical essay at the end of this volume. It is a history as fascinating as the literary form it purports to describe and is largely inextricable from it. In fact, it could be argued that the history of the romance theory of American fiction ought to precede the reading of the literary texts. In many ways, critical practice determines our interpretation of literary texts. As contemporary theorists such as Frederic Jameson have made us keenly aware, genre definitions cannot be divorced from sociopolitical and economic concerns. Like other institutions of human society, including literature itself, literary criticism performs cultural work. It affirms and reconstitutes social values, oftimes inexplicitly, even surreptitiously, as much through its implicit assumptions as through any overt or covert themes or subjects.[8] No definition of genre, then, can proceed without registering what it means to talk about genre in the first place. This is doubly the case with the 19th-century American romance, especially since, as recent critics have pointed out, it produced a very skewed literary canon, consisting almost exclusively of white male authors.

Furthermore, as its name already insists, this genre, unlike others (the lyric poem, for example, or the epic or the gothic novel), cannot be defined apart from considerations of national literary history. When we speak of the 19th-century American romance we are speaking of the writings of a particular group of authors, all of whom wrote in a particular place at a particular time. If we wish to discuss the genre that Poe, Hawthorne, and Melville produced, we must also consider why they might have chosen this literary form and not another. And if we wish to argue further (as have many critics) that their writings represent the best of American literature in the 19th century, we are going to have to try to understand what this claim means and what it implies about power relations within the world of literary studies, on the parts of both authors and critics. What historical, social, cultural, and economic factors may have contributed to, perhaps even determined, the form of American writing in the 19th century? Similarly, what factors pertained to the canonization and interpretation of the romance tradition in our own century?[9]

As I have said, I will leave the second part of this question for the bibliographical essay. I mention the challenges to the tradition at this point, however, in order to suggest that for the critic of the 1990s it has become imperative to ask anew the question, Is there something distinctive about the fiction of Poe, Hawthorne, and Melville, and, if so, exactly how might we define this difference from other forms of 19th-century fiction, American and non-American? However we want to define the American romance, there is something striking in the way that Poe, Hawthorne, and Melville gravitate toward certain shared themes and, even more pertinent to the question of genre, toward a common mode of representing those themes. Following are some of the most famous lines in American literature:

> I cannot, for my soul, remember how, when, or even precisely where, I first became acquainted with the lady Ligeia.—Edgar Allan Poe, "Ligeia" (1838)

> During the whole of a dull, dark, and soundless day in the autumn of the year, when the clouds hung oppressively low in the heavens, I had been passing alone, on horseback, through a singularly dreary tract of country; and at length found myself, as the shades of evening drew on, within view of the melancholy House of Usher.—Edgar Allan Poe, "The Fall of the House of Usher" (1839)

> A throng of bearded men, in sad-colored garments and gray, steeple-crowned hats, intermixed with women, some wearing hoods, and others bareheaded, was assembled in front of a wooden edifice, the door of which was heavily timbered with oak, and studded with iron spikes.—Nathaniel Hawthorne, *The Scarlet Letter* (1850)

Call me Ishmael.—Herman Melville, *Moby-Dick* (1851)[10]

Although these lines bear relations to other literary traditions (from German romanticism to British gothicism) and in various ways distinguish themselves from one another, they also bear striking affinities. However we might want to interpret them, or identify their compositional strategies, they do not encourage us to see them in straightforward relation to a clearly defined, pre-existent social world that the text is actively figuring forth. It is almost as if no world exists prior to the words of the text: the text expressly refrains from saying where we are in these lines or when or with whom (what "throng?" what "edifice"?).

The texts, in other words, go about the business not so much of representing a world but of creating one, ex nihilo. "Call me Ishmael," Melville begins, immediately raising the question in our minds of who it is, if not someone named Ishmael, who is speaking these lines. The narrator's identity seems more a matter of mutual agreement between writer and reader (the imperative voice serving as an appeal to the reader) than a verifiable, existential fact. Who the narrator may really be seems to matter less than what he is to become in the course of the text as a consequence of the story he tells.

Nor is the world in which this Ishmael exists any more concrete and certain than the identity of its major character. Hawthorne's "throng of bearded men . . . intermixed with women" is notable more for the atmosphere created by these unidentified and indistinguishable men and women than for any recognizable personalities (fictional or historical) among them. As in Poe's fiction of gothic castles and decaying old mansions, peopled by figures more ghostlike than fleshly, the world Hawthorne creates seems more diagramatic, self-consciously representational, than real. It is populated not by people but by hats, hoods, ghosts, and phantoms, which achieve a life and a specificity of their own, often at the expense of the "real" people who in "real" life inhabit the garments of this world. The people are faceless, but the door is heavily timbered with oak and studded with iron spikes: personality has shifted from the human being to the objects of human manufacture. Furthermore, even in the midst of civilization, Poe's and Hawthorne's and Melville's worlds are outside civilization as we know it—in fantasy castles of the mind, on the margins of the wilderness between country and forest, on the sea—anywhere and consequently nowhere. This is not to say that no sociopolitical, economic world informs these texts or stands behind them. But the texts figure forth and comment on the socioeconomic, political world in a certain way, which is described by the writers themselves and by later critics as romance.

Whatever the location of American romance, it is not the social and geographical place of the dominant tradition of 19th-century British fiction or, for that matter, of the sentimental or melodramatic fiction being written in the United States in the same period. Compare, for example, the openings of four of the works that, in F. R. Leavis's view, define the "Great Tradition" of the English novel:

Emma Woodhouse, handsome, clever, and rich, with a comfortable home and happy disposition, seemed to unite some of the best blessings of existence; and had lived nearly twenty-one years in the world with very little to distress or vex her.—Jane Austen, *Emma* (1816)

1801—I have just returned from a visit to my landlord—the solitary neighbour that I shall be troubled with. This is certainly a beautiful country! In all England, I do not believe that I could have fixed on a situation so completely removed from the stir of society.—Emily Brontë, *Wuthering Heights* (1847)

My father's family name being Pirrip, and my Christian name Philip, my infant tongue could make of both names nothing longer or more explicit than Pip. So, I called myself Pip, and came to be called Pip. —Charles Dickens, *Great Expectations* (1860)

Miss Brooke had that kind of beauty which seems to be thrown into relief by poor dress. Her hand and wrist were so finely formed that she could wear sleeves not less bare of style than those in which the Blessed Virgin appeared to Italian painters; and her profile as well as her stature and bearing seemed to gain the more dignity for her plain garments, which by the side of provincial fashion gave her the impressiveness of a fine quotation from the Bible,—or from one of our elder poets,—in a paragraph of to-day's newspaper.—George Eliot, *Middlemarch* (1871–72)

Or compare the openings of these American texts, which, though far more melodramatic and sentimental than the British texts cited, are nonetheless not romance fictions:

"Mama, what was that I heard papa saying to you this morning about his lawsuit?"

"I cannot tell you just now. Ellen, pick up that shawl, and spread it over me."

"Mama!—are you cold in this warm room?"—Susan Warner, *The Wide, Wide World* (1850)

It was growing dark in the city. Out in the open country it would be light for half an hour or more; but within the close streets where my story leads me it was already dusk. Upon the wooden door-step of a low-roofed, dark, and unwholesome-looking house, sat a little girl, who was gazing up the street with much earnestness.—Maria Susanna Cummins, *The Lamplighter* (1854)

Hurricane Hall is a large old family mansion, built of dark, red sand-stone, in one of the loneliest and wildest of the mountain regions of Virginia.

Major Ira Warfield, the lonely proprietor of the Hall, was a veteran officer, who, in disgust at what he supposed to be ill-requited services, had retired from public life to spend the evening of his vigorous age on this his patrimonial estate. Here he lived in seclusion, with his old-fashioned housekeeper, Mrs. Condiment, and his old family servants and his favorite dogs and horses.—E. D. E. N. Southworth, *The Hidden Hand or, Capitola the Madcap* (1859)

One could point to similarities between the English and American texts or between American romances and sentimental fictions. Like the American romance fictions cited above, Brontë's *Wuthering Heights* and Southworth's *Hidden Hand* take place at a clear remove from society, while Cummins's *Lamplighter* and *Wuthering Heights* take place in darkness and shadows reminiscent of all three romancers. Like Melville's *Moby-Dick*, Dickens's *Great Expectations* begins with a character's naming himself. And both Austen's *Emma* and Eliot's *Middlemarch*, along with all of the American women's novels above, focus, like Hawthorne's *Scarlet Letter*, on a woman's discovering, through her relationship to a man, both her own inner consciousness and her place in the world. These similarities, among many others, exist and are important. The differences, however, are just as striking, and, insofar as literary texts distinguish themselves in their uniqueness from other texts, the differences bear more markedly than the similarities on our interpretations of these texts.

The most insistent of the differences is the way in which the British and sentimental texts, as opposed to the romance fictions, position themselves vis-à-vis the "real" world of social inter-course. This is the difference that Hawthorne himself notes in his preface to *The House of the Seven Gables* and that is remarked upon by Henry James, Richard Chase, and a host of other Americanist critics. The works of British and sentimental fiction quoted above—even in the cases of the least realistic of these fictions (Dickens's *Great Expectations* and Emily Brontë's *Wuthering Heights*)—maintain, to some significant degree, a "very minute fidelity . . . to the probable, and ordinary course of man's experi-ence." This is the case, most obviously, in *Emma* and *Middlemarch,* which not only proceed through various depictions of their heroines' social conversations but which themselves conduct their relation to the reader through the conversational mode of everyday commentary and description. The authors of *Emma* and *Middlemarch* chart the probable courses of their very proba-ble heroines to resolutions that are just as probable as the prob-lems that their heroes confront. It is also true, however, of the more melodramatic fictions of Warner, Cummins, and Southworth, which, for all their implausibilities, record a daily life eminently mundane and unremarkable.

In a similar fashion, for all its tugging against realistic modes of representation, *Great Expectations* does not depart dramatically from the world of social interaction. Pip may name himself, but he does so through the most natural of processes. Nor is his name pure invention or literary allusion. Family name and Christian name conspire to determine what Pip will call himself and how others will come to call him. This is not the same as Ishmael's "call," which is addressed directly to the reader, to be named, through a name that (like the name of the other major protagonist, Ahab) imports into the text a whole other biblical and historical context. Even *Wuthering Heights,* the most gothic of the four works of British fiction cited and therefore the one clos-est to the origins of the American romance in the epic and gothic romance traditions, keeps the experiential "course" of human affairs in view, even as it violates it.

In *Wuthering Heights,* in other words, as in *Emma, Great Expectations,* and *Middlemarch,* as well as in *The Wide, Wide World, The Lamplighter,* and *The Hidden Hand,* the "stir of society" is a given, a factor to be reckoned with, both in time (1801) and place

(Britain). By "stir of society" I take Brontë to mean not simply the existence of other people in one's world but the complex, formalized network of relations through which social structure realizes itself. It is this "stir of society" that is attenuated in the 19th-century American romance. In the fiction of Poe this attenuation is the most extreme. Poe's is a world virtually without people, let alone sociopolitical and economic institutions. "I cannot, for my soul, remember how, when, or even precisely where, I first became acquainted with the lady Ligeia," says the solipsistic and quite likely deranged narrator of "Ligeia"; "During the whole of a dull, dark, and soundless day in the autumn of the year . . . as the shades of evening drew on," begins the equally isolated narrator of "The Fall of the House of Usher." No time, no place, no consciousness other than the narrator's penetrates the barren stillness of Poe's world. For Hawthorne and Melville, the quotidian world exists in somewhat greater materiality. But for these writers as well the world is deeply saturated in the subjectivity of individual perception. It exists more as something to be resisted or as background for the more important explorations—the explorations of self and consciousness—than as the literal world itself.

The textual features that distinguish the fiction of Poe, Hawthorne, and Melville are in evidence, in more muted form, even earlier in American writing. James Fenimore Cooper, Washington Irving, and Charles Brockden Brown already exhibit the tendency of Poe, Hawthorne, and Melville to swerve away from the depiction of social reality toward the evocation of a country of the mind. This is the opening of what may be American fiction's most famous short story, certainly one of its earliest productions:

> Whoever has made a voyage up the Hudson, must remember the Kaatskill Mountains. They are a dismembered branch of the great Appalachain [sic] family, and are seen away to the west of the river, swelling up to a noble height, and lording it over the surrounding country. Every change of season, every change of weather, indeed every hour of the day, produces some change in the magical hues and shapes of these mountains; and they are regarded by all the good wives, far and near, as perfect barometers.—Washington Irving, "Rip Van Winkle," *The Sketch Book* (1819–20)

And this is the beginning of James Fenimore Cooper's equally famous *Deerslayer* (1841):

On the human imagination events produce the effects of time. Thus, he who has traveled far and seen much is apt to fancy that he has lived long and the history that most abounds in important incidents soonest assumes the aspect of antiquity. In no other way can we account for the venerable air that is already gathering around American annals.

What these two works have in common with the fiction of Poe, Hawthorne, and Melville, and therefore what seems to define a dominant impulse in American fiction in the 19th century, is a self-conscious literariness, an explicit concern or an express intention not to ignore reality but to remember that imagination and language are the vehicles through which we comprehend, represent, and, therefore, largely create the world of sociopolitical and economic fact.

The Politics of Literary Form

How might we understand this self-conscious literariness of 19th-century American romance? In other words, what purposes—sociopolitical, economic, cultural, and literary—might the form of 19th-century fiction serve, and, therefore, how might we want to understand this genre in relation to competing literary genres, both in America and abroad?

As I have already suggested, the term *19th-century American romance* is as much a historical definition as it is a genre definition. In order, therefore, to arrive at a reasonable working definition of this genre, and to move forward from that definition to perhaps an even more meaningful one, one has to retrace some elements in American cultural and intellectual history. These elements include, of course, the sociopolitical and economic events of the time—including the slave controversy, westward expansion, and the various economic and political conflicts, many of which provide the subject matter and background of 19th-century fiction. They also include the sheer differences between the newly established republic and the old world from which it had separated.

As Leslie Fiedler puts it,

To write . . . about the American novel is to write about the fate of certain European genres in a world of alien experience. It is not only a world where courtship and marriage have suffered a profound change, but also one in the process of losing the traditional distinctions of class; a world without a significant history or a substantial past; a world which had left behind the terror of Europe not for the innocence it dreamed of, but for new and special guilts associated with the rape of nature and the exploitation of dark-skinned people; a world doomed to play out the imaginary childhood of Europe. The American novel is only *finally* American; its appearance is an event in the history of the European spirit—as, indeed, is the very invention of America itself.[11]

To the sociopolitical specificity of the American experience, however, and to its inevitable differences from European experience, one must also add as a critical factor in the development of American literature a self-consciously evolving national consciousness.

This consciousness is, of course, inextricably linked to the sociopolitical and economic controversies of the day and to the relation to Europe: it both determines and is determined by the configuration of events in the world in which the writers exist. Therefore, it is perfectly legitimate, even necessary, to understand Cooper's books (the Littlepage and Leatherstocking tales, for example) as contemplating American economic development and the relationship between the Native and European inhabitants of the land; or to read a book like Hawthorne's *House of the Seven Gables* as dealing with capitalism and the reform movements of the 19th century. And, indeed, much of the criticism on Cooper, Hawthorne, and Melville, throughout the 20th century, has tried to understand these writers within their socioeconomic context.

Nonetheless, the 19th-century authors also wrote within a more self-conscious world of national self-definition. And this context is just as important as the actual events transpiring in their everyday realities. To wit, it may be that the *form* of the 19th-century texts, the romance strategies cited by Hawthorne, et al., were determined by what the writers understood to be the necessary literary—that is, cultural and intellectual—implications of the socioeconomic and political issues they were addressing.

Like any other nation, the United States of America had to cope with a variety of social and moral problems. But, unlike other countries, the U.S. also had to produce a culture different from the culture from which it had derived. (It also had to distinguish itself from the Native American cultures that had existed for thousands of years before Europeans began to arrive in the Americas.) Unlike the nations of Europe, in other words, the United States did not arrive in the 19th century after a centuries-long evolution toward modernity. Rather, its origins constituted a historically locatable moment of rupture with another cultural and political entity. The colonization of America meant more than putting an ocean between the new country and the Old World. Despite economic, social, and geographical differences (which, as Fiedler suggests, would likely have produced literary consequences of their own), the colonies and later the nation could well have decided to pattern themselves on the nations from which the original settlers had come. But almost from the beginning, America began to define itself not only as different from England (and Spain and France) but as in opposition to Europe, so that addressing social and political issues was at best a very self-conscious enterprise for the 19th-century American.

As Benjamin T. Spencer has pointed out, this "quest for nationality" in America predates the emergence of the nation.[12] In imagining themselves not only a New England but a New Israel, the Puritans, for example, were already entering the process that would continue to define one strong impulse in the nation, both north and south, during the 18th and 19th centuries. For the colonists of Salem and Massachusetts Bay, the New World represented a chance for human history to begin virtually anew. The idea of the American as a new kind of human being—whether a new Israelite, a new Adam, or merely a new man or woman (depending on one's religious disposition)—permeates American writing in the 17th and 18th centuries.

The following is one of the most famous and definitive 18th-century statements of this American self-conception:

> Here are no aristocratical families, no courts, no kings, no bishops, no ecclesiastical dominion, no invisible power giving to a few a very visible one . . . no great refinements of luxury. The rich and the poor are not so far removed from each other as they are in Europe. Some few towns excepted, we are all tillers of the earth. . . . What then is the American, this new man? He is either a European or the descendant of an European, hence that strange mixture of blood, which you will find in no other country. . . . *He* is an American, who, leaving behind him all his ancient prejudices and manners, receives new ones from

the new mode of life he has embraced, the new government he obeys, and the new rank he holds. . . . Here individuals of all nations are melted into a new race of men, whose labors and posterity will one day cause great changes in the world. . . . The American is a new man, who acts upon new principles; he must therefore entertain new ideas, and form new opinions.[13]

One must immediately acknowledge that for the writer of the above lines, Jean de Crèvecœur, who was a British sympathizer during the American Revolution and who returned to his native France after the war, there was no necessary contradiction between being uniquely an American and also a British subject. "May not and ought not the children of these fathers rightly say," William Bradford had written in one of the first of America's great histories, "'Our fathers were Englishmen which came over this great ocean, and were ready to perish in this wilderness; but they cried unto the Lord, and He heard their voice and looked on their adversity.'"[14] Though Bradford, like many other Puritan authors, perceived the Puritan departure from England as an exodus like that of the Israelites from Egypt, over an ocean that was for them like a desert, still he could acknowledge the English origins of the American self—to paraphrase the title of an important study of these issues of national self-identity.[15]

For many Americans, however, independence required a revolution in culture—in particular, literary culture—no less absolute than the revolution that produced independent nationhood. To begin with, it was distressing and baffling to 19th-century American intellectuals that America seemed to produce so little literature of value. Critics located many different reasons for this failure of American literature. Not least of these was America's prosperity as a commercial nation, which seemed to mediate against literary productivity (see, for example, Francis Calley Gray, "An Address Pronounced before the Society of Phi Beta Kappa"—1816).[16] This sentiment was shared as well by another 19th-century figure, who in 1809 declared American egalitarianism and commercialism the villains of the American spirit (Fisher Ames; Spiller, 73–87). It was expressed, most famously perhaps, by Alexis de Tocqueville in *Democracy in America*, when he wrote, "[I]t must be acknowledged that in few of the civilized nations of our time have the higher sciences made less progress than in the United States; and in few have great artists, distinguished poets, or celebrated writers, been more rare." This fact about America, de Tocqueville concluded, was not necessarily the consequence of democracy but of what was peculiarly American in American democracy, which had "singularly concurred to fix the mind of the American upon purely practical objects."[17]

But precisely because of what America had accomplished in other areas of human endeavor, it seemed to her writers and critics imperative that the nation develop a first-rate national culture, including a major literature. That literature, furthermore, would express uniquely American values and concepts. As one critic succinctly remarked, "[T]he proudest freedom to which a nation can aspire, not excepting even political independence, is found in complete emancipation from literary thraldom" (Solyman Brown, *An Essay on American Poetry,* 1818; Spiller, 187); America, declared Noah Webster, "must be as independent in *literature* as she is in *politics*" (Spencer, 27).

William Ellery Channing, in "Remarks on National Literature" (1830), details why this is so:

> Literature . . . is plainly among the most powerful methods of exalting the character of a nation, of forming a better race of men. . . . Do we possess . . . what may be called a national literature? . . . We regret that the reply to these questions is so obvious. . . . On this point, if marks and proofs of our real condition were needed, we should find them in the current apologies for our deficiencies. Our writers are accustomed to plead in our excuse our youth, the necessities of a newly settled country, and the direction of our best talents to practical life. Be the pleas sufficient or not, one thing they prove, and that is, our consciousness of having failed to make important contributions to the interests of the intellect. . . . The question is, Shall Europe . . . fashion us after its pleasure? Shall America be only an echo of what is thought and written under the aristocracies beyond the ocean? . . . [A] foreign literature will always . . . be foreign. It has sprung from the soul of another people. (Spiller, 347–57)

The consequence of America's literary independence would be nothing less than the birth of the nation and of a new human being to go with it. Writes Ralph Waldo Emerson in *The American Scholar,* "[W]e have listened too long to the courtly muses of Europe. The spirit of the American freeman is already suspected to be timid, imitative, tame. . . . We will walk on our own feet; we will work with our own hands; we will speak our own minds . . . [A] nation of men will for the first time exist."[18]

For most of the early critics of American literature, the essential problem with American writing was not the temper of the American people or the materials with which they had to work (writes one critic, "It has been said that one reason why we have not produced more good poems was owing to the want of subjects . . . [but] the early history of illustrious nations has been the source of the great master pieces of poetry"—William Tudor, 1815; Spiller, 132–33). Rather, the problem seemed to be America's continuing dependence on British and European literary models, so that however many texts the new nation produced, even if those texts treated American landscapes and subjects, a native, national literature as such could not be said to exist.

Consider, for example, the following statements:

[T]here are two things to be deplored. The first is that, while so many books are vended, they are not of our own manufacture. . . . The second misfortune is that Novels being the picture of the times, the New England reader is insensibly taught to admire the levity and often the vices of the parent country. (Royall Tyler, preface to "The Algerine Captive," 1797; Spiller, 23)

Our literary delinquency may principally be resolved into our dependence on English literature. We have been so perfectly satisfied with it that we have not yet made an attempt towards a literature of our own. (Walter Channing, "Reflections on the Literary Delinquency of America," 1815; Spiller, 123–24)

It is impossible to recur to the history of our literature without remarking that since the settlement of America, while the ancient states of Europe have produced generation after generation of illustrious writers, we cannot boast one worthy of immortality. . . . [O]ur language, our literature, our taste are English, and we determine the merit of our literary productions by comparing them with those of men who enjoy better means and stronger motives for the cultivation of letters than America affords. (Francis Calley Gray, "An Address Pronounced Before the Society of Phi Beta Kappa," 1816; Spiller, 166–70)

With respect to the prevailing style of poetry at the present day in our country, we apprehend that it will be found, in too many instances, tinged with a sickly and affected imitation of the peculiar manner of some of the late popular poets of England. . . . [W]e desire to set a mark on that servile habit of copying which adopts the vocabulary of some favourite author and apes the fashion of his sentences and cramps and forces the ideas into a shape which they would not naturally have taken and of which the only recommendation is, not that it is most elegant or most striking, but that it bears some resemblance to the manner of him who is proposed as a model. (William Cullen Bryant, "Essay on American Poetry," 1818; Spiller, 204–5)

It is clear that to the critics quoted above American national independence demanded literary independence as well. Without such cultural independence America could neither consolidate its own unique identity nor communicate that identity to the world at large. But how, exactly, did a country produce a native literature, especially when the nation derived both its cultural tradition and its language from another, now very dissimilar nation to which it had set itself in direct sociopolitical and economic opposition?

As Michael Kramer has pointed out, language emerges as a key factor in almost all of the early criticism of American literature.[19] "As an independent nation, our honor requires us to have a system of our own in language as well as in government," declared Noah Webster, producer of the first American dictionary (*Dissertations on the English Language*, 1789; Spencer, 55–56; Spiller, 59). Or as James Kirke Paulding put it, in terms especially useful to keep in mind in relation to Hawthorne's most famous novel, America must "'make a French revolution among the alphabet' . . . to demote the 'aristocratic A' and 'put honest Z in its place'" (Spencer, 57).[20]

Such statements are typical of a group of comments put forward in American essays and lectures of the early 19th century. "National literature seems to be the product, the legitimate product, of a national language," argued Walter Channing in his "Essay on American Language and Literature."

If then we are now asked, why is this country deficient in literature? I would answer, in the first place, because it possesses the same language with a nation totally unlike it in almost every relation; and in the second, delights more in the acquisition of foreign literature than in a laborious independent exertion of its own intellectual powers. (Spiller, 113)

The Language of Democracy

American romance fiction, I suggest, was an effort by a group of writers to produce what Noah Webster called an "American tongue." It was the attempt to encode within language itself the specifically American features of the new sociopolitical and economic reality known as the United States. The call for nationality, repeated from the Puritans through the leaders of the American Revolution to the leading lights of the new republic, emphasized a difference between America and Europe. That difference had fundamentally to do with America's political, economic, and social institutions. In other words, it concerned a powerful ideological difference between Europe and America, a difference between aristocracy and democracy, between the hierarchical dissemination of power and pluralism. Whatever our evaluation of America's success in realizing its aspirations (and given such realities as slavery, the extermination of Native Americans, the denial of women's rights, and the exploitation of labor, we have severe reservations about that success), a certain self-conception and design did characterize American literary culture in the 19th century. One can no more ignore the American idea of itself than one can ignore the sociopolitical and economic events that also contributed to the production of American society.

In the readings that follow, I suggest that the 19th-century American romancers—Cooper, Poe, Hawthorne, Melville, and James—all glimpsed (each in his own way) a relationship between a certain way of telling stories and authoritarianism. Therefore, they each set out to create a new mode of storytelling that would work to further the expression of pluralism and democracy. This mode of storytelling could not (in the manner of realistic, sentimental, or epistolary fiction) thematize values or ideas—as if there were a social or moral or even psychological "truth" out there that was the writer's responsibility to encode. Instead, like democracy itself, it would have to permit the play of conflict and controversy. It would have to accommodate multiple and even contradictory systems of belief, to produce a text that, poised on a question, would demand the interpretative skills and active involvement of the reader. Only such a text, in the views of the romance writers, could contribute to creating a culture hospitable to, supportive of, and capable of realizing the values of democracy and pluralism.

Nineteenth-century American romance fiction is the story of an evolving literary aesthetic and cultural philosophy based on an idea of what Kenneth Dauber calls democratic poetics.[21] This poetics proceeds from an idea of the subjectivity of human perception and therefore the necessary tentativeness of all human statements. Romance fiction is philosophically skepticist. It questions whether the world exists and whether we can know the world and other people, and it therefore examines how human beings can and must act in a world shrouded in doubt. Though romance fiction (especially the tales of Edgar Allan Poe) seems, at times, to dissolve reality for the sheer fun of what James calls cutting the cable, its objective is not to shake free of a world of sociopolitical and economic impingement but to reconstruct the relation between the individual and reality on terms other than those of knowledge. Romance fiction is a fiction of what philosopher Stanley Cavell calls "acknowledgment" or "affirmation" whereby human beings discover their way back to the world and to other people through decisions they make and articulate despite the fact that they cannot prove the existence of any one or anything.[22]

In the romance tradition, especially as it is embodied in the writings of Hawthorne and Melville, the world is a place not of transcendent truths (religious, philosophical, moral, or otherwise) but of human manufacture, in which human beings must take responsibility for a world that they alone create and validate. In this way, romance fiction is a literature of democracy, of, for, and by the people for whom it is written. Although the romances of Cooper, Poe, Hawthorne, Melville, and James all exhibit the prevailing characteristics of the tradition, including its concern with storytelling and its skepticism, the chronological development of these writers, in relation to each other, nonetheless reveals an ever strengthening impulse in American writing toward greater and greater intellectual, philosophical, and literary sophistication.

Therefore, I begin with the fiction of James Fenimore Cooper, in particular one of the Leatherstocking Tales. *The Prairie* can be thought of as a precursor text in the romance tradition. It begins to put some of the pieces in place—in particular the tendency toward mythological and allegorical representation and the self-consciousness about storytelling. It does not, however, go the whole distance toward the philosophical skepticism that defines romance as a genre. In *The Prairie*, Cooper raises as a major subject of the text the question of how the story of America will be told: as myth, as religious type, or as purely social and political history, no different from the history of any other nation and with no larger, informing meanings beyond those to which the history itself points. And it concludes that the story of America will constitute an endless crossing of boundaries among different narrative forms, and between the reader and the writer, so that the story will be as much the product of the American reader who takes up Cooper's text as of the author himself.

The gothic tales of Edgar Allan Poe are less obviously culturally contextualized than Cooper's (or Hawthorne's or Melville's). They are less explicitly concerned with the nation in which they are written. They are also more purely theoretical and abstract. They do not so much investigate storytelling as they call into question whether a world even exists, about which stories might be told. And they conclude (with genuine fear and horror) that perhaps there is not, and, if there is, then our desire to narrate it may be desperately at odds with the possibility of either its survival or our own. Like Cooper, Poe shifts the burden of narrative meaning from author to reader. But in producing narrative fictions that are likely the insane fantasies of madmen, Poe does not so much put the reader in control of the fictive world as cause him or her to fall under the suspicion of mental instability. Poe's is a skepticism that tends toward the answer that, no the world does not exist, nor the individual in it. Thus Poe produces a text that screams out in anguish and defiance of everything it believes to be true as it tries (unsuccessfully) to convince its narrator and its readers that the world does indeed exist.

The fiction of Nathaniel Hawthorne participates in the skepticist inquiry of Poe's writing. But Hawthorne does not abandon his narratives to the horror of unanswered questions or of intimations that the answers may be more terrible still. Rather, accepting the question of knowledge as indeed not susceptible to solution except through the self-conscious manufacture of human answers, Hawthorne depicts a world of human intercourse—of love and desire, of affirmation and acknowledgment, of life. Though Melville is less optimistic than Hawthorne, he, too, recognizes the way in which skepticism can return us to, rather than divide us from, the physical world. Therefore, in his masterwork of romance fiction, *Moby-Dick*, he balances highly speculative philosophical inquiry with literalistic, almost scientific, natural description, suggesting how the divorce of one from the other (as achieved by many a Poe narrator) destroys not only the world of human invention (both material and verbal) but the world itself. Hawthorne and Melville are America's two great romancers. Their fiction consummates the genre and establishes its centrality in the American literary tradition.

For Henry James, the culminating figure in this tradition in the 19th century, the issues of romance fiction come to take their place alongside another set of issues—those of the everyday communication of individuals within a real and recognizable fictional world. Henry James, as the master of American realism (both sociological and psychological), provides the moment of transition when the genre of American romance is absorbed by differing forms of 20th-century fiction, including postmodernism, magical realism, and science fiction—although in some 20th-century writers (notably William Faulkner) the genre of American romance continues to have an uninterrupted existence. Although James's realism will always remain tinged with the legacy of romance, his fiction subordinates the question of philosophical inquiry, which so preoccupies Hawthorne and Melville, to the more unexceptional demands of everyday life.

I begin my story of the unfolding of the genre of American romance, then, with James Fenimore Cooper's *Prairie*.

Chapter 2

THE ROMANCE OF STORYTELLING: JAMES FENIMORE COOPER'S PRAIRIE

To begin a study of a uniquely American literary genre with the writer who was called during his own lifetime the American Sir Walter Scott might seem to undo the argument for American exceptionalism even before it is presented. But, as I have already suggested, the designation *American romance* in no way denies the origins of American fiction within British fiction, nor does it disclaim the affinities between varieties of American, British, and German romance. In fact, all three of America's earliest romancers—Washington Irving, Charles Brockden Brown, and the writer who will concern me in this chapter, James Fenimore Cooper, bear close relationships to British and even European literature. Washington Irving quite deliberately and unself-consciously set out to adapt German folktales to the American scene (Irving's most famous stories, such as "Rip Van Winkle" and "The Headless Horseman," fit into this category), while Charles Brockden Brown's novels (*Ormond*, 1793; *Wieland*, 1798; *Edgar Huntley*, 1799; *Arthur Mervyn*, 1793–1800; *Clara Howard*, 1800; and *Jane Talbot*, 1801) have much in common with the gothic, epistolary, and sentimental traditions of the British novel.[1]

No debt is more profound than Cooper's to Sir Walter Scott. Therefore, one must begin the description of 19th-century American romance with its connections with the literary form from which it eventually achieved its independence: the 18th-century British novel and the gothic and historical fictions of such authors as Walpole, Radcliffe, and Scott himself. In fact, one way of thinking about the 19th-century American romance tradition is as repeating, at a time lag of several decades, features of the historical development of British fiction. Just as the 18th-century British novel of Henry Fielding, Laurence Sterne, and Daniel Defoe self-consciously experimented and played with transforming epic and legend into a formally constituted literary genre, so the American writers a century later found themselves not simply telling stories in prose fiction but investigating the materials of their newfound art. Though *The Scarlet Letter* is no *Emma* or *Middlemarch* in terms of its depiction of society and therefore needs to be differentiated from these competing novelistic forms, it is no less realistic, which is to say no less sensationalistic and experimental, in its rendering of the world than *Moll Flanders* or *Clarissa*.

Nonetheless, even as American authors like Cooper, Irving, and Brown looked to British models and European traditions in order to devise their own form, they were already responding to the different conditions of America, not only in terms of geographical place and native history but also in relation to the designs and expectations of the new nation vis-à-vis the development of its literary culture. As William Cullen Bryant put it in a poem, aptly enough titled for our purposes "The Prairies": "These are the gardens of the Desert, these / The unshorn fields, boundless and beautiful, / For which the speech of England has no name— / The Prairies." (I will return to certain features of Bryant's imagery in a moment.) How America would "name" itself, how it would give itself significant literary voice is, as I have already suggested, very much an issue in America in the 19th century, no less for Cooper, Irving, and Brown than for the many intellectuals and critics who addressed this issue more discursively in the literary journals of the period.

Whether the literature these writers produced succeeded in declaring its full independence from British fiction remains to be seen. That it self-consciously took the first steps toward creating a literary form for which the speech and literature of Europe had no name seems very clearly a part of each of these writers' enterprises. As John P. McWilliams Jr. notes of Cooper, Cooper himself defined his literary function in *Notions of the Americans* as "elucidat[ing] the history, manner, usages, and scenery, of his native land" with an eye to America's "mental independence." Cooper was, in his own words, an "American who wishe[d] to illustrate and enforce the peculiar principles of his own country, by the agency of polite literature." He desired, McWilliams explains, to "serve as spokesman and guardian for the unformed republic."[2]

Let me designate, then, as a primary feature of American romance from its origins in Cooper, Irving, and Brown to its final flowering in Poe, Hawthorne, Melville, and James a self-consciousness about literary form, especially in its relation to creating a uniquely American literature. This self-consciousness made the literary text not simply the vehicle of their expression, concerning one theme or another, but its subject as well. For the romance writers the text would be anything but transparent. It would itself constitute matter for thought, as much so as any idea presented in or through it. Whether their fiction was constructed by them with a clear and self-acknowledged view to developing a certain interpretative relationship between the writer and the reader (as critics such as Edgar Dryden and Kenneth Dauber have suggested),[3] or whether it only seems that way to later audiences who were already schooled in the fiction of these writers, may be impossible to determine. Suffice it to say that to many critics the romance texts seem to distinguish themselves from other 19th-century fictions in the way that they issue a challenge to the reader to understand the structural or formal constituents of the work. Although Cooper's romances do not achieve the full-blown skepticism of the writings of Poe, Hawthorne, and Melville, nonetheless a certain doubtfulness seems to hover over the text, which calls into question apparent meanings and interpretations and which therefore also sets the stage for the active involvement of the reader in the construction of textual meaning.

The skepticist demeanor of romance fiction, I have suggested, is one of its salient characteristics. So is the relationship that the text tries to create with its reader. While these aspects of the romance only receive their fully mature expression in the writings of Poe, Hawthorne, and Melville, they are already apparent and important in many of the novels and short stories of Irving, Brown, and, in particular, Cooper. Cooper's most famous novels are not adventure stories or melodramatic, sentimental fictions, celebrating (however warily) the westward expansion of the United States. Nor are they allegories of American destiny (whether affirmative or cautionary), though as allegories they would already *not* constitute novels as such and thus set the stage for the later fictional evolutions of Poe, Hawthorne, and Melville. Rather, Cooper's Leatherstocking Tales—the five books concerning his American frontiersman Natty Bumppo—attempt a new form of literary composition, in which the burden of authorship is largely shifted from writer to reader. The series includes *The Pioneers,* 1823; *The Last of the Mohicans,* 1826; *The Prairie,* 1827; *The Pathfinder,* 1840; and *The Deerslayer,* 1841. It constitutes neither an historical nor a mythical telling of the story of America, having a certain didactic intention. Rather, it self-consciously stages a mutual interrogation of such historical and mythical renditions of "America" in order to complicate and, perhaps, even deconstruct the difference between such varieties of narrative.

In so doing, the texts issue in a fictional form in which the story told is no more important than the process of storytelling as such. The subject of Cooper's fiction, in other words, is largely the degree to which myth and history—which is to say imagination and subjectivity on the one hand and the world of sociopolitical and economic fact on the other—are inseparable from our perceptions of the world and from our representations of those perceptions in writing. The texts do not so much expostulate this subject as enact or embody it. In this way, they encourage the reader to acknowledge the degree to which culture is driven and created not by something outside of culture (such as truth or God or morality) but by culture itself. Culture, however, is not simply materially determined by the socioeconomic and political details of our everyday lives. Rather, it is as much formed by our stories or myths or fictions of ourselves and of our history.

Like other romances in the tradition, Cooper's Leatherstocking Tales treat culture as a place of distinctly human manufacture. The moral force of this is palpable. For, in a world that we as human beings create by ourselves and for ourselves, responsibility for everything that is or happens in that world can lie nowhere but in our own hands. This idea of assuming such a responsibility had, for the romance writers, specifically American implications. As a nation founded on principles of democracy and equality, the United States of America depended for its continuing existence on the constant and active involvement of all of its citizens in the construction of the nation.

The Trappings of Plot

The Prairie is the third of the Leatherstocking Tales in order of composition; the fifth, and last, in terms of the internal chronology of the tales. Its plot is fairly straightforward and not difficult to understand. It consists, more or less, of an amazing number of captures and escapes with very little other significant action in between and with little or no conversation to intrigue or divert us from the bare bones of the plot. In fact, the plot is so uncompelling, one might even say uninteresting, as immediately to alert us to the fact that, if this book has any merit whatsoever, the source of its interest must lie elsewhere. One might recall here Richard Chase's observation that, in the romance, plot will tend to be more important than character and that it will, rather, illustrate an idea more than be meaningful in its own terms. This certainly seems to be the case with *The Prairie,* though, as opposed perhaps to Poe's short stories or a novel such as Melville's *Moby-Dick,* even the plot seems woefully thin.

In many ways, *The Prairie* reads like a modern-day prime-time soap opera. The many separate stories, all of them highly melodramatic and superficial, dip into and out of each other, occasionally converging in a kind of epiphany of heightened sensationalism. But what the climax of the plot is meant to suggest is very hard to determine. For the most part the plot, though it makes a lot of fuss about itself, goes nowhere. It is difficult to take any of it seriously.

And yet *The Prairie* has become a classic of American fiction. It not only appealed to 19th-century readers, both in England and in the United States, but it has continued as basic fare both of American youth and of the college curriculum. How is one to understand the appeal of so apparently silly a text? Does it cater to some deep need on the part of American readers to believe in a fantasy of the American West? Or is there some other satisfaction that it provides, some other subject that the novel introduces that is, perhaps, inextricably part of our American consciousness, even in our contemporary period of radically changed literary sensibilities? Even though some critics have felt the need to redeem Cooper's novel from the oblivion of modern taste, the fact is that the novel has persisted rather well in holding an honored position in American literary history. The question is, Why?

Since plot is so fundamental to the structure of this novel, dominating any other interest in people or places or large historical consequences, let me begin my exploration of this prototype of an American genre by isolating the individual narratives that the book weaves together and putting the question, Why this textual structure?

1. There is first and foremost the story of Leatherstocking himself, in this novel referred to only as the trapper. The story spans not only this book (bringing the trapper finally to his death) but the other four books in the series as well. This story is referred to self-consciously within *The Prairie* when the trapper and Middleton discover the close relationship between the trapper and Middleton's grandfather and together reconstruct part of their joint histories. In this novel the story of the trapper has basically to do with his helping the other white members of the cast, and occasionally an Indian associate, to escape from each other and from the Indians, who are the avowed enemies not only of the whites but of other Indian tribes as well. There are no radical transformations in the nature or attitudes of the trapper, no major events to impress themselves either on his consciousness or our own, except, of course, for the event with which the book ends, the trapper's death.

2. A second primary story is that of Ishmael Bush and his family as (almost anticipating Mark Twain's Huckleberry Finn) they escape from the constraints of community and convention into what they imagine to be the unoccupied expanses of the American prairie. Though this story portends large significance both for the Bushes and for the nation, it hardly gets the characters or the book anywhere at all, since the action revolves around a stationary and static rock on which Bush builds his temporary fortress. Bush and his family, we are told at the end of the novel, will have no impact on American history. They will disappear from the annals of the nation as if they had never been.

3. Then we have the love story of Paul Hover and Ellen Wade, Ellen Wade constituting as well a part of the Ishmael Bush story, as does

4. Inez in the fourth story: the love story of Middleton and his wife, who has been abducted by Ishmael's brother-in-law Abiram White. Both of these stories are, each in its own way, also stories of American expansion and settlement (both Paul and Middleton will eventually become important political and military figures in the new nation); they are also stories of conflict with authority and tradition, in particular the authority and tradition of family. But, since the lovers are already committed to each other when the story begins, very little happens in the course of these stories, except, in the case of Ellen and Paul, for their receiving permission to marry and, in the case of Inez and Middleton, for their reunion. These stories do not so much progress as retreat, recovering lost moments of happiness and union.

5. Last but by no means least, we have the stories of the Pawnees and

6. the Sioux, whose individual tales also constitute a joint story of Indian persecution by whites and of intra-Indian warfare. These stories, too, are nonstories, the situations of the Indians vis-à-vis the whites and each other changing almost not at all from the beginning of the book to the end.

What becomes obvious as one lists these separate stories is, first, how little actually occurs in Cooper's novel and, second, that the stories are not in fact wholly separable from one another. Each story depends upon the others. Each one generates the others. And what this yields is another set of stories, which are similarly static and nonprogressive. These stories might be summarized as follows:

1. the story of the white settlement of America—the story that includes the story of the border settlers (like Bush and White) and therefore the stories of Paul and Ellen, on the one hand, and of Inez and Middleton, on the other, with the trapper representing both an alternative and an ally to this settlement, and

2. the story of the Indians, of their conflict with the whites and of their conflicts with each other. This is the story of the historical evolution of the Indian nations under the pressures of both internal and external interference.

Indeed, in the final analysis, there is a way of locating in this book a single unified and coherent story, though (crucially) this story contains two different focuses and is therefore susceptible to two different interpretations. This is the story of "America," where the Bushes and the trapper and all of the other white and Indian characters become part of the narrative of America's westward expansion. In this unified telling of the novel, however, one could place either Ishmael Bush and family or the trapper in the central position, coordinating the other various elements beneath them, so that the novel could emerge either as what one critic has called "social allegory"—i.e., an allegory of the social, political, and economic realities of westward expansion—or as what a previous generation of critics defined as "myth," the idealized vision of an America immune to the social and historical conditions that pertain to ordinary, everyday life.[4]

This final possible consolidation of the novel into a single plot, which is itself susceptible to two very different interpretations (one sociohistorical, one mythic), gives us the major issue of the text in exactly the interpretive form that Cooper, I believe, intends it. The question that this text raises (the question raised by the very mundaneness of its plot) is not, What is the story that this novel is telling? Rather, the question is, What *kind* of story is this book telling, and how are we going to understand not only the story but the manner in which it is being told? Is Cooper's fiction historical narrative, directly reflecting and bearing upon sociopolitical reality? Or is it a verbal picture of an idea, a myth as it were, with no necessary reference outside itself to a world that exists in historical, sociopolitical fact? Or is the book something else entirely?

What makes Cooper's *Prairie* a romance and not a novel is that its major concern is neither the sociopolitical, economic reality that the text figures forth nor the myth of America but rather the relation between the socioeconomic-historical and the mythic as they interact to produce both fact and fiction. In Cooper's text, neither the world of historical fact nor the world of literary invention exists independent of the other; each is infused with and determined by the other; and the telling of one will necessarily involve the telling of the other.

For this reason, the separate plots out of which this novel is constructed are made to converge not only literally (in the ways in which events determine and are determined by one another) but formally or structurally as well. That is, just as the several plots through which the narrative unfolds intersect with one another (suggesting that no event exists autonomous of other events), so the larger sociohistorical and mythic structures of meaning interact (suggesting that no way of conceptualizing reality can fail to cut in two directions). Universalist, absolutist assumptions about truth and meaning as much characterize the attitudes and aspirations of the history-oriented Ishmael Bush (and company) and the two Indian communities as they do the ahistorical or transhistorical trapper. Similarly, the trapper is no less pragmatic, practical, and historically attuned and contingent than the more historically oriented figures, like Bush. To put this matter still differently, the texture of Cooper's novel is as much created by an intermingling of types and levels of representation as the world depicted within the novel is the consequence of competing lifestyles and philosophies. There is, in this book, no place outside either history or storytelling, either for the white or Indian man or woman or for the reader of this text.

History Versus Myth

The book goes out of its way to break down the very distinctions between history and myth that, on some level at least, it is also drawing. Take, for example, the story that, of the two plots (Bush vs. trapper), seems to be the more sociohistorical and less mythic. Bush's very name—Ishmael—already signals to us the mythic and religious dimensions of his story, both from Cooper's and our own point of view and, perhaps even more significantly, from Bush's own perspective. Nineteenth-century readers of Cooper's novel would be readily conscious of the play of its rhetoric here. The era of the Revolution and the period following had revived an earlier Puritan discourse that had imagined America as a new Israel, its inhabitants as Israelites escaping over an ocean that was for them a desert, in an exodus led by leaders variously refered to as their Joshuas and Moseses.[5] Cooper, like Bryant, does not accidentally or loosely refer to the prairie as a desert in this book. Nor is his constant reference back to the ocean on the east coast of the United States any less meaningful in this context.

The flight of the Bush family across the desert/prairie recalls an American typology of exodus, not so very different from that which characterized a previous generation of American settlers, to which the book also makes constant reference. Even Bush's family name recalls the Moses figure so central to the mythic retelling of American history as an exodus. That Ishmael Bush's brother-in-law Abiram bears a version of the name Abraham strengthens the biblical allusiveness of the text. As Bush's own statements suggest, he and his family are on a mission of westward migration.

But, of course, as the name Ishmael suggests and as the events of the story confirm, Ishmael is no more a patriarch than Abiram. Traditional typology had very firmly held the reins controlling the relationship between type and antitype (i.e., between history preceding and following the crucifixion of Christ and the crucifixion itself). Puritan typology tended to loosen those reins, confusing America and Israel and making of the New World a new promised land (Bercovitch 1975).

Cooper's story of the "wandering" "tribe" of Ishmael does not, therefore, record a Christian allegory or myth.[6] Instead, it rebukes that allegory. The Bushes' trek across the "desert" harbingers no fulfillment of Christian goals. Bush and Abiram White are definitely *not* the chosen people. If anything, "wandering" as they do, they are more Jewish than Christian. Cooper makes use here of a convention within Christian representation that identified the Jews with Ishmael, the Christians, which is to say the true chosen people (from the Christian point of view), with Isaac. The name Abiram reenforces the direction of the text toward identifying the Bush clan, not with the forward movement of Christian history properly conceived, but with the backward movement of Puritan Christianity, which had aimed at recovering an old Israel (Melville will repeat this move in his long poem about pilgrimage to the Holy Land, *Clarel*). By more closely recalling the name *Abram*, which was Abraham's name before God's covenant with him, Abiram is not only a Jewish precursor of a Christian, he is a pagan precursor of a Jew.

Cooper is clearly subverting a Christian myth of America. Is he asserting his own romantic myth of a prelapsarian world—represented either by the Indians or by the trapper or by both? Let me complicate further the Ishmaelite reference. We are not very far into the novel when Cooper refers to the Indians as the

"Ishmaelites of the American deserts" (38). Even if one of the major characters in this novel were not also called Ishmael and his family were not referred to, within a page of the reference to the Indians, as "the tribe of wandering Ishmael" (39), the phrase would demand interpretation. But the conjunction of the two references cannot help but make us consider the one tribe of Ishmaelites in relation to the other.

On the one hand, to call the Indians Ishmaelites is simply to acknowledge their excommunication within the white world that America was fast becoming. It affirms the general racist prejudice that saw the whites as chosen, the Indians (and Africans) as descendants of the excluded and accursed (Ishmael, in this case, and Ham, in the case of the blacks). On the other hand, and as any experienced reader of the biblical text would immediately recall, God promises Ishmael that he, like Isaac, will become the leader of a great nation. Cooper's novel does not forget the full implications of the biblical text. As Cooper's trapper never tires of saying, the Indians are a great people. If the white Christian settlers have their biblical injunction, this text seems to say, so do the Indians.

But, as I have just been arguing, the white Christian settlers, according to Cooper, at least as they are represented by Ishmael Bush, do *not* have any divine promises. And neither do the Indians. Or, if they do, and if they are, as the trapper insists, a great nation, then so perhaps is that other tribe of Ishmaelites, the Bushes. By identifying both the Bushes and the Indians with Ishmael (and thus with each other), Cooper both constructs a mythic basis for America and withdraws it. Both of these groups of prairie settlers simultaneously are and are not instruments of American destiny, and in the same way and to the same degree. Neither is less chosen, neither more.

At the same time (and with important implications for later American fiction), Cooper blurs the difference between the races. Both red skins and white—Abiram White—play essentially the same roles in the human drama of American settlement. That Abiram's last name is carefully chosen to represent white racism is made clear in the following statement: "I know a man who is called Abiram White.—I believe the knave took that name to show his enmity to the race of blacks"—(189); earlier in the text we are told that White is a "dealer in black flesh"—(100). Both Christians and Indians suffer from the same delusion: that they are the land's chosen people (a delusion that will concern a lat-terday romancer, William Faulkner, a century later); they are the divinely designated receptacles of all power and grace (hence the conflict not only between white people and red people but between Pawnee and Sioux). But, in the pattern of ironic half-allusions that characterizes this text, Hard Heart, the "good" Indian, who becomes a son to the trapper, is only an ironic pharaoh. He hardens his heart—not to enable a divine miracle but to transform a delusion of exodus into a process of human-ized settlement.

Like the references to Ishmael, the name Hard Heart, which tentatively and inversely recalls the story of the Exodus, is impor-tant for the way this book works. Cooper specifically does not abandon the world of myth and allegorical reference. But by iden-tifying the Bushes and the Indians as Ishmaelites rather than as Israelites, the Indians with good pharaohs, Cooper produces an antimythic myth, a myth that only ironically and indirectly achieves its purposes as it comes into contact with and is made to accommodate historical realities. (In *Moby-Dick,* a book that looks back to Cooper's *Prairie,* Melville plays a similar game with myth and antimyth through the same figure of Ishmael.) Cooper's world is a fallen, human, historically conditioned world. It is post-lapsarian and postbiblical both. Myth and allegory, therefore, though they have no more disappeared than has the divine author of those myths and allegories, exist only at one remove from their original meanings or promises. Such covenants of nationhood as are now in effect are at best secondary and com-pensatory (like the original covenant given to Ishmael), existing in the shadow of what has become only a vision or a memory of cho-senness and promise, not to be mistaken for the genuine article.

Cooper infuses the historical narrative of the Bushes and the Indians with mythical elements, which both do and do not corre-spond to the contours of their historical situations. He represents the Bushes and the Indians as imagining themselves in mythic terms—as patriarchs and saviors; and he renders their dramas in his own set of antithetical mythic terminologies (as Ishmaels and pharaohs), which ironically sustains aspects of their mythic imaginings (i.e., that they will complete an exodus and become a great people) by severely undercutting and rewriting them.

A similar process of paradoxical revision pertains to the sec-ond axis of the book's narrative, the more purely mythical plot enacted by the trapper, which the book redirects away from myth and back toward historical contingency. If the object of Cooper's revision in the Ishmael image is a Christian allegory of America, his object here is not only biblical myth but the equally problematical romantic allegory of America as Eden, which, at the beginning of the 19th century, replaced the Christian allegory.

Cooper's romance of *The Prairie,* in other words, exposes the fallacy not only of Christian typologizing in the New World but of the pantheistic romanticism that took its place in the early years of the new republic. The opening lines of Bryant's "The Prairies," for example, published several years before Cooper's novel, do not so much reject the Puritan conception of America as a new Israel as they replace that idea with a claim even more radical. "The gardens of the Desert," "unshorn . . . boundless and beautiful," continue the backward-moving, historical unraveling of the Puritan conceit in order to discover, beyond the desert, the garden, in all its prelapsarian lushness. Early American romanticism, such as Bryant's, rather than correcting the basic mode of Puritan typology, intensified it. By imagining America not as Israel, but as Eden, the writers of the new nation backed out of history even further.

It is this backward, mythologizing motion of American ahistoricism that Cooper is resisting in his portrayal of what emerges as a decidedly postlapsarian Eden. Cooper's America is a world not so much new as in the process of discovering how much history it already has and must work through, before it can, indeed, sufficiently break with the past to declare a measure of newness in its undertaking. Like Ishmael and the Indians, the trapper, we discover, is *in* history, driving it forward, being driven by it, in this book to his death, which is the death of a certain myth of America as well—though it is by no means the death of American myth as such.

Thus the trapper's death (like the death of Christ) both does and does not represent a covenant-producing moment of ascension. "Nearly motionless for an hour," the old man suddenly rises "upright to his feet" and, in clear imitation of such biblical figures as Abraham, Isaac, and Moses—all of them types of Christ—he declares, "Here!" (452). Significantly, the trapper is enfolded by an Indian and a white man—Hard Heart to one side of him, Middleton to the other. Throughout the novel the trapper has represented a relationship between two nations, each of which has both its own history and destiny and also the history and destiny it shares with the other nation. But the trapper does not then emerge as the common myth or savior binding these two peoples. The trapper's revulsion at the stuffing of his dog Hector makes clear that he will not have them, in defiance of the laws of nature and history, preserve him. Rather, he will have them lay him to rest, with a simple headstone listing only the bare facts of his life and the warning, which Middleton adds to this: "*May no wanton hand ever disturb his remains!*" (453).

This tombstone inscription cuts two ways. The trapper remains an informing figure, a myth, by which Americans (red and white) can define themselves. This is the "spot where a just White man sleeps" (453). But dead and buried, a man and not a god, the trapper is also not to be resurrected. His remains are as mortal as they are mythic, and, as such, they must never be disturbed. Such future as succeeds the trapper is in the hands of others, who are not even his genetic heirs, such as Middleton and Inez and Paul and Ellen and the Indians, and, most importantly, their children. Their stories, into succeeding generations, are now the story of America. They constitute its history, its reality.

Hence, the section immediately preceding the death of the trapper contains the future histories of these two couples. By chapter 33 the novel has no more time for indulging the particulars of the many repeating scenes of conquest and escape. It summarizes the major events, delivering the novel firmly into the lap of historical narrative. "The local importance Middleton had acquired, by his union with the daughter of so affluent a proprietor as Don Augustin, united to his personal merit, attracted the attention of the government. He was soon employed in various situations of responsibility and confidence" (441). Similarly, Paul "soon became a landholder, then a prosperous cultivator of the soil, and shortly after a town-officer. . . . Paul is actually at this moment a member of the lower branch of the legislature of the state where he had long resided" (441).

Whatever the mythic dimensions of *The Prairie*, there is an historical consequence toward which this story is moving. The histories of Paul and Middleton, however, are only the penultimate ending of the book. Reversing the chronology (as if in imitation of the whole series of Leatherstocking Tales, which dispense with chronology), the book ends with the death of the trapper. It ends with the mythic figure that dominates one reading of the novel. Or, rather, it ends with the death of that myth, the myth now catapulted into the status of a new kind of myth: a romance, in which the historical and the mythic, the factual and the purely subjective and imaginative, are yoked together in a process of mutual interrogation in which the reader becomes the arbiter of meaning.

Words and Worlds

Cooper's *Prairie* is thus a romance largely because of the self-conscious self-reflexivity of its form, specifically the way in which it comprises a narrative both quasibiblical and historical. The book expressly eschews the domain of historical fiction, preferring melodrama and sensationalism over realistic representation and infusing the entire narrative with an allegorical, mythic, biblical dimension. And yet, through explicit reference back to a sociopolitical, economic, historical reality, it constantly, quite vividly, subverts the allegorical, mythic dimension of the text. The objective of this strategy is to position the text between worlds or, more precisely, at the points of intersection between them. For Cooper in *The Prairie,* the world is as much a linguistic construct as it is an external, sense reality. Therefore, much depends for him on how we "name" this world, especially in the case of this new entity known as America.

Therefore, when Cooper turns his thoughts in one of the more discursive passages of the book, to defining the new nation, he proceeds through a series of wordplays that as much reconstruct the English language as assert the difference between America and England:

> The Anglo-American is apt to boast, and not without reason, that his nation may claim a descent more truly honorable than that of any other people whose history is to be credited. Whatever might have been the weaknesses of the original colonists, their virtues have rarely been disputed. If they were superstitious, they were sincerely pious, and, consequently, honest. The descendants of these simple and single-minded provincials have been content to reject the ordinary and artificial means by which honors have been perpetuated in

families, and have substituted a standard which brings the individual himself to the ordeal of the public estimation, paying as little deference as may be to those who have gone before him. This forbearance, self-denial, or common sense, or by whatever term it may be thought proper to distinguish the measure, has subjected the nation to the imputation of having an ignoble origin. (68)

Cooper begins this passage in very familiar territory. He locates the origins of America in its explicit rejection of Europe, specifically of Europe's celebration and embodiment of history. America, as Cooper presents the nation, is doubly antihistorical. It imagines itself exempt from the implications of European history, and it sets about removing the accretions of privilege and power, historically determined, that define society in the Old World. Of course, in so recording America's break with European history and manners, Cooper is producing his own history of America and his own set of social principles. This is part of Cooper's point: that America exists in history and culture as surely as does any other nation. *But*—and this is equally important to Cooper—unlike European history and culture, American civilization is conditioned by an antihistorical impulse. It is informed, from the first, by a desire to subvert or undo history and its trappings.

This antihistorical impulse may be no more than a dream, an American myth of itself, but as myth, as dream, it exists as surely as if America had realized its desire in literal, historical fact. For in a world of human manufacture (a world created as much by our telling ourselves the story of our history as by that history itself), how we articulate our reality will be just as important to the world we create as any events that occur in that world. The very commonplace familiarity of Cooper's statements in this passage, like the simplicity of his plot in the book as a whole, alerts us to the fact that as important as what we say or do is how we say and do it. The objective of Cooper's long, discursive statement concerning the promise of America is to redefine the language of human culture and to locate as one of America's primary roles this rewriting and revitalization of human discourse.

Take, for example, Cooper's point concerning the charge against America that it derives from "ignoble" origins. In the first instance, Cooper's defense of America is as historical as what it is resisting; it does nothing more than imitate, with certain differences, the system of values that Cooper is claiming that America rejects, thus substituting America for Europe in the hierarchy of human civilization: "Were it worth the inquiry," he tells us,

> it would be found that more than a just proportion of the renowned names of the mother-country are, at this hour, to be found in her ci-devant colonies; and it is a fact well known to the few who have wasted sufficient time to become the masters of so unimportant a subject, that the direct descendants of many a failing line, which the policy of England has seen fit to sustain by collateral supporters, are now discharging the simple duties of citizens in the bosom of this republic. (68)

But, as the statement clearly stipulates, this kind of historical genealogy is not worth the inquiry. What is worth exploring, according to Cooper's text, is the concept of nobility itself. Cooper's text cracks open the words *nobility* and *ignoble,* in order to question not whether America is noble, but whether what Europeans take to be nobility, in the purely aristocratic sense, has anything whatsoever to do with nobility, in the moral sense. Indeed, Cooper suggests, such nobility as exists in Europe might better be termed *ignobility.*

Significantly, the passage does not itself produce the word ignobility. Rather, it pushes the reader toward articulating it. Cooper examines the discourse of European thought not simply to locate where definitional confusions have crept in and to reverse the terms of the equation but to locate in America, and specifically in the American reader, the place where terms of nobility and ignobility can now, at least tentatively, be defined and redefined, in an unending process of unraveling and reconstructing what exactly these terms ought to signify.

Cooper initiates the project that will most definitively come to characterize the writings of Henry David Thoreau and Ralph Waldo Emerson some decades later as they set out to renew and to keep open to constant renewal the language through which Americans will define themselves. Thus, in Cooper's wordplay, "forebearance" is not just a moral quality that Americans embody; it is exactly what is lacking, what has gotten lost, in the European worship of forebears, and what America recovers as an original intention of European culture. Similarly, "self-denial" is not to be understood merely as selflessness—though selflessness is clearly an important value that Americans embody. Rather, in the context of a discussion of "families" and inheritance, self-denial is a willingness to let go of past and future both, to deny oneself as central the way one is in European aristocracy, and thereby to grant to the next generation the same freedom from genealogy as one claims for oneself. Finally, "common sense" is not just practical wisdom but a form of the "ordinary," which is not (as in the system of patronage and privilege) "artificial" but rather sensible, logical.

What America has to offer, Cooper seems to be suggesting, is not an absolute break with the past. There is no way, according to Cooper, that America can fail to inherit its European origins. But insofar as culture is language, America does have the power to redefine its terms, retrieving meanings and intentions that—through disuse and habituation—have gotten lost as much in the language of culture as in its everyday institutions. Even more important, by writing language in a certain style of self-consciousness, America can keep language, which is to say the linguistic construction of culture, ever open to endless redefinition—so that America will not metamorphose into a simple replication of the past (with only an alteration of the terms of the equation) but will preserve its capacity for renewal and revision.

Cooper is under no illusions that this process of linguistic reconstruction is precarious, likely to result in a further repetition of European manners and mores, as the best European families take up residence in the New World. England, Cooper suggests, again in conformity with one large myth of America, is the "hive" that has "remained stationary" while its "numerous and vigorous swarms . . . are culling the fresher sweets of a virgin world," i.e., America:

> The hive has remained stationary, and they who flutter around the venerable straw are wont to claim the empty distinction of antiquity, regardless alike of the frailty of their tenement and of the enjoyments of the numerous and vigorous swarms that are culling the fresher sweets of a virgin world. But as this is a subject which belongs rather to the politician and historian than to the humble narrator of the home-bred incidents we are about to reveal, we must confine our reflections to such matters as have an immediate relation to the subject of the tale. (68–69)

These "swarms" are, we are told in the previous sentence, former Britishers. They now thrive, however, as simple citizens of

America, who dwell within the "bosom" of the American republic. But the American difference is not so easy to maintain. One of the major characters in the novel is a beekeeper, whose specific function has been to fill the American wilderness with hives. Soon America will be as hivelike as England, with all of the positive, but also negative, implications of this condition, each nation or hive sending out its bees (B's, as in Bushes?) as emissaries of what is, in the final analysis, a colonizing queen.

The image of both America and England as hives reenforces the sense created earlier in the passage that the two nations are structurally more similar than dissimilar. The difference between them is one that exists only in the continuing construction of that difference on the part of the American nation. The virgin world, Cooper reveals, seeming to contradict himself but making good on the logic of his text, is no virgin. It is, as Cooper states directly in his very next paragraph, a world already fallen; and "although the citizen of the United States may claim so just an ancestry," whereby "ancestry" Cooper has already indicated that he means both the English and the original American settlers, "he is far from being exempt from the penalties of his fallen race" (69). In fact, the American "swarms" (such as the Bushes and the Indians) "swarming" about like so many snakes, worms, reptiles, and other loathesome creatures, may not represent an alternative at all preferable to the static but at least harmonious and civilized decorum of the hive.

And yet America, in Cooper's view, is neither a replication of Europe nor a simple continuation of European history—or, at least, it does not have to be either one of these two things. If life in America is, like life anywhere else, always in the middle of history, it is also always in the middle of its self-conception:

> The march of civilization with us, has a strong analogy to that of all coming events, which are known "to cast their shadows before." The gradations of society, from that state which is called refined to that which approaches as near barbarity as connection with an intelligent people will readily allow, are to be traced from the bosom of the States, where wealth, luxury and the arts are beginning to seat themselves, to those distant and ever-receding borders which mark the skirts and announce the approach of the nation, as moving mists precede the signs of the day. (69)

As if echoing John Milton's *Paradise Lost,* for Cooper the postlapsarian world is all "before us." That is, it is our past as well as our future; indeed, it is our past in the act of becoming our future, and, conversely, our future or present, in the moment of its coming into being, immediately dissolving back into pastness.

As Hawthorne puts it in his famous definition of the romance in his preface to *The House of the Seven Gables*: "The point of view in which this Tale comes under the Romantic definition, lies in the attempt to connect a by-gone time with the very Present that is flitting away from us" (2). For Hawthorne reality exists for us only in our consciousness of reality. Therefore, reality is always in the process of a relocation, out of the world itself (such as it exists) into our minds, where it is instantaneously transformed into memory.

For Cooper the situation is essentially the same, though in Cooper's metaphor the relocation of world into mind is more spatial than temporal. Where is the "bosom" of America, the text inquires; where are the "skirts" or margins? The text had earlier maintained that "the direct descendants of many a failing line [in England] are now discharging the simple duties of citizens in the bosom of this republic" (68), suggesting that the "bosom" of this nation is where its simple citizens perform those duties that are not in the domain of its aristocratic forebears, i.e., on the prairies or what Cooper later identifies as the "skirts." And yet later in the passage, Cooper places "the bosom of the States, where wealth, luxury and the arts are beginning to seat themselves" (69) as if the bosom is America's inheritance of and continuity with European civilization.

In this second formulation, the nation thus defined only approaches "those distant and ever-receding borders which mark the skirts and announce the approach of the nation, as moving mists precede the signs of day" (69). Indeed, Bush, we are informed at the end of the passage, will never become a citizen of the "bosom" of the nation. He will pass "the whole of a life of more than fifty years on the skirts of society" (70). The impasse that this confusion of "bosom" and "skirts" creates is undone only by further confusion that the passage seems to introduce, between before and after. The distant borders, we are told, are "ever-receding." "The march of civilization," like "all coming events," "cast[s its] shadows before." The march of civilization, in other words, is not linear. Rather, it sweeps like a lady's skirt, foreshadowing and yet preserving what has been, "coming" in the double sense of now happening and about to come.

Cooper's image of America is of life always in the middle of creating and articulating itself. Past and present, in Cooper's view as in Hawthorne's, are inseparable, present always in the process of becoming past, past always kept in mind as an eternal present. The centers and margins of civilization are always in interrelated flux, making it impossible to distinguish the one from the other.[7] There is no progress in Cooper's story of America toward some fulfillment of the goals of civilization (as imagined and developed either in Europe or in America) or toward a recovery of some authentic paradise or promised land, such as the American colonists and settlers might have proposed. The shadows "before" precede but have already been cast before events that are "coming" in the future and are already in the process of realizing themselves (becoming) in the present. We have only the world we have, but this is largely a world of our own making.

Out of Space, Beyond Time

Hawthorne and Melville will directly inherit Cooper's attempt to construct a romance of American history in which the terms of storytelling are as vital to the creation of the nation as any sociopolitical or economic institutions. But when Hawthorne and Melville set about writing their own romances of America, the American writer's self-conscious concern with the construction of the world through language will have passed through a far darker and more troubled mind than Cooper's. Still basking in the glow of English enlightenment and the optimistic romanticism of the early 19th century, Cooper produces a romance that yokes history and myth in a process of mutual interrogation in which neither world nor mind dominates over the other. Meaning emerges through the collaborative effort of the two. Edgar Allan Poe will not be so confident about the possibilities of the human intellect. Indeed, Poe will so relentlessly question the mind's access to the world as veritably to make the world disappear, with terrifying consequences. His tales of the grotesque and the arabesque heighten the consciousness of the writers who follow him in the tradition. This matter of subjectivity and of the construction of the world through language, which Cooper so valiantly and confidently dramatizes, is not without its dangers, Poe warns. For, if pressed to its ultimate logic, it may deliver us not only out of both mythic and historical renditions of reality, both of which preserve an idea of the possibility of the mind's knowing and recording the world, but out of the world altogether. The world comes to seem completely inaccessible, even through words.

Hawthorne and Melville will recognize Poe's insights concerning the dark side of subjectivity, and American romance fiction will never return to Cooper's comforting melodramas. But having taken Poe's warning that the worlds of idea and fact, if kept separate, may never discover their way back to each other, the fiction of Hawthorne and Melville will propose modes of reconciliation between the two. Hawthorne and Melville will recover a real world in their fiction, and they will enforce upon the reader the implicit message of Poe's fiction: the necessity of keeping the physical world in mind, even if "in mind" is the only place where we can be sure a world exists.

Chapter 3

The Romance of the Word: Edgar Allan Poe's "Fall of the House of Usher"

As anyone familiar with contemporary trends in literary criticism will have recognized, a principle informing my reading of Cooper is what is currently called deconstruction. I did not deconstruct Cooper's text. Nonetheless, my reading followed what seemed to be not the apparent unities or truths of the text but its deviations from such unities or truths. Though deconstruction as a philosophy and as a strategy of reading is a fairly recent phenomenon (as deconstructive critics themselves emphasize), the qualities of the text that it traces are nonetheless as ancient as writing itself. These qualities are very much in evidence in Cooper's novel.

In saying this I do not in any way want to suggest that a deconstructive or deconstructively informed reading is the only permissible reading of Cooper's novel (or, for that matter, of romance fiction). As will become clearer in the chapters that follow, my own philosophy of reading differs in many ways from that of deconstruction. Nonetheless, deconstruction has something powerful to offer in unlocking the power of Cooper's novel. In fact, as a system of skepticist thought, deconstruction recalls features of the romance theory that canonized Cooper (along with Poe, Hawthorne, and Melville) in the first place. It has been argued that one of the reasons that deconstruction has become so popular in the American literary establishment is that American writing—in particular the 19th-century tradition—lends itself so readily to this kind of analysis.[1] One might even go so far as to say that American romance as a genre is to some significant degree defined by what deconstructionist critics have called the decenteredness or indeterminacy of the text, the ways in which the text actively prevents the consolidation of a single, unified meaning. Romance is certainly characterized by a self-consciousness concerning language, a heightened awareness of language as the not entirely stable and controllable medium through which the text proceeds.

This is not to say that American texts have no meanings. As I have argued in relation to *The Prairie*, Cooper brings myth and history into a mutually interrogatory, even antagonistic, relationship, not in order to cancel out the validity of either one of them but rather to show how each of them is a humanly organized construct or fiction and not an essentialist truth. By saying this, I do not mean now to posit a new unity to Cooper's text, as if its "truth" were either the "truth" of deconstruction (i.e., that meaning is never stable) or the "truth" of the inevitable (even if temporary) reconciliation of opposites—a truth that, for want of a better term, we might call symbolism. Rather than declare the text "true" in any one of these ways, I want instead to highlight as an important feature of Cooper's enterprise, which is relevant to the romance tradition as a whole, an investigation of the limits both of the decenteredness of language and of its potential for the unified reconstitution of meaning.

This investigation was not without immediate, practical significance to the nation just setting out. In the early and mid-19th century, when the romancers wrote, the country might well have seemed to have an abundance of myth (much of it biblical) with very little history; from another perspective, it could easily have appeared to have a lot of history with extremely little cultural coherence. That a dualism or dialectic between reality and fiction should arise in the minds of early American intellectuals is hardly surprising.

Allegory and Symbol

The terms *symbolism* and *deconstruction* are crucial to any definition of the American romance tradition. These terms describe a major tension in romance fiction—a desire, on the one hand, for unity and fullness of meaning and, on the other, a resistance to such unity and fullness. Both symbolism and deconstruction may be thought of as responses to philosophical skepticism. That is, they are both ways of responding to the doubt about whether the world exists; whether the individual can ever "know" reality, if indeed it does exist; and, if the individual could know reality, whether such knowledge could be conveyed in language. The argument concerning skepticism was palpable in the early 19th century in America. It is therefore quite natural that American texts written during this period should provide reflections both of and on this philosophical debate.

When I get to Hawthorne's *Scarlet Letter* I will add another term into the discussion of romance fiction that also has to do with the relationship between fiction and philosophical reflection in America. This is the word *aversion*. Stanley Cavell adapts it from the writings of Ralph Waldo Emerson in order to describe a language-mediated, skeptically informed relationship between the individual and his or her society.[2] For the moment, let me stay with the terms symbolism and deconstruction as two forces within the romance text that help give it its definitive character. These forces, as we shall see, reconstruct a skepticist problematic. They also offer potential responses and even penultimate solutions to the problem of knowledge, though they do not, finally, go the whole distance in defining the skepticist romance text.

The original generation of romance critics took their sense of the term *symbolism* from Charles Feidelson's 1953 *Symbolism and American Literature.* For these critics, romance fiction as a genre was defined not only by a symbolic relation, which is to say a self-consciously language-mediated as opposed to a "realistic" relation to America and American history, but by a philosophy of symbolic consciousness. In this philosophical system, language was empowered to convey a wholeness to human experience that, in the real world outside language, could never really exist. As Feidelson puts it, in a definition of the romance tradition that built heavily on Hawthorne and was to influence Richard Chase and others strongly:

Whereas the novelist was limited to "the probable and ordinary course of man's experience" [Hawthorne's phrase in the preface to *The House of the Seven Gables*], the romancer tried to create a realm midway between private thought and the objective world. This doctrine . . . betrayed an intellectual as well as a literary problem. Hawthorne was anxious not merely to draw the literary distinction between the novel and the romance . . . but also, and more fundamentally, to fix the status of the romance in an almost metaphysical sense. . . . [H]e was trying, in effect, to say what kind of reality his own work had. . . . The natural outcome of [his] theoretical indecisiveness was Hawthorne's allegorical method; by this means, consciously or not, he evaded the issue with which he was confronted. For it is in the nature of allegory, as opposed to symbolism, to beg the question of absolute reality. . . . Yet his underlying purpose was always "to open an intercourse with the world," and out of this purpose arose not allegory but symbolism. (7–9)

"Symbolism," Feidelson continues, "is an attempt to find a point of departure outside the premises of dualism—not so much an attempt to solve the old 'problem of knowledge' [i.e., skepticism] as an effort to redefine the process of knowing in such a manner that that problem never arises" (50).

In Feidelson's terms, allegory evades the problem of knowledge by creating a text that is a transcript of the world or of certain ideas about the world, without considering the question of whether this world does or does not enjoy phenomenal existence. Allegory, we might say, proceeds on the basis of a kind of parallelism to this world, whether or not it exists. It reconstructs ideas about this world through analogies or likenesses to it. Symbolism, on the other hand, does not evade the problem of knowledge so much as reconstruct the relationship between world and mind in such a way that the problem does not arise. The literary work as symbol, the symbol as word, makes language the place where mind and world intersect. In language the mind knows the world because it is the creator or re-creator of this world. For this reason, Poe celebrates "The Power of Words," as he calls it in one essay. As I will suggest in my next chapter, Ralph Waldo Emerson shares much of Poe's faith in language, though he is much more restrained about it even as he is more optimistic about the world generally.

In the view of Feidelson and other critics of the 1950s and '60s, "to consider the literary work as a piece of language is to regard it as a symbol, autonomous in the sense that it is quite distinct both from the personality of its author and from any world of pure objects, and creative in the sense that it brings into existence its own meaning" (49). Of course, as Feidelson immediately goes on to say, not all "modern theorists and writers" would agree with this generalization about the symbolic status of the literary text. This is especially the case in the 1990s, 40 years after Feidelson published his book, making him not only an apt critic of his times but a rather prophetic one as well. But, even if the critical establishment concurred in thinking about literature itself as symbolic, Feidelson's purpose in discussing symbolism and American literature is in any case to make a claim that goes well beyond that of the generally symbolic status of the text as text. Rather, he wants to argue for the American tradition as a special and insistently self-conscious symbolic tradition. For Feidelson, as for most of the other romance critics, American literature was not only symbolic in the sense in which all literatures are (perhaps) symbolic, but it was by philosophical commitment symbolic. It embodied a philosophy of symbolic relations.

It is no coincidence that in resisting the premises of New Criticism the deconstructionists have returned to the idea that language (literary and otherwise) is allegorical rather than symbolic. Nonetheless, in stressing verbal play and the instability of the text, deconstruction, in a curiously paradoxical way, repeats New Criticism's own move in relation to allegory. By reversing the standard prioritization of symbolism over allegory (classically expressed by Samuel Coleridge in the *Biographia Literaria*), prominent deconstructionist critics like Paul de Man had hoped to dislodge the logocentric poetics of Formalist Criticism. Language, de Man and others argued, whether literary or otherwise, is not symbolic but allegorical. That is, as a purely human construct, having no absolute or necessary relationship to reality, language can tell us nothing about reality or reality's relationship to mind. Instead, it exists only within a system of its own self-referentiality, in which words tell us only about themselves and about the linguistic constitution of the minds that generated them.

In so stressing the autonomous world of language, however, deconstruction reconstructs a basic premise of the New Criticism—that the text exists apart from the sociopolitical and economic world of its manufacture. Even more importantly, by imagining language as its own reality, deconstruction, like New

Criticism (and unlike classical allegory), does venture a response to the question of knowledge. If the New Critics, subscribing to a symbolic philosophy of language, respond to the question of knowledge by affirming a place, namely language, where mind and world intersect, the deconstructionists, while in no way either affirming or denying the existence of reality, do deny the possibility of the mind's access to reality. To the question, Can we know reality? deconstruction answers, No, we cannot. All we can "know" is the word, and the word is a purely human, social contrivance. It has no basis within any world outside itself.

The major point of convergence between New Criticism and deconstruction, which makes both of them of major relevance to the definition of American romance fiction, is their emphasis on language as opposed to the social, political, psychological, economic, or even literary-historical contexts that go into producing any literary work. For the New Critics and the deconstructionist critics alike, the text is a self-consciously linguistic artifact. Romance, we might say, is such self-conscious literariness writ large. Though for recent critics like John Carlos Rowe, Gregory Jay, and Evan Carton the self-conscious literariness of American romance in no way affirms a tradition of confidence in language (indeed, for them the situation is quite the reverse), it nonetheless testifies to a primary interest in language as such.[3] The major point of disagreement between the symbolists and the deconstructionists has to do with how the text relates to the question of knowledge that it raises: Does the text answer in the affirmative, providing itself, through its construction of symbols, as evidence of the mind's relationship to the world? Or does the text respond in the negative, demonstrating through a deconstruction of its terms that it is no more than a verbal fabrication of the world, and a disunified, incoherent, and decentered fabrication at that? Or does romance fiction offer some other, quite different response? An investigation of the fiction of Edgar Allan Poe—which plays with the possibility both of symbolism and indeterminacy—will help us answer this question.

The Literal Versus the Allegorical

Given the correspondences and divisions between the romance critics and the deconstructionists, it is not surprising that a central figure in recent debates has been Poe, whose "Purloined Letter" has become a locus classicus in deconstructionist poetics as it once was in the symbol school of American criticism.[4] Let me turn, then, to Poe, whose literary reputation has been nothing less than a roller-coaster ride of celebration and dismissal and who is at this moment in American literary history emerging once again as a dominant figure. Poe best exemplifies the linguistic orientation of the romance tradition, the self-conscious literariness of his texts being of such a pure and rarified form as veritably to exclude from the text almost any subject other than the textuality of the text itself. At the same time, Poe's stories point in the direction that the romances of Hawthorne and Melville will take: toward scrutinizing the implications of answering the question of knowledge, either in the affirmative (through symbolism) or in the negative (as deconstruction). The horror of Poe's fiction, its gothicism, is largely the consequence of the narrator's failure fully to register the implications of the metaphysical game he is playing in his own narrative.

I focus my discussion on one of Poe's most famous short stories, "The Fall of the House of Usher," which seems to be about nothing so much as what one critic calls Poe's "world of words," his linguistically oriented universe.[5] I could as easily, however, discuss a dozen similar stories, such as "Ligeia," "The Purloined Letter," "The Black Cat," "The Tell-Tale Heart," "The Imp of the Perverse," "The Descent into the Maelström," "The Pit and the Pendulum," "William Wilson," or "The Masque of the Red Death." All of these texts seem, on some level, no more than casual tales of terror, horror stories intended to thrill the reader with the bizarre and the grotesque. But each of these tales is deeply philosophical and self-consciously literary. The stakes turn out to be nothing less than the existence of the world and of ourselves in it.

Since I will be pressing very hard in my discussion of Poe for the self-conscious literariness of his fiction, let me begin my reading with the opposite claim. As it turns out, this reversal of direction is in any case where the self-conscious literary reading will take us. There is nothing in "The Fall of the House of Usher" to prevent a reader from taking the story literally, at least in the first instance. There is nothing, for example, to stop us from imagining that the narrator has been summoned to the house of Usher by his boyhood friend, who is suffering a deep depression as a result of the mortal illness of his dearly beloved sister. Nor is there anything to undermine our understanding that his sister subsequently dies and is laid in the family vault.

At this point, the barrier to formulating a literal interpretation becomes a bit more sizable but hardly insurmountable. It may be that Madeline succeeds in coming back from the tomb for the simple reason that she was not actually dead when the narrator and her brother put her in the family vault. This possibility is clearly raised by the text, when Usher informs the narrator of Madeline's death and

> state[s] his intention of preserving her corpse for a fortnight, (previously to its final interment,) [sic] in one of the numerous vaults within the main walls of the building. The worldy reason, however, assigned for this singular proceeding, was one which I did not feel at liberty to dispute. The brother had been led to his resolution (so he told me) by consideration of the unusual character of the malady of the deceased, of certain obstrusive and eager inquiries on the part of her medical men, and of the remote and exposed situation of the burial-ground of the family. (409)

Of course, the possibility that Madeline is not actually dead also raises the possibility of accusing Roderick (and, perhaps, the narrator as well) of intentionally burying the still-living woman. The text goes on to emphasize (409–10) the smallness, dampness, and inaccessibility of the vault in which they place the "dead" Madeline, hardly the kind of location designed to protect her from a premature burial. Even if Madeline is dead when the narrator and Usher bury her, we can still take the text literally if we either imagine the terms of the natural world in this text to be different from those with which we are familiar or if we accept that within our own natural world apparently supernatural or unnatural events can and do occur.

There is one further way in which we can take the story literally, and that is if we understand the narrative as recording the narrator's hallucination of the events of the story. In other words, even if we do not accept the events recorded within the story to be "true" in the sense of actually having occurred in a verifiably "real" world, nonetheless the story itself (the story of a deranged narrator's bizarre fantasy) may be true. The narrator may well have imagined these terrifying and highly implausible events. The story, then, may represent a later moment of lucidity, when the narrator records his strange hallucination. Or the story, fully endorsing the events it records, may be understood as a continuation of that hallucination and a further manifestation of it. The story, in other words, may be true as a record of the mind, as a transcript of the mind's construction of reality.

Of course, every readerly instinct (not to mention plain common sense) cautions us against reading the story as a straightforward, literal account of real events. Still, taking the story literally is not only permissible but necessary. As literal narrative, even before it launches us into more theoretical relocation of the text in the world of the narrator's mind, this text seems to be raising a set of interrelated questions on the nature and knowability of the world. These are the same questions raised more directly and self-consciously if we take the story (again, in some sense, literally) as the narrative of a hallucination. The questions are: What constitutes the natural world, and how do we, as human inhabitants of this world, differentiate the real from the unreal, the plausible from the implausible, and the implausible from the impossible? Is the natural world sufficiently large and flexible as to include a range of events that, though infrequent, are far from nonexistent? Or does the natural world place a firm, recognizable border between the natural and the unnatural or supernatural? And, in either case, what is our relationship to these events? How do we perceive and understand them?

These questions lead ineluctably into the second "literal" reading of the story. What, the story forces us to ask, is the status of a hallucination in the natural world? Or, for that matter, what is a fiction, whether that fiction is self-generated and out of control (as in a hallucination) or whether it seems to be firmly authored and thus authorized by a consciousness as rational as our own? (And how rational is that, given how powerfully we respond to tales of madness and terror?) Does fiction tell us about the world? Or is fiction always self-fabricated and self-referential, telling us only about fiction itself?

In other words, even when we take the story as literal in either of the ways I have proposed, "The Fall of the House of Usher" leads in the direction of large, metaphysical, psychological questions about the nature of reality and our knowledge of it. The fiction, therefore, immediately comes to seem more theoretical and self-conscious, more philosophical, than immediately sociopolitical or even psychological. As in Cooper's novel, plot dominates over any other feature of the text. And, also as in Cooper, the plot is anything but minutely (which is to say socially or psychologically) nuanced. Here, however, the similarities between Poe and Cooper cease. Whereas Cooper's plot goes almost nowhere through a series of vivid captures and escapes, Poe's goes a maximal distance (to death and horror) without anything significant really happening along the way. And it is accompanied, at every moment, by philosophical speculations on one subject or another.

These differences between Cooper and Poe are as important as the similarities. By staying closer to events (however nonprogressive and meaningless they are), Cooper, even as he is raising questions about how we narrate events in this world, preserves a fairly recognizable relationship between the world and his text. Whether he is writing history, myth, or romance, Cooper intends us to take the events of his story as having some literal relationship to the world outside his text. Poe, by producing an almost eventless plot, with endless explications of it, transforms his work from a description of the world to a mind's meditation concerning it. It is not clear what Poe would have us do with this meditation, except scare ourselves to death. Poe does not write history or myth or the kind of historical, mythic romance that Cooper writes. Rather, he seems to write what we would have to call allegory. That is, the events of a typical Poe story are not so much interesting and compelling as themselves but rather as agents of other issues and ideas, which the events represent.

In a moment I will contest the allegorical reading of Poe, in order to suggest that what seems to be conventional allegory is, in Poe's fiction, what I have been calling romance. First, however, let me sketch the dimensions of the tale's allegorical narrative. In parallel with the first of the two literal readings, this allegory may be unself-conscious. That is, it may not be about allegory as such but may have as its intention a statement that it wishes to make, allegorically, about the real world. On the other hand, in parallel with the second literal reading, Poe's may be an allegory about allegory; it may self-consciously intend to reveal how words can be about nothing but words, all words proceeding within their own self-contained universe, with no possibility of verification outside themselves. This is allegory as hallucination.

For the moment let me collapse the two allegorical dimensions of the tale into each other and only keep separate the different plots that the allegory seems to unfold—although it is necessary to keep in mind, throughout, the way in which this story exponentially proliferates interpretive options: whether we take the tale as literal narrative or allegory, unself-conscious allegory or self-conscious allegory, will, of course, change our understanding of any particular plot or set of ideas we identify in the story's details. This feature of the text's exponential proliferation of meaning is of prime importance in considering it a romance and not simply an allegory, for the story resists, with every fiber of its existence, being flattened out into one explication or another. The story is no less than dizzying, a quality that the text replicates in its culminating paragraphs.

Nonetheless, putting aside for the moment what kind of allegory this is (if it is allegory at all), the story it plots seems susceptible to at least two interpretations. In the first the story seems to record a conflict between two faculties of the intellect: reason and the imagination, where the imagination may be synonymous with insanity or may represent some divinely instituted capacity of human understanding, loftier than reason (as in Poe's Dupin stories, for example "The Purloined Letter"). In the second, which may be a version of the first, the story dramatizes a struggle either between an instinct for survival and a death wish or between the physical body and the human mind, including, of course, the imagination and reason, which, as I have just suggested, are themselves in some opposition and conflict.

Proceeding through the first of the narrative options (i.e., the story as an allegory of two mental faculties, reason and the imagination), the story seems to concern three characters—the narrator and the two Ushers—with the Ushers either enjoying the same ontological status as the narrator or being imaginative fabrications or projections of his mind. As a rational everyman, somewhat given to fears and superstitions but always trying to pull back from that tendency within himself in order to put things back into rational perspective, the narrator is drawn into a world of mystery and terror and the irrational, either against his will or because of his own predisposition to insanity. This narrator, whom we meet at the beginning of the story quite sanely studying the house of Usher and its "remodelled and inverted images" (398) and trying to understand what, precisely, accounts for the "sense of insufferable gloom" (397) that it shadows forth, endeavors throughout the story to break the pull toward insanity, whether this insanity is external to him (in a person named Usher) or inherent within his own disposition (and therefore embodied, in his imagination, in a fantasy named Usher). Thus, throughout his stay with Usher and especially in the final moments of the tale, the narrator seems to do everything in his power to resist, and to help Usher to resist, the "anomalous species of terror" to which Usher is a "bounden slave" (403). In fact, one way of understanding the end of the story is to conclude that the narrator does indeed succeed in saving himself, even though he cannot save Usher.

In this reading of the story, whether Usher is real or imagined, he represents terror and superstition. That Usher is closely associated throughout the story with the arts—music, painting, and literature—is not incidental. Terror and superstition are largely products of the imagination. Like literature and art, they transgress the boundaries of the real and knowable world. They create realities divorced from the natural world of quotidian fact. In the case of Usher, this tendency of art and the imagination is carried to painful extremes. Writes the narrator,

> An excited and highly distempered ideality threw a sulphureous lustre over all. . . . From the paintings over which his elaborate fancy brooded, and which grew, touch by touch, into vaguenesses at which I shuddered the more thrillingly, because I shuddered knowing not why;—from these paintings . . . I would in vain endeavor to educe more than a small portion which should lie within the compass of merely written words. By the utter simplicity, by the nakedness of his designs, he arrested and overawed attention. If ever mortal painted an idea, that mortal was Roderick Usher. (405)

This is art with a vengeance. The morbidity (406) of Usher's art is matched only by the morbidity of his temperament. And both conspire in his giving way to the world of imagination over the world of reason.

In this contest between reason and the imagination (between the narrator and Usher, whether Usher is a person or an aspect of himself), it is by no means clear what or who triumphs at the end. Let me quote the end of the story, to which I will be returning at various points in my argument:

> As if in the superhuman energy of his utterance there had been found the potency of a spell—the huge antique panels to which the

speaker pointed, threw slowly back, upon the instant, their ponderous and ebony jaws. It was the work of the rushing gust—but then
without those doors there did stand the lofty and enshrouded figure
of the lady Madeline of Usher. There was blood upon her white
robes, and the evidence of some bitter struggle upon every portion of
her emaciated frame. For a moment she remained trembling and
reeling to and fro upon the threshold—then, with a low moaning
cry, fell heavily inward upon the person of her brother, and in her
violent and now final death-agonies, bore him to the floor a corpse,
and a victim to the terrors he had anticipated.

From that chamber, and from that mansion, I fled aghast. The
storm was still abroad in all its wrath as I found myself crossing the
old causeway. Suddenly there shot along the path a wild light, and I
turned to see whence a gleam so unusual could have issued; for the
vast house and its shadows were alone behind me. The radiance was
that of the full, setting, and blood-red moon, which now shone
vividly through that once barely-discernible fissure, of which I have
before spoken as extending from the roof of the building, in a zigzag
direction, to the base. While I gazed, this fissure rapidly widened—
there came a fierce breath of the whirlwind—the entire orb of the
satellite burst at once upon my sight—my brain reeled as I saw the
mighty walls rushing asunder—there was a long tumultuous shout-
ing sound like the voice of a thousand waters—and the deep and
dank tarn at my feet closed sullenly and silently over the fragments
of the *"House of Usher."* (416–17)

As the narrator stands reeling over the tarn, just as moments
before Madeline has stood trembling and reeling on the threshold of the room, it is not clear whether he, like Usher, will suc-
cumb "a corpse, and a victim to the terrors he had anticipated,"
or whether, as the fragments close over the tarn at his feet, he
will survive and (as it were) live to tell the tale. In fact, whether
the narrator lives or dies, it may be impossible to determine
whether imagination (Usher) has triumphed over reason (the
narrator) or reason over imagination: for, if Madeline is still alive
(as Usher suspects) or, even more so, if she is resurrected from
the dead, then Usher, not the narrator, is the most reasonable of
men, and his reason has triumphed (in death) over the flimsy
imagination of the narrator, who cannot begin to fathom the
strange universe in which he exists.

The climax of the story makes us vividly aware of a feature of
the story that operates throughout: that, even as Usher and the
narrator represent different, antithetical faculties of the mind,

they also replicate each other. As the end so powerfully witnesses for us, Usher is no less in touch with the reality of his world than the narrator. He may not be a madman at all. Indeed, if we assume the events of the story actually to have occurred, then Usher is a far better register of those events than the narrator. Throughout the story the narrator dismisses supernatural events, which turn out to be accurate descriptions of what is going on. In the final scene, when Madeline reappears, there is every reason to believe that Usher and not the narrator has been right about what constitutes the ordinary and probable course of human events in this tale. In this tale it is Usher and not the narrator who is the "rational" man, the individual who "knows" how reality works, since the world that exists in this story may not be an external reality but a translocated universe of the mind.

Similarly, the narrator is hardly a rational person. This is, after all, a first-person narrative, and our narrator is the artist. He is the one telling a story, and for all we know, he is responsible for making a purely natural scene horrible, he who is hallucinating an encounter with a man gone mad and a woman resurrected ("*Madman*," Usher calls him at the end of the story) (416). "The whole of a dull, dark, and soundless day in the autumn of the year, when the clouds hung oppressively low in the heavens" (397) has no existence outside the first-person narrative of this text. There is no way of verifying the narrator's perceptions, no way of knowing whether the narrator sees and interprets the world accurately or instead projects it according to his own warped and gloomy (Usherlike) imagination.

In other words, if, in one direction of the story, Usher plays madness to the narrator's rationality, his madness is uncannily reasonable in its ability to register the truths of the "unreasonable" world in which he exists, making the narrator, by contrast, mad. Usher is quite correct that he and the narrator have put Madeline living in the tomb. He is absolutely accurate in his prediction that he and she are soon to perish, and he is right on target when he registers the sounds of her return. Usher, in other words, is as sane as the narrator, or as insane. In fact, by the end of the story there seems to be very little difference between them. After the two of them have deposited Madeline in the tomb, Usher yields completely to the "mental disorder" (410) that has characterized him from the start. So does the narrator:

It was no wonder that his condition terrified—that it infected me. I felt creeping upon me, by slow yet certain degrees, the wild influences of his own fantastic yet impressive superstitions.

It was, especially, upon retiring to bed late in the night of the seventh or eighth day after the placing of the lady Madeline within the donjon, that I experienced the full power of such feelings. . . . I struggled to reason off . . . nervousness . . . [b]ut my efforts were fruitless. (411)

When Madeline finally appears at the door of the narrator's room, he will see her as clearly as does Usher. There is no way of deciding, in Poe's story, whether the narrator is sane and Usher mad, or vice versa; or whether they are both mad or both sane, since there is no inside or outside to this text, no place from which to judge the essential nature of reality and therefore to determine what constitutes a rational response to it. Like the several plots in Cooper's *Prairie*, the different narratives produced by "The Fall of the House of Usher" blend into each other. They determine and are determined by each other, breaking down rather than yielding distinctions and differences between them.

Skepticism, Indeterminacy, and the Woman

The collapse of Usher and the narrator into each other as figures of the same quality of mind or, at least, as both figures for the mind, either rationally or irrationally disposed, perhaps mutually contradictory and therefore mutually annihilating, produces the second conflict that the story seems to embody: that of the body versus the mind; of the physical self versus the spiritual or emotional or psychological or intellectual self. It is this conflict, not within the mind but between the mind and the world, that disqualifies Poe's story as allegory (either straightforward or self-conscious) and moves it in the direction of romance. This definition of the tale as romance depends upon the figure who, till now, has received scant attention in my reading: Madeline Usher.[6]

The virtual absence of Madeline from my interpretation is not without justification by the story itself. Though Madeline is instrumental in the events in the story—indeed, even though without her the story could not take place—she is, throughout, largely marginalized. Of course, one could ignore the proportions of the text and reinsert Madeline into the drama as a full participant in the story that the text records. In this case, we could do one of two things. We could see Madeline as alternately reenforcing either the figure of the narrator or of Usher, representing therefore either the powers of reason or the powers of imagination. That is, insofar as Madeline twins her brother, Roderick (we are told that Madeline and Roderick are identical twins and that "sympathies of a scarcely intelligible nature had always existed between them"—[410]), she is, as he is, a figure of the imagination, who threatens to seduce and thus destroy the narrator. However, insofar as she resists Roderick and is his victim, she might seem to double the narrator.

Madeline unsettles the neat allegorical structure of this story in two ways. First of all, by alternately or simultaneously doubling *both* major characters, she disrupts the neat allegorical pattern, unpredictably and erratically disrupting the balanced opposition between reason and the imagination. She also introduces a second competing allegory. Madeline occupies the same ontological plane as her brother. Therefore, she represents, like him, a mental construct. Nonetheless, she figures the body, the desire for physical existence in this world. If Usher embodies the desire to escape material reality and to make the mind all the reality there is, Madeline, quite the contrary, images an equally cerebral will to physical survival. She embodies the desire simply to live, which means to preserve her existence in the world as a physical entity. In this way, Madeline replicates the narrator, who is, in some sense, the "house" of Usher and whose physical existence in the world is as much threatened by Usher as is Madeline's. But in order to represent the narrator, Madeline has to cross ontological barriers. In so doing, Madeline again disrupts the allegorical structure of the tale. She pierces the self-enclosure of allegory (its way of evading the question of its relation to the world, so that it is only words about words) by making the purely mental issue nothing less than the survival of the physical individual within the physical world.

In the second allegory, Madeline, like her twin brother, represents a mental construct, a feature of the narrator's mind. She does not, however, threaten his sanity (madness is not the issue here) so much as his relation to the world as such. Madeline, we might say, ups the ante. She shows us that what is at stake in the conflict between Roderick and the narrator is *not* simply whether we will perceive this world sanely or insanely, as a product of the imagination or of the reason—which may, in any case, be the same thing. Rather, the issue she raises is whether this world is an invention of the mind (sanely or insanely disposed, reasonable or fantastic) or is physical and fleshly—of the body and not of the mind at all. And if it is physical and real, then what is the mind's relation to it? And what are the consequences of this relation between mind and world?

Madeline, in other words, provides an antithesis both to the narrator and to her brother, whether the narrator represents reason and Roderick imagination or vice versa or whether both of them represent reason and/or insanity, i.e., the mind. Whereas the narrator (insofar as he is telling us this story) is physically real, occupying the same ontological plane as the reader, Madeline, like her twin, is pure fabrication, an idea. But Madeline, in contrast to her brother, does not image the desire to escape the world of matter into the world of mind. On the contrary, she reverses Usher's implication and moves in the opposite direction.

In so opposing both the narrator and Usher (even as she duplicates aspects of them), Madeline does more than provide an additional allegorical meaning for the story, which now seems to be about the conflict between the physical and the mental. Rather, she unsettles the allegorical structure of the story as such. Madeline's experience in Poe's story shows the allegorical relocation of reality into a world of words itself to be the problem. Such relocation in Poe's tale is tantamount to the death of the world, which, insofar as it contains the world of the mind, means also the annihilation of the mind.

The virtual undecidability of the end of the story—and the urgent necessity of deciding how to read it—crystallizes the issue raised by Madeline throughout the story. By the time Madeline comes to claim her brother, it matters very little whether imagination has triumphed over reason or vice versa. What looms large at the end, in the body of Madeline herself, is the struggle between the life force that she represents and the tendency toward murder, suicide, and death exemplified by both her brother and his accomplice, the narrator. In the internal world of the narrator's mind (or in the fictional reality created by this text) that battle seems to be decided in Madeline's favor: she is the one who (like Ligeia) returns from the grave, to vanquish what

Poe calls in that story the conqueror worm, death. The consequences of her triumph, however, are fatal, for as Madeline's
body/corpse (is Madeline dead or alive?) collapses in on her
brother's, she kills both of them as surely as her brother has
killed or tried to kill her.

In the final moments of the story, the triumph of life over
death becomes indistinguishable from the triumph of death over
life. This indistinguishability is replicated in the situation of the
narrator himself. We cannot say whether the narrator survives
the deaths of the Ushers and the collapse of the house or
whether he, too, yields. The narrator's would not be the first
voice Poe represented in his fiction as coming from beyond the
grave: "MS. Found in a Bottle" is one example of such a story.
And indeed, the collapse of the house does not augur well for
the narrator's survivability, since, insofar as he is the body containing the Ushers, he himself is that house. Though we cannot
decide whether imagination or reason triumphs, it does seem
fairly clear that death triumphs over life, even if the finality of
that death is held off until the moment following the actual conclusion of the text. Throughout the story the narrator has battled
to keep insanity and death at bay. In the end he is defeated by
both because he chose to pursue the course of imagination.

In other words, the end of the story dramatizes, through
Madeline, the way in which the retreat into the mind, into the
world of language and ideas, is itself suicidal and can result only
in death. Madeline deconstructs the flat, allegorical, self-reflexive
self-containedness of the story and makes manifest its implications for the real lives of real human beings in a real world.

The Power of Words

Before I bring forward the symbolic reading of Poe's story, which
dominated interpretations of Poe in the 1960s and '70s, let me
intensify even further the sense in which this story resists the
autonomy of allegory and (horribly, terrifyingly) breaks through
into the world as such. In the text itself, it is Madeline who
crosses ontological borders, producing both the emotional
impact of the story (its horror) and its intellectual message. In the
world of authors, texts, and readers, it is the reader who performs this function. For if, as the text seems to be claiming, the

world of words, which the text produces, is nothing less than fatal, than this text *as text* (whatever its story) is a very dangerous commodity, to say the least, and its victims will be its readers.

Of course, it is highly unlikely that any reader has ever died from reading Poe's story, though probably more than a few have been "scared to death." Still, the implications of its dangers are real and relevant. In fact, a major part of the action of the story concerns the telling of gothic tales of horror (such as this one) and its consequences. Poe images the status of his own text vis-à-vis the issue of the self-referentiality of language in the text within the text, "The Mad Trist of Sir Launcelot Canning." This story not only encapsulates features of Poe's own art but also dramatizes aspects of the reader-writer relationship, which break down the hermetic seal around the story's self-conscious self-reflexivity.

Here one must pause to note that, like "Usher," almost all of Poe's fictions are first-person narratives that address themselves directly and insistently to the reader. If "Usher" records the call of one character to another to save him from insanity (or the self-directed call of the individual to save himself), the story itself enacts this call as the narrator turns to the reader to perform much the same service. (Melville, as we shall see, will repeat this move quite closely in *Moby-Dick*.)

At first glance "The Mad Trist" might seem to be the final nail in the coffin of deadening, allegorical repetitions, which seem to constitute the frame narrative. The story itself is even more prosaic than "Usher." The events it records seem to have only a single, allegorical purpose (to parallel Madeline's escape from the coffin) but no intrinsic meaning. And yet this story, of which "there is little in its uncouth and unimaginative prolixity which could have had interest for the lofty and spiritual ideality of [Usher]" (413), is exactly the vehicle through which the unfathomable events of Madeline's escape from the tomb are made real, first for Usher, second (and more importantly) for the narrator, and finally and most importantly for the reader. As unimaginative and uncouth as the words of this story surely are, they reach out to its audience, in order to produce nothing less than a total transformation of that audience's perception of reality; indeed, of the reality itself:

> At the termination of this sentence I started, and for a moment, paused; for it appeared to me (although I at once concluded that my

excited fancy had deceived me)—it appeared to me that, from some very remote portion of the mansion, there came, indistinctly, to my ears, what might have been, in its exact similarity of character, the echo (but a stifled and dull one certainly) of the very cracking and ripping sound which Sir Launcelot had so particularly described. It was, beyond doubt, the coincidence alone which had arrested my attention; for, amid the rattling of the sashes of the casements, and the ordinary commingled noises of the still increasing storm, the sound, in itself, had nothing, surely, which should have interested or disturbed me. I continued the story. (414)

This process of correspondence between the words of the story and the events transpiring outside the narrator's door, with the narrator's disputing this correspondence and attempting to explain it away, continues through several phases, until, finally, Usher articulates for the narrator the convergence of text and action, and, the door being thrown open, reveals to the narrator the bodily resurrected Madeline:

'Not hear it?—yes, I hear it, and *have* heard it. Long—long—long— many minutes, many hours, many days, have I heard it—yet I dared not—oh, pity me, miserable wretch that I am!—I dared not—I *dared* not speak! *We have put her living in the tomb!* . . . And now—to-night— Ethelred—ha! ha!—the breaking of the hermit's door, and the death-cry of the dragon, and the clangor of the shield!—say, rather, the rending of her coffin, and the grating of the iron hinges of her prison, and her struggles within the coppered archway of the vault! . . . *Madman! I tell you that she now stands without the door!'*

As if in the superhuman energy of his utterance there had been found the potency of a spell—the huge antique panels to which the speaker pointed, threw slowly back, upon the instant, their ponderous and ebony jaws. It was the work of the rushing gust—but then without those doors there *did* stand the lofty and enshrouded figure of the lady Madeline of Usher. (416)

Throughout the final pages of the story, then, words are represented not simply as describing events but as producing them. Indeed, what Usher has been experiencing, in the days following the burial of Madeline, are the sounds of her escape. Her emergence in the room, in fact, is first represented more as the uttering of a word than as a solid event: a rushing gust proceeding through the jaws. The story of Ethelred translates the story of

Madeline into terms that recover the link between the word and the world and bring the word once again to bear upon the world.

The words of Poe's story—both the frame text and the internal text—function in a similar way. Insofar as they shock and horrify the reader, they reach out of the world of words on the page (in the text as in the tomb) and, like a gush of air, rush into ours. Of course, ours is also a world of words. But it is also a world of feeling and response, a world of at least as much phenomenal substance as we are.

"The Fall of the House of Usher" is a horror story. It frightens us in direct proportion to the degree to which its argument is not purely intellectual. It uses language, therefore, not to produce other words but to produce something that is exactly not verbal or intellectual. This something is emotional, even, perhaps insofar as fear produces physiological consequences, physical. The moment that the tale exceeds the world of the house of Usher, the world of words, which is purely a mental construct (whether of Poe's or of the narrator's), it takes on the consciousness of the physical world, of the world outside language, which has been excluded from this world. The death of Madeline, her resurrection, and her murderous and suicidal redeath convert the stakes of the language game from a matter of play to one of life and death. She warns the reader that on our ability to penetrate the allegorical veil that language throws up between us and the world depends the very existence of that world and of ourselves.

Like Madeline the reader is outside the dynamics of the narrator-Usher dyad; the reader is only the instrument through which the story proceeds, outside the action of the story proper. But like Madeline, and like the house, which is also a counterpart of Madeline as it is of the narrator, the reader is the direct object of the story's aggression. Mind-boggling, the story threatens to do just that: boggle the mind, to tie it down and annihilate it in a welter of indecipherable, undecidable evidences. Can the reader resist the story's pull into deadening allegorical repetition? That is, can the reader refuse the world of purely linguistic construct that Usher and the narrator represent? Can the reader be scared, not to death (either literally or symbolically) but back to the life of language, world, and emotion, out of which Usher and the narrator (as either allegorical figures or symbolic ones) have escaped?

Symbolism and the Indeterminate Text

The symbolic reading of Poe, as exemplified by major studies in the field by Edward Davidson, Allen Tate, and Richard Wilbur, recognizes the degree to which the mind and the world are intertwined in Poe's conception of language. Nonetheless, in imagining Poe's world (either intellectual or physical or as the symbolic reconstitution of the two) as unified, as bringing together (potentially at least), within language itself, sets of dualisms—such as body versus mind, reason versus imagination, sanity versus insanity, and so on—the symbolic reading gets stuck at the same point of undecidability at the end of the story that also snags the allegorical reading. For the end of this story seems as deadly in the symbolic reading as in the allegorical one.

Let me give the symbolic reading its full play. In this reading "The Fall of the House of Usher" is about reconciliation or reunion, as warring and apparently irreconcilable alternatives of mind and consciousness (madness and reason, in one line of the story's thinking, or a desire for death and a desire for life in the other) are thought back into wholeness, in language, either by the mind of the narrator or by the mind of the author. The story, in other words, seems to be about dualisms that have to be reconciled into unities, if not within the physical world then within the linguistic one. This is true both in the external drama involving three characters, all of whom enjoy the same ontological reality within the story—which is, of course, the projection of the author's imagination—and in the internal drama within the narrator's mind (which replicates the situation of the writer: i.e., Poe is to the narrator and the Ushers as the narrator is to the Ushers). In all of these dramas, as they cut across and complicate each other, the individual must integrate opposing principles, reason and imagination, mind and body, world and self.

Of prime importance to this reading of Poe is his *Eureka,* a "prose-poem" or "romance," as he calls it, published the year before his death. In *Eureka* Poe puts forward his theory of the origins of the universe. In this neo-Platonic cosmology, the physical universe is a materialization and fragmentation of the original idea (which existed in immaterial and undifferentiated form in the mind of God) with which the universe began. Human beings represent a part of this fragmentation and materialization of the cosmos. Simultaneously, however, they contain large elements of the original divine unity. As such, human beings are able to think the world back to immaterial unity again and, through language, to reconstitute it, albeit imperfectly and temporarily.

For the symbol critics, the plots of most Poe stories and much of their imagery tell this essential drama of the disunification, fragmentation, and materialization of the originating idea, the torturous consequences of this process, and finally, in the stories' concluding epiphanies, the moment when the human mind, through language, reconstructs the lost idea or ideal. Thus, in "The Fall of the House of Usher," Roderick and Madeline (as identical twins) or the narrator and the Ushers (as aspects of each other) represent fragments of a once shared unity. The plot of the story, then, records the effects of disunity, moving toward a reunion that reconstitutes the unity before creation—before birth (in the case of the twins) or at least before adulthood (in the case of the Ushers and the narrator; the narrator and Usher, recall, are childhood friends). This narrative structure is reproduced within the textual imagery, for example in the depiction of the house itself. Facelike, the house is scored by a "fissure . . . extending from the roof of the building in front [and making] its way down the wall in a zigzag direction, until it became lost in the sullen waters of the tarn" (400), which, we are told earlier in the description, produced a "remodelled and inverted" (398) image of the house. In the final moments, the house splits along this line of division only to merge with its image in the tarn, reconstituting unity in the moment of destruction.

This idea of division and reunification can be made to explain as well the relation between the two primary stories that "Usher" seems to enact—the first concerning the three characters (the Ushers in relation to each other and in relation to the narrator), the second concerning the Ushers as mental constructs of the narrator. As the narrator moves out of harmony with his internal projections of himself and his world (i.e., his imagination) he suffers the wrenching effects of psychological and emotional disintegration. By recommitting himself to the world of the mind, however (by reentering the house of Usher, as it were), he reintegrates the warring components of self, achieving—at least temporarily—the wholeness and integrity he has lost. This process is doubled in the dramas of the divided Ushers, who are reunited moments before the narrator's reunion with them.

Indeed, it may be that what makes possible the narrator's escape from the literal devastation of the house at the end, thus saving him from the Ushers' fate, is the drama that he there witnessed. In this case, whether the story involves three characters or only one, the experience of the Ushers (as a real, witnessed event or as an internal, psychological process) serves as a warning to the narrator. It provides him with a lesson essential to his physical and/or psychological survival. Either because he witnesses through the Ushers' drama the consequences of the separation of mind from body or because he experiences this separation internally, the narrator recognizes the need for unity. He also, however, comes to recognize the consequences of literal as opposed to symbolic reunification. Therefore, the narrator only thinks back together again, in his own mind, the warring components that threaten to destroy each other and thus himself.

Though the narrator, at the end of the tale, is tottering on the brink of an abyss, he will not, in this reading of the story, fall into it. He has discovered, for the moment at any rate, the unity that transcends fragmentation and that offers at least a temporary stay against its implications—the unity achieved in language, in the reproduction of the mind's world as text. Hence the final words of the story reproduce its title, with the significant omission of the word *Fall*. The "House of Usher" survives—not merely as text (the text, after all, is "The Fall of the House of Usher") but even more importantly as a figure for the narrator or author, who survives because of the mind's ability to translate reality into idea and experience it where its implications are purely verbal, intellectual.

Of course, the problem with this reading is that, as I have already suggested, it is not at all clear that the narrator survives the end of the story, or, if he does, for how long. The symbolic reading of the story excels over the allegorical reading in that it acknowledges that the stakes in the story are nothing less than our life in the world. Still, it provides no reassurance that the symbolic relocation of the world in the text will in any way save us from the story's implications. Indeed, it suggests that to find the place where mind and world intersect, in language, is to ensure the ultimately self-annihilating collapse of world and mind both.

Thus, another story, "The Mad Trist," precipitates the tragic events of the story's finale, while the house itself is not spared the deaths of its inhabitants. These features of "The Fall" are related to, or perhaps are the consequence of, another, more fundamental problem with the symbolic reading, which is that the dualisms or oppositions of which the story seems to consist do not at all line up with each other to form a single coherent or unified bifurcation or division. I have already suggested that Madeline resists consolidation to the allegorical reading of the story, making the issue between the narrator and Usher nothing less than the difference between life and death, reality and unreality. Madeline also, however, disturbs the unity of the text so necessary to the symbolic reading, for however much Madeline duplicates one or another force of division in the story, she also duplicates its opposite.

Thus Madeline is both sanity and madness, reason and imagination, the mind of the world and the world of the mind. And as she slips and slides, she makes it impossible to stabilize a set of oppositions that the story might be thought to reconcile. In the symbolic reading, as in the allegorical one, Madeline, even as she is rendered an image or symbol or construct by the story, seems to resist the process of intellectualization itself, reminding the reader that there is no place of language outside the physical universe that can survive language's dematerialization of the world.

The Death of a Beautiful Woman

To read the story symbolically is not to read it allegorically. Unlike the allegorical reading, the symbolic reading insists on a relationship between the world and the words that we use to analyze and experience that world. The symbolic interpretation, as Feidelson suggests, posits a place of intercourse between the world and the mind, in language. Yet if we return to the end of the story and ask again the question whether the narrator lives or dies, we realize the limitations of the symbolic reading. For the place of the symbolic where reality and mind intersect no more guarantees the survival of the individual than does the allegorical evasion of this place, our divorcing the world from the mind and making fiction the place of language in disrelation to the world. Nor do we know anything more about where this place of intersection is than if we had decided either that it does not exist or that we have no means of verifying its existence.

The story, then, does not answer yes to the questions, Does the world exist, and can I know it? Nor does the story evade these questions. Rather, it explores the consequences of both answering and evading the question of knowledge. If we think of symbolism as an X, positing a point of intersection between mind and world in language, and allegory as a set of parallel planes, one the world, one the mind, where there is no necessary relation between the two and neither can verify the other (though each, as it were, can verify itself), then Poe's "House" constructs a box or house, which figures a bipartite, material-spiritual universe itself, in which sets of parallel planes touch each other at infinity, i.e., at their imaginary limits. One can assign different names to the parallel planes, such as reason and imagination or mind and world. But without the cross filaments linking them to each other and to the other pairs of parallel planes, they vanish, taking with them the space of human thought and action: the world itself.

This world—the place of matter and action, thinking and living—is imaged for Poe, not accidentally, as the physical woman, who has been excluded from the house of masculinist (abstract, intellectual) construction or, more precisely, buried alive in it. Madeline's gender is important in this story, for to talk about life (in the middle of this tale of death) is also to talk about home and family (in the middle of this house of Usher that ushers in no home, no family). "The stem of the Usher race," we are told,

> had put forth, at no period, any enduring branch; in other words, . . . the entire family lay in the direct line of descent, and had always, with very trifling and very temporary variation, so lain. It was this deficiency, . . . perhaps, of collateral issue, and the consequent undeviating transmission, from sire to son, of the patrimony with the name, which had, at length, so identified the two as to merge the original title of the estate in the quaint and equivocal appellation of the 'House of Usher'—an appellation which seemed to include, in the minds of the peasantry who used it, both the family and the family mansion. (399)

The death of Madeline, Usher's "sole companion for long years, his last and only relative on earth," "would leave him," he tells the narrator, "'the last of the ancient race of the Ushers'" (404).

If nothing else, this passage suggests the way in which "The Fall of the House of Usher," like several other of Poe's female-related stories ("Ligeia," "Morella," "Berenice," "Eleanora," and perhaps even "The Purloined Letter"), may contain an important sociopolitical critique of patriarchal culture. But the passage, I contend, goes even further than this. It suggests the way in which, in Poe's view, a certain poetics of the intellect precludes and destroys the possibility of home and family, which depend upon the physical (as much as the intellectual) relations between men and women. Whether "The Fall of the House of Usher" symbolizes reunification or death or whether it unsettles such fantasies of symbolic wholeness, allegorizing instead a world of endlessly shifting words, there is no place in this house for a home. And, therefore, as procreativity is sacrificed to a purely mental creativity, the house collapses, producing no one and nothing—except horror—in its wake. When William Faulkner later sets out to tell the story of slavery, racism, and the American South, he will remember Poe and redirect this moment of the end of history to very precise sociopolitical and historical ends.

Poe's idea of the mind's infatuation with itself as an end to human intercourse is even more powerfully set forth in "Ligeia." "Ligeia" differs from "The Fall of the House of Usher" in that it dispenses with the doubling of the male narrator. Instead, it dwells upon the single all-defining male consciousness that, Usherlike, either passively, painfully, suffers the death of its female counterpart or actively kills her off, only to discover that without her he cannot survive. The plot of "Ligeia" is also susceptible to symbolic and allegorical interpretations. In the first, we have a narrator who was once in perfect unity with his Ligeia, who, as something between a mother, a wife, and a version of self, represented knowledge, beauty, power, and psychological wholeness. But Ligeia dies, and the narrator, as a consequence, suffers severe psychological and physical disorientation, not so very different from what afflicts Usher. In this story, however, the bereaved husband (as in "Eleanora" and "Berenice") marries again, a woman of the more purely earthly world who represents none of the things that Ligeia represented (in "Morella" the plot is somewhat different, with Morella's daughter representing the new relationship with the flesh that the narrator establishes). Through his new wife, Rowena, the narrator conjures his lost love, Ligeia.

But, as in "Usher," the implications of completion and unity are not so simple. Like the conclusion to "Usher," the climax of

"Ligeia" yields to multiply antithetical readings. On the one hand, it may be that, having successfully caused Ligeia to reemerge through Rowena, the narrator restores the unity and harmony he has lost (if only momentarily). He does this by destroying the material world (represented by Rowena) and permitting the spiritual world (Ligeia) unencumbered existence. Or it may be that, having resurrected Ligeia, he realizes that unity is death; by thinking together the material/spiritual in Rowena/Ligeia he collapses the difference between them and makes the world disappear. In thus allowing the spiritual to exist at the price of the material, he produces a reality that is only death. It could be, too, that the narrator only hallucinates Ligeia's reemergence. This in turn may exemplify the narrator's final surrender to insanity. Or, insofar as Ligeia's return would (if literally enacted) represent the triumph of her will over death and thus the destruction of the material world, it may be that his only hallucinating her return preserves the natural world and thus saves the narrator, even in his insanity, from Ligeia's triumph.

Like "Usher," "Ligeia" both lends itself to unified readings and resists such readings. One might even go so far as to say that these stories resist reading itself: it is not only the narrator who is shaken to his foundations at the end of these fictions but the reader who also experiences the horror that, as Poe tells us in "The Conqueror Worm," is the soul of the plot. In both works, Poe unsettles symbolic and allegorical assumptions both, the tale reaching out of its world of words into the world of the reader.

Just as one can reintegrate Madeline into her story, so one can reintegrate Ligeia into hers, the story coming either to symbolize something like the indissoluability of the male-female bond or to deconstruct the idea of the essential difference between male and female. But, as I suggested in relation to "Usher," the woman, in these stories, is multiply disruptive. She disturbs not only the separable symbolic and/or allegorical readings but the ideas of symbolism and allegory themselves. The Ligeia/Rowena who emerges at the end of this story is no more a woman than is either Ligeia or Rowena separately. She is, like each of them, a construct of the male imagination as it alternately fantasizes the woman as the perfect elimination of all earthly embodiment (the idealized Ligeia of the opening pages of the story) and as the perfect embodiment of all material restriction (Rowena). One might even say that the woman (whether as an essential way of being in the world or as a mere indicator of gender difference) is that which exists nowhere in the world of Poe's fiction, that no matter how hard his narrators try to get her right, she resists the efforts of the male imagination to reconstruct the world on its own terms. Madeline Usher and Ligeia and even the royal personage in "The Purloined Letter" exist outside the telling of the story, coming in only as vehicles through which male narrators (and/or protagonists and/or consciousnesses) attempt, and fail, to clarify their own meanings.

Here we do well to expand the frame around this story to its fullest, to include Poe the author as well as each of his created narrators. I have already suggested that a "literal" reading, in which each of the characters possesses equal quotidian realness, yields one kind of interpretation; a reading that makes the narrator the only real person and all of the other characters figments of his imagination produces another kind of interpretation. By recognizing beyond the text the author Poe and by imagining the text as a language field in which all of the characters are equally and simultaneously real and purely verbiage, we are in a position to press the text even further for its self-consciously literary meaning. Whether as a rather uncontrolled projection of authorial consciousness (Poe's own fantasy or hallucination) or as a willed piece of writing (whether or not all of the elements of the text fully obey the writer's will), Poe's fiction seems to have to do with the relationship between language and the mind—the way in which the mind, whether it wants to or not, expresses itself in words at the same time as, no matter how hard it tries, it fails wholly to express one meaning or another.

Poe's women are crucial here. Try as he may to incorporate them within the economy of his fiction, they inevitably wrestle loose. Like Madeline's or Ligeia's coming to reclaim the man in her life, the female spirit, in Poe's fiction, in a kind of return of the repressed, arrives at the end, in the form of the reader, to reclaim the text. Whatever the intellectual argument of Poe's tales (whether an affirmation of transcendent unity or its denial), Madeline and Ligeia determine the emotional impact of the tales. That emotional impact is what stays, long after the intellectual apparatus of the story has faded from view. The reader can no more escape it than can the narrators within the stories Poe tells.

In the final analysis, the reader of Poe's fiction (very possibly unlike his narrators, whose fate is hardly guaranteed, and more, instead, like his female protagonists) remains to decide what the story will signify. Like Hawthorne's narrator in "The Custom-House" sketch, which prefaces *The Scarlet Letter*, and like Melville's Ishmael in *Moby-Dick*, Poe's fiction directly addresses itself to the reader. This call (like Usher's summons to the narrator) brings us into treacherous terrain. It also, however, affords us the opportunity to witness, first-hand, the dynamics of a universe in which we are always already implicated in the dissolution of individual consciousness and control but also always already in a position to pull back and escape. Like "The Mad Trist," which the narrator reads to Usher in order simultaneously to distract him from his madness and to ensure its ultimate triumph, so Poe's stories self-consciously force us to the brink of consciousness and language in order to enable us to experience and articulate for ourselves the shifting dimensions of an inexpressibly unknowable world.

And yet this horror, insofar as it is a horror of the barrenness and sterility produced by our self-abandonment in a world of words, cuts through the mental construct of this world. It bares the exclusion of the physical, which is also to say of the feminine. It reveals the house to be empty. And it suggests that, are we ever to cut through the soul of this plot, we will have to abandon the segregation of world from text. Though Poe himself never dramatizes the reentry of the self into the world, except to record how the self destroys the world and is destroyed by it, Hawthorne, in such romances as *The Scarlet Letter*, does. Not accidentally, this is a story about a woman, who is also a mother.

The Impulse to Self-Destruction and Philosophical Skepticism

Before I turn to Hawthorne's great masterpiece of romance fiction, let me trace one final aspect of Poe's writing that defines his special place within the romance tradition. This pattern exists within the group of stories I have already discussed. It is even more prominent in another group of stories, which one might want to label Poe's tales of self-destruction. This group includes "The Imp of the Perverse," "The Tell-Tale Heart," "The Black Cat," and "William Wilson." The essential plot of these tales has to do with a narrator who either wantonly or senselessly kills someone (often someone he loves), gets away with the murder, and then (perversely, to pick up Poe's term in "The Imp of the Perverse") confesses to the crime and is punished.

How are we to understand these strange narratives of crime and confession, which flesh out an element of so many of Poe's stories—the self divided against itself, luring itself into endless enactments of self-destruction? Stanley Cavell, in an essay comparing Poe with Ralph Waldo Emerson, suggests that "The Imp of the Perverse" (and the other tales in the group) acts out a form of philosophical skepticism that substitutes for Descartes' "I think, therefore I am" formula (the formula that Emerson, in Cavell's view, adapts in his writing) the proof "I am killed, therefore I was."[7] The stories, we might say, proceed as follows: the isolated individual (like so many of Poe's narrators) attempts to prove his existence, and the existence of the world, by striking out against the world. He kills some other person in a desperate attempt to have some concrete effect on the world outside himself, so as to make certain that the world outside exists. In fact, he kills someone close to him—the beloved old man in "The Tell-Tale Heart"; the cat and then the wife in "The Black Cat"—as if the emotions of sympathy and love that define his relationship to the other threaten to dissolve his individual, private self. By killing the other, the narrator is also winning back or preserving his unique identity. But, having killed the other, the narrator discovers that striking out against the world can in no way assure one that the world exists, since the drama of murder may, like any action (benevolent or violent), be one more figment of one's own, isolated imagination. The narrator then confesses his deed, in order to create a witness who might thereby verify both the existence of a world outside the self and the existence of the self itself. The cost of such proof, however, is the destruction of the self, for having confessed the crime of murder, the individual is sentenced to hang.

In such a reading of these stories, Poe's fiction becomes skepticist in a deeply emotional way. The texts do more than play with the boundaries between self and other, text and world. They imagine the consequences of the dissolution of these boundaries. They record the experience of realizing the dream of nonexistence, which becomes nothing less than the nightmare of skepticism. Is it possible to explore the issue of knowing without yielding to the terrifying possibility of self-dissolution? Is it, indeed, possible to give the skepticist reading of the world its full range of significance and yet reaffirm the existence of the world and of a self that is committed to a life in that world? In *The Scarlet Letter*, Hawthorne's great romance of history (and of family and community), Hawthorne, following Emerson, does just this. Let me turn now to that novel.

Chapter 4

THE ROMANCE OF HISTORY:
NATHANIEL HAWTHORNE'S
SCARLET LETTER

In *The Fictive and the Imaginary: Charting a Literary Anthropology,* Wolfgang Iser understands the act of literary production as an effort at self-knowledge. Through fiction, human beings cross ontological boundaries to gain a perspective outside the self from which the self can be brought into view as an object of its own perception.[1] Poe's fiction can be understood as dramatizing and exploring such boundary crossing, where the border crossed is disastrously forgotten or canceled out. Poe does not dissolve the boundaries between the material and the ideal or between the self and the other in order to escape the limitations of a fragmented material world—as it might at first appear. Rather, he dissolves these boundaries to expose the ultimately self-destructive human desire for such impossible transcendent and boundless existence. In so doing, he also demonstrates how language, while relocating the terms of the human dilemma from the apparently external world of physical barriers and restraints to a more malleable linguistic one, in no way avoids the problems posed by the skepticist question.

As the narrators of "The Imp of the Perverse," "The Tell-Tale Heart," and "The Black Cat" discover, too late, to confess may prove one's existence and one's relation to the world only at the cost of self-extinction. In these stories, the self is destroyed with the same finality as it is by the retreat into the linguistic realm, dramatized in other Poe stories such as "The Fall of the House of Usher" and "Ligeia." Poe's is a damned-if-you-do, damned-if-you-don't and damned-if-you-say, damned-if-you-don't-say world, in which extremes of self-assertion and self-destruction fold onto each other, producing the only kind of certainty there is—the certainty of death.

Though Poe's response to the skeptical dilemma might seem one more proof of the extreme fragility of Poe's sanity (which has always seemed questionable), it is possible to read in Poe a considerably rational response to 19th-century American transcendentalism, at least as it was articulated by its most important spokesperson, Ralph Waldo Emerson. Poe's stories of self-destruction and self-dissolution often seem direct glosses on Emerson: for example, on the famous image in *Nature*—the transparent eyeball. Though Emerson seems to intend this image to capture a moment of epiphanic unity of self and other, it nonetheless verges on the grotesque as the self disappears, leaving behind only a large and grossly overmaterialized eyeball. Is this eye, when one thinks about it or when one tries to imagine it, any less terrifying than the eyes of Ligeia that peer out through the sockets of the resurrected Rowena? Is it any less a provocation to fear and terror than the single remaining eye of the cat in "The Black Cat" or of the old man in "The Tell-Tale Heart"?

Stanley Cavell has argued that Emerson himself in his writing did not intend a transcendental stance outside of or in defiance of the world but a dialectics of presence and absence, self and other, individual and community. Far from turning away from the world in order to discover his own ineffable essence, Emerson, according to Cavell, used himself, and in particular his writing, as the instrument through which he discovered his relatedness to the world and to other people. Emerson, Cavell maintains, takes on the challenge of skepticism. When he writes in the essay "Self-Reliance" that "[m]an is timid and apologetic; he is no longer upright; he dares not say 'I think,' 'I am,' but quotes some saint or sage," he intends nothing less than an allusion to Descartes. Descartes's famous statement, popularly reproduced as "I think, therefore I am," corresponds quite closely to Emerson's rendering of it: "*I am, I exist* is necessarily true every time that I pronounce it or conceive it in my mind" (1989, 106–7).

In Cavell's reading, pronouncing or conceiving identity is for Emerson a primary objective of writing. In this sense, Poe and Emerson are very similar writers. The difference between them, however, is nothing less than definitive. For Poe the cost of self-conception is self-destruction. For Emerson it is possible not only to maintain or preserve the self in its self-conceiving but to convert the self into a medium of communal affirmation. It is possible, in other words, to use self-conceiving and boundary-crossing as a way of forging a relationship between the self and the world.

For Emerson, language is not the place where the skeptical situation repeats itself, endlessly (deconstructively) to reassert the impossibility of knowing. Rather, writing is the instrument through which a relationship of selves and others, framed by skepticism and characterized by acts of acknowledgment and affirmation, establishes itself. Cavell identifies this quality of writing as part of the aversive strategy of Emerson's thinking:

> The relation of Emerson's writing (the expression of his self-reliance) to his society (the realm of what he calls conformity) is one, as "Self-Reliance" puts it, of mutual aversion: "Self-reliance is the aversion of conformity." Naturally Emerson's critics take this to mean roughly that he is disgusted with society and wants no more to do with it. But "Self-reliance is the aversion of conformity" figures each side in terms of the other, declares the issue between them as always joined, never settled. But then this is to say that Emerson's writing and his society are in any unending argument with one another—that is to say, he writes in such a way as to *place* his writing in his unending argument (such is his loyal opposition)—an unending turning away from one another . . . hence endlessly a turning *toward* one another.[2]

This turning away that is also a turning toward and the affirmation that emerges through doubt characterize as well the achievement of Nathaniel Hawthorne. They distinguish Hawthorne's brand of romance fiction from Poe's. In *The Scarlet Letter*, which contains some very specific allusions to Poe's fiction (including to "The Purloined Letter" and "The Imp of the Perverse") and which shares both the self-consciousness of Poe's (and Cooper's) fiction and its self-reflexivity, Hawthorne discovers an aversive mode of writing that has direct implications for the continuity of the romance tradition into the 19th century, specifically in Henry James but also in some of the 20th-century women romancers, such as Flannery O'Connor, Toni Morrison, and Grace Paley.[3] Among the many other meanings that one might ascribe to the scarlet letter A, aversion seems to me another salient valence of its signification.

The World as Text

The title of Hawthorne's novel (reminiscent of Poe's "The Purloined Letter") could not more self-consciously or self-reflexively point to the subject of language as a primary issue in this text. A major feature of the story is the competition for control over the meaning of the letter. And while most readers clearly prefer Hester's artful embroidery of the A to the Puritans' rigid and fanatical, punitive and literalistic use of it, it is by no means clear whose interpretation of the letter triumphs in the end.

In order to understand what the Puritans mean by the A— which is to say as well what they mean by branding Hester with the letter—it is necessary to recover some of the historical backgrounds of Hawthorne's text. Hawthorne clearly places his story in time and place, however allegorically or symbolically. The references in the opening chapter to Isaac Johnson and Ann Hutchinson, as well as the general references to Puritanism's establishment of itself in the New World, would almost seem to make this more an historical narrative than a romance fiction. And, in fact, historical knowledge of the Puritans is, as I have just suggested, imperative to adequately interpreting this text.

But no sooner than one has noted the historical frame of the novel than one has to concede how very ahistorical, allegorical, and symbolic these references to the past are. The prison and the cemetery are less particular places than lightly veiled metaphors for sin and death. The rose bush and the world of nature that the rose bush figures forth may represent antitheses to such sin and death, but they are no less a part of the text's allegorical unfolding. The characters who people this world (Hester, Dimmesdale, Chillingworth, and Pearl) and the events that punctuate the plot (letters in the sky and letters on people's bodies) further emphasize the nonrealistic strategy of the text. At the very least this novel seems (like Poe's fiction) to have more to do with the inner workings of the human psyche (Dimmesdale's guilt, Chillingworth's vengefulness, Hester's pride, Pearl's innocence) than with the historical facts of a concrete sociopolitical place. Early reviews of the book, as well as many later interpretations, understood the work in just these psychological or moral terms.

Furthermore, the story is clearly concerned with itself as text. As Hawthorne nears the end of the very short opening chapter, he accomplishes a blurring of the distinctions between world and text not so very different from what Poe achieves in many of his fictions. "Finding [the rose bush] so directly on the threshold of our narrative," writes the narrator, "which is now about to issue from that inauspicious portal, we could hardly do otherwise than pluck one of its flowers and present it to the reader" (48). Hawthorne's narrative does not so much refer to a rose bush that exists outside it, in the real world, as it creates a rose bush to occupy the same epistemological field as the text itself. The portal and threshold of the world are indistinguishable from the portal and threshold of the narrative—recalling the "jaws" in Poe's "Fall of the House of Usher," which are both doors within the tale but also the mouth of the narrator and author, which is to say the "jaws" of the story itself.

When Hawthorne's narrator, therefore, plucks one of the roses and presents it to the reader, he is offering nothing more, though also nothing less, than his own words. The narrator's reaching out of the text to the reader replicates the collapse of the distance between external reality and text: just as the "rose" as object is drawn into and made inseparable from the "rose" as word, so the reader, who receives this word, is drawn back by the word into the text, to become one more element in the linguistic universe that the work is constructing. To note such boundary-crossing is not, of course, to decide whether such a crossing of thresholds and collapsing of borders is what the text is endorsing or problematizing or even rejecting. It is, however, to suggest that a feature of this text is its recognition of the possibility that there is no world outside the text, no world that is not mediated by words. And yet the historical facts remain. How does one understand the relationship in this opening chapter between these historical, social, and natural references and the allegorical, symbolic strategy of the text? Might there be an intrinsic connection between Puritan history and the text's formal representation of that history?

One possible way of understanding the relationship between the explicit historical allusions and the literary structure is to imagine Hawthorne's subject as something like historical consciousness itself. The historical world, Hawthorne suggests, is as real and authentic a world as any that exists. And yet we know this world only through the story of the past. The possibility that the romance raises is that our access to contemporary reality is no less mediated by the narrativizing, fictionalizing imagination. Yet, reality, the book suggests, may be no less real for that mediation. By rendering the historical world allegorical Hawthorne accomplishes a double purpose. He enforces the idea (fundamental to Cooper and Poe as well) that there is no knowledge of reality except what the mind produces. But, more in the mode of Cooper and, later, James, he also insists that the mind's intervention does not necessarily mean that we can answer the question of knowledge in the negative, that, no, we can never know the world or (even more problematical) that the world, because it is unknowable, for all intents and purposes does not exist.[4] In reading the story as preserving the skeptical question, the specific historical setting of the romance is less important than the fact that the book is historical fiction. The work's romance argument is an argument about historicity, about our consciousness of reality, past and present.

But Hawthorne's purposes do not stop here, and the particular world in American history that the book conjures forth matters very much. For the Puritans the world of the human and the natural, on the one hand, and, on the other, the world of God are completely incommensurate and separate realms. Nor is there any doubt in the Puritan mind as to which of these realms is fallen, which sacred. But the world of the human and natural, they believed, however fallen, inevitably pointed to the realm of God. It was nothing less than a reflection or embodiment of divine meanings. One might even say that, for the Puritans, the world existed for no other purpose than to communicate divine meanings; it was merely the theater in which divine purposes might be played out. (In many ways, though with significant variations, Poe's cosmology in *Eureka* is very close to the Puritan theology I have just outlined.)

Furthermore, the scenario of life, for the Puritans, enacted in this symbolically arrayed universe had a clear plot. Following very closely the premises of Calvinistic Christianity, the Puritans understood human-divine history to have consisted of three major events: the fall of humankind in the garden of Eden, which left all human beings depraved and in a state of sin; the temporary covenanting of God with humanity on new terms, first through Abraham and then through Moses; and, last, the final redemption of humankind through the covenant of grace, which God instituted through the death and resurrection of Christ, His son. For the Puritans, as for the Calvinists, the covenant of grace was an absolute, nonnegotiable convenant, in which God decided who was to be saved and who not; it was a covenant made from the beginning of time to the end of time, and human beings could in no way affect or alter it.

This theology of the covenant of grace was a primary feature of American Puritanism, as it was of British Puritanism and of Protestantism in general. For this reason, the Puritans, like the Protestants during the Reformation, objected to the Roman Catholic conception of a church, in which a powerful figure like the Pope served as the central authority (with lesser authorities arrayed in hierarchical descent) and in which any and all who sought church membership were admitted into the church. For the Puritans the church had to be, as nearly as possible, a reflection of the covenant of grace. That is, it had to consist primarily, if not exclusively, of those individuals to whom God had decided to bestow grace. Of course, how human beings were to know whether they or other human beings were saved was hardly a simple matter. Roman Catholicism had opened church membership to the masses because the Church perceived such discriminations impossible to make. But for a variety of historical reasons, the Puritans, especially after their arrival in the New World, began to evolve a theology in which such discoveries of saintedness were rendered possible.[5]

In the American colonies, Puritanism evolved in the direction not only of making the church covenant synonymous with the covenant of grace but, even more astonishingly, of producing a society that would also reflect or even replicate both of these more primary covenants. Fundamental to this project of what was called federal theology was the idea of visible sanctity—that the inner sanctity, the savedness or saintedness, of an individual could be made visible, and that on the basis of such visible evidence of the soul's salvation, one could construct not only a church but a state.

In this context, I think, not only Hawthorne's strategy of representation in this book but also the Puritans' (and perhaps even Hawthorne's) use of the A become clearer. For the Puritans the human and natural world was intrinsically symbolic. It figured forth the history of the human-divine relationship and the condition of the individual soul. When the Puritans brand Hester with the A, they do so because they believe that the letter, which for them stands for one thing and one thing only—adultery—correctly and absolutely labels Hester. She is an adulteress. She is a sinner. Furthermore, it is essential for the proper functioning of Puritan society that Hester's sin be publicized in this manner. Since the Puritans' federal compact was to include only those who were saved, it was of vital importance to identify and exclude those individuals who were not saved.

Hester's crime is particularly troubling to the Puritan community for two reasons. First, Hester herself, once presumably a member of the community in good standing or, at least, an immigrant to the New World on her way to becoming such a member of the community, now raises problems about the accuracy of the Church's determinations concerning who should or should not be within the body politic. Second, in producing an illegitimate offspring, she raises similarly distressing questions about her daughter, and, perhaps even more disturbing, about the unknown, unidentified father of her child. Somewhere in Salem, the colony's elders know, there is another adulterer, whom the community may be presuming to be a saint but who might be, in fact, no less a sinner than Hester. That this sinner should be none other than the community's own minister is one of the great ironies of the book.

Hawthorne's strategy, then, might be understood as simultaneously representing and subverting the Puritans' way of perceiving the world. Hawthorne, we might say, writes an anti-allegorical allegory or an antisymbolic symbolic text. He exposes the ways in which methodologies such as the Puritans' pretend to harmonies and unities of meaning that do not actually exist and make claims to knowledge to which human beings cannot actually acceed. He reveals as well the cruelty to which such philosophies of natural and divine correspondence might lead. But Hawthorne does not intend this critique to relate only to Puritan society. In focusing the problem of visible sanctity on the issue of adultery, Hawthorne also suggests the way in which the rigidity and authoritarianism of the Puritans exemplify a more generalizable human tendency. In a sense, the doctrine of visible sanctity and the federal covenant that it produced are responses to the old question of knowledge. The Puritans, Hawthorne suggests, would settle and resolve all doubts concerning everything from what events mean to the essential condition of an individual human soul. By branding Hester with the A, the Puritans declare that they do know and that they can unequivocally represent what they know.

For this reason, perhaps, the elders of the community prefer to stigmatize Hester rather than execute her or expel her from the community—both of which are legal options. So long as she remains within the community, Hester serves as a confirmation of their certainty. She testifies to the possibility of knowing and naming. "'A wise sentence!'" remarks Chillingworth. "'Thus she will be a living sermon against sin. . . . It irks me, nevertheless, that the partner of her iniquity should not, at least, stand on the scaffold by her side. But he will be known!—he will be known!— he will be known!'" (63). But as testimony to the certainty produced by naming, and as the adulterous mother whose illegitimate child is the cause of that naming, Hester also suggests how this desire for knowledge characterizes not only the Puritan patriarchy but patriarchal societies in general. The terms of human reproduction, Hawthorne understands, in which a man's knowledge of his biological link to his children can never absolutely be affirmed, necessitates a system (a system of monogomous marriage, for example, which restricts the woman's access to sexual relations with other men) in which the male can attain as closely as possible the certainty that his children are his own.[6]

In exposing the presumption and cruelty of the Puritans' A, Hawthorne, then, is also providing a critique of patriarchal culture. Women, Hawthorne suggests, introduce doubt into human history. Men try to reduce, if not eliminate, that doubt through various institutions (like marriage), which restrict the woman's freedom. The consequence of this male effort to achieve certainty and knowledge is, as Hawthorne presents it, nothing short of punishing the woman and her children. The letter A, as its place of origin in the Custom-house would suggest, stands in Hawthorne's novel in condemnation of Puritan patriarchy as surely as the Puritans' A stands in condemnation of Hester.

Is there any difference between Hawthorne's A and the Puritans' aside from whom or what they condemn? In other words, does Hawthorne share or reject the Puritans' symbolic consciousness of language and the world?

Language and Silence

At first Hawthorne's A would seem, like that of his protagonist, the *a*ble *a*rtist Hester Prynne, to represent a total subversion of the Puritans' letter:

> When [she] stood fully revealed before the crowd, it seemed to be her first impulse to clasp the infant closely to her bosom; not so much by an impulse of motherly affection, as that she might thereby conceal a certain token, which was wrought or fastened into her dress. In a moment, however, wisely judging that one token of her shame would but poorly serve to hide another, she took the baby on her arm, and, with a burning blush, and yet a haughty smile, and a glance that would not be abashed, looked around at her townspeople and neighbours. On the breast of her gown, in fine red cloth, surrounded with an elaborate embroidery and fantastic flourishes of gold thread, appeared the letter A. It was so artistically done, and with so much fertility and gorgeous luxuriance of fancy, that it had all the effect of a last and fitting decoration to the apparel which she wore; and which was of a splendor in accordance with the taste of the age, but greatly beyond what was allowed by the sumptuary regulations of the colony. (52–53)

But as the description of Hester's defiance already begins to suggest, subverting the *A* may not be so simple. And it may repeat rather than resist major elements of the Puritans' use of the A.[7]

Hester's letter, for all its gold and glitter, is still the token of shame that the Puritans have commanded that she wear, so that Hester's haughtiness is more pretense than genuine rebellion. Furthermore, the "fertility" of the letter suggests the way in which the two "tokens"—the letter and the child—are inseparable. By converting the letter into a weapon against Puritan society Hester transforms her child as well into a subversive artistic object. This transformation of the living child into artistic emblem is picked up again later in the text: "[L]ittle Pearl was not clad in rustic weeds. Her mother, with a morbid purpose that may be better understood hereafter, had bought the richest tissues that could be procured, and allowed her imaginative faculty its full play in the arrangement and decoration of the dresses which the child wore, before the public eye" (90). Pearl, we are told, is "the scarlet letter in another form; the scarlet letter endowed with life! The mother herself . . . had carefully wrought out the similitude, lavishing many hours of morbid ingenuity, to create an analogy between the object of her affection and the emblem of her guilt and torture" (102).

If the problem with the Puritans' A is that it converts a human being into a "living sermon," then Hester, for all her artistic designs, in no way evades the logic of Puritan literalism. For her, Pearl is no less a living text than she herself is for the Puritans. And just as for them Hester will come to have a "part to perform," so for her will Pearl. Pearl serves her mother in the same way that Hester serves the community—as symbol and token and as punishment.

For all its apparently subversive expression, Hester's A, then, in many respects quotes the Puritans' A. As quotation, it repeats rather than subverts the Puritans' offense. At the same time, however, insofar as Hester's symbol wrestles free of the restriction of meaning that the Puritans intend for it to ensure, it introduces another problem as well. As endlessly multivalenced, infinitely meaningful (signifying *able, angel, artist,* and so on) the letter A does not mean anything in particular at all. It threatens not to enter into the language system of words and sentences and utterances but to remain always a letter, always a potential vehicle or component of meaning, meaningless in itself.[8] As in the initial scene, in which both the reader and the community view the letter for the first time, it is not even clear whether the letter, as Hester employs it, represents her shame or her defiance. And its ambivalence makes it less an appropriate or effective counterweight to the Puritans' quite clearly overdetermined letter than a self-subverting and therefore powerless sign.

This powerlessness of Hester's letter to speak, which is to say to communicate genuinely and forcefully with the community, is mirrored in Hester's silence throughout most of the novel. This silence is most notable in relation to what Hester refuses to say to the one person to whom she might well communicate the most: her daughter, Pearl. "'Mother, dear,'" asks Pearl, no fewer than three times in one very compact, very tense scene, "'what does this scarlet letter mean?—and why dost thou wear it on thy bosom?'" (179). Hester knows that Pearl is likely "seeking to approach her with childlike confidence ... to establish a meeting-point of sympathy" (179). She knows, in other words, that the relationship between them depends to an important degree on their communicating about the letter. But Hester refuses to answer Pearl's questions. She refuses to speak. "'Hold thy tongue, naughty child,'" Hester finally responds, "with an asperity that she had never permitted to herself before. 'Do not tease me; else I shall shut thee into the dark closet!'" (181).

This silence reaches a point of absoluteness in the forest scene when Dimmesdale and Hester finally decide to flee New England altogether: "'Let us not look back,'" Hester says to Dimmesdale.

> "The past is gone! Wherefore should we linger upon it now? See! With this symbol, I undo it all, and make it as it had never been!"
> So speaking, she undid the clasp that fastened the scarlet letter, and, taking it from her bosom, threw it to a distance among the withered leaves. The mystic token alighted on the hither verge of the stream . . . glittering like a lost jewel. (202)

By throwing away the letter, Hester would undo all and make it as if it had never been. But in thus attempting to erase the past, Hester also effectually erases the existence of her daughter, Pearl, who becomes the "glittering . . . lost jewel" her mother discards.

It is no wonder, then, that Pearl refuses to come to Hester and Dimmesdale until Hester has replaced the letter on her bosom. The problem is not only that "another inmate had been admitted within the circle of the mother's feelings, and so modified the aspect of them all, that Pearl, the returning wanderer, could not find her wonted place, and hardly knew where she was" (208). Rather, in throwing off the letter and undoing her identity, Hester has thrown away and undone the identity of the child as well. Pearl says to Hester, after Hester has put the letter back on, "'And I am thy little Pearl.' In a mood of tenderness that was not usual with her, she drew down her mother's head, and kissed her brow and both her cheeks. But then . . . Pearl put up her mouth, and kissed the scarlet letter too!" (211–12).

Hester does not take this kiss well. "'That was not kind,'" she says. "'When thou hast shown me a little love, thou mockest me!'" (212). But for Pearl, the A, whether Hester likes it or not, is a part of her mother's identity. It is a part of what defines her mother. It is also a part of what defines their relationship to each other. Though Hester is unwilling to make this explicit either to her daughter or to herself, the letter, which she would discard, as much symbolizes the relationship between Hester and Pearl (the mother-daughter relationship of love and devotion) as it does the adulterous relationship between her and Dimmesdale, with the accompanying punishment by the community. What Pearl forces Hester to realize is that she cannot have the love without the consequences, that she cannot be the mother without having sexually, biologically produced the child and that the letter cannot mean and cannot cease to mean whatever it is that Hester (or for that matter the Puritans) wants it to mean (or not to mean). Meaning is a contract between two individuals (mother and daughter, man and woman, citizen and state) who, to paraphrase a statement of Stanley Cavell's in relation to Henry David Thoreau, agree to meet upon the word, to engage in and experience the human conversation that ensues.[9]

Through the major portion of the novel, Hester's letter wavers unproductively between being an ironic duplication of the Puritans' letter to being so underdetermined as to collapse under the force of the Puritans' convictions, to refuse the burden of meaning and communication altogether, even with her daughter. Is Hawthorne's letter similarly a reaffirmation of Puritan perspectives? Is it, like Hester's, indeterminate and self-subverting? A refusal to speak? Or, perhaps, is Hawthorne's *S/scarlet L/letter* (both the symbol and the novel) what we might call, following Emerson, aversive? Does it, perhaps, turn away from society in order to turn back toward it and to reaffirm, in language and not without dissent, the community (past, present, and future) in which the author exists?

Ideology, Consensus, and Consent

In the 1950s and '60s *The Scarlet Letter* was by and large interpreted by critics as celebrating individualism and human aspiration. Both Hawthorne's A and Hester's were understood as images of the power of art to defy cultural coercion. The book, in other words, was read as a critique of Puritan society, and, per-haps, of 19th-century American culture, as well. It was seen as resisting ideology, in the sense of the particular political and reli-gious beliefs of the time, and as placing the power of moral deci-sion making firmly in the hands of individuals, who would cre-ate reality according to their private, personal moral lights. This, according to the critics, was the American message of Hawthorne's text (as it had been, we might add, of Cooper's): that the American individual, defying social norms, would create a new society, based on the individual's resistance to society as such.

In a more recent reading of the book, Sacvan Bercovitch has overturned this view of Hawthorne's novel. By illuminating some of the more coercive strategies of the book, he has permit-ted us to see how the text takes place within an environment of political constraints that it does not explicitly acknowledge, aim-ing at goals it does not fully confess. Like its heroine, Hester Prynne, Bercovitch suggests, *The Scarlet Letter* may not be the embodiment of resistance or rebellion as generations of readers have assumed. Rather, concealing its ideological function, whether intentionally or not, the book may serve instead as an "agent of socialization."[10] Neither open-ended nor decentered, *The Scarlet Letter* socializes the reader to the dominant American ideology it incorporates. The book, writes Bercovitch, "is a novel of endless points of view that together conspire to deprive us of choice" (20); "it employs sentimental themes and gothic tech-niques in order to mediate between utopian and dystopian reso-lutions, and . . . its return to cultural origins speaks to the threat of fragmentation [as evidenced in the revolutions in Europe] while proposing the benefits of gradualism" (87). It compels our participation in a social compact that it only minimally exposes to view.

This process, according to Bercovitch, is both dramatized and effected at the end of the novel, when Hawthorne (almost inex-plicably) has Hester return to New England and once again take up the scarlet letter, "of her own free will, for not the sternest magistrate of that iron period would have imposed it" on her (263). The moment of Hester's "silent" return is pivotal for Bercovitch's reinterpretation: "[T]he silence surrounding Hester's final conversion to the letter is clearly deliberate on Hawthorne's part. . . . It [serves to] mystif[y] Hester's choice by forcing us to represent it through the act of interpretation" (91–92).

Bercovitch's reading of *The Scarlet Letter* locates what it is that makes this text a romance. To force representation, Bercovitch explains, is not to determine meaning. Rather,

> having given us ample directives about how to understand the ambiguous ways in which the letter had not done its office and having set out the ironies that thread the pattern of American consensus from 1649 to 1849, Hawthorne now depends on us to recognize—freely and voluntarily, for his method depends on his seeming not to impose meaning—the need for Hester's return. In effect, he invites us to participate in a free enterprise democracy of symbol making. (92)

The key terms in Bercovitch's reading are *plurality, process,* and *interpretation,* i.e., *both/and,* a formula that he consistently develops from his *American Jeremiad* (12) to his more recent *The Office of the Scarlet Letter* (9–13). These terms imply relationship. They suggest that American consensus consists as much of a dynamics of meaning-making as of shared beliefs. In other words, Hawthorne's novel exposes and clarifies (albeit darkly and complexly) the ideology it incorporates.

If we grant the ideological underpinnings of Hawthorne's text, as Bercovitch identifies them, the questions we must ask are: What does it mean to consent to a consensus of which one is already a part? How can an ideology of interpretation not become, finally, a contradiction in terms, interpretation ultimately reduced, under the pressure of ideology, to a process of reformulating or allegorizing social or political events and beliefs? *Interpretation,* as Bercovitch uses the term, can mean two very different things. It can simply mean explaining something, restating an idea in different, perhaps easier and more readily accessible language or concepts—thus reconstituting the problem of repetition and unity. Or the term can indicate a more personal and creative act, construing according to one's beliefs, realizing (as in a dramatic performance or a work of art) a private vision.

By emphasizing words like *process* and *plurality,* Bercovitch seems to move interpretation in the direction of creative perception. Yet by linking interpretation to ideology—to "process as closure" (90)—he retreats from this more open conception.

Interpretation so linked, for all its show of freedom, seems incapable of escaping from the tautological conditions of ideology. Is there a way of understanding Hester's return, and specifically her resumption of the letter, in a more Emersonian, Cavellian mode? Can we take it as exemplifying the aversion of conformity, in which, turning away from society, Hester returns to it once more in order to reestablish a broken intimacy and to assume the responsibilities of both speaking and listening?

The question that Hester's return poses is why Hester chooses to return and why, having so chosen, she also chooses to resume the letter and to speak through it. The text does not tell us exactly why Hester returns. Nonetheless, Hester and the letter are anything but silent at the end of the book. Bercovitch argues quite persuasively that the letter does not figure Hester's withdrawal from society (her rebellion or resistance). Yet it also does not signify her subordination to Puritan speaking (her silent consent). It figures instead Hester's free and uncircumscribed, aversive speaking. At the end of the book, Hester is exactly not silent in the way that she was earlier in the book, when, according to Hawthorne, the scarlet letter did *not* do its office (166).[11]

Hester's return to speech is twofold. In the first place, she speaks literally. She returns to New England, Hawthorne tells us, as a counselor and an articulator of American values. By way of further acknowledging this, Hawthorne attributes the penultimate words of the story to Hester: "So said Hester Prynne, and glanced her sad eyes downward at the scarlet letter" (264). Having learned to speak for herself, Hester becomes the voice of the text. In order to emphasize that this speaking is uncoerced, Hawthorne positions Hester's return in relation to her daughter's decision not to return to New England. Of course, Hester's earlier decision to remain in New England also represents a choice (itself affirming the possibility of consent). Hawthorne is explicit that Hester is "kept by no restrictive clause of her condemnation within the limits of the Puritan settlement." She is "free to return to her birthplace, or to any other European land" (79). Choosing to remain and choosing to return, however, emerge as two different orders of choice, not merely two different choices. Staying is distinguished from leaving and returning by the force of return itself, which produces a special kind of speaking.

When Hester returns to New England and chooses to speak, the text emphasizes that her speaking is not only vocal, direct to her audience, but also oblique and cryptic, through the letter. As important as Hester's decision to return to her community and to language is where she places her words in relation to her audience. From the beginning of the story, the community's eyes are on Hester. Her placement, at the end, of the A on her breast redirects the public gaze there and acknowledges her shame in the eyes of the settlement's inhabitants. In glancing downward to her breast, she also confesses that she sees herself as they do. But by placing the A on her breast, Hester also accuses and resists the public. She exposes the community's shamelessness when it refused to avert its gaze from her body. Hester, then, involves the community members in a form of aversive seeing. By averting her own glance from them, she both sees herself as they see her and confesses to them that she so sees herself. But as her seeing is upside down, her viewers also perceive that she redirects toward them their accusatory glances. She reverses what they see and reflects or turns the image back to them.

Furthermore, in averting her eyes from her audience (creating a line of obliqueness that replicates the letter's own diagonals), Hester does not focus attention exclusively on the meanings that her words directly or indirectly convey or conceal. Rather, she defines lines of relationship with her audience. Hester's A establishes that the "issue" between her and the Puritans is, as Cavell says about Emerson, "always joined, never settled," in an "unending argument" between them. The ideological power of Hester's letter serves the purposes of consent (and not of conformity) when individuals, recognizing that they will never settle the issues between them, nonetheless choose to meet upon the word (as Cavell puts it in *Senses of Walden*), to turn simultaneously away from and toward each other, allowing themselves to catch and deflect, to brave and be embarrassed by, each other's gazes.

This aversive seeing eschews the direct articulation of any sociopolitical ideology. But its indirection is turned as much toward as away from community, and it issues forth in a kind of speaking that does not simply define or inform but establishes relations of commitment and acknowledgment. This speaking participates in and encourages listening.

Hester's letter at the end of the book declares itself communally serviceable in the way it converts the silence of her resistance into a way of speaking. For Hawthorne, consent is no simple statement of affirmation, like a pledge of allegiance or a declaration of independence or the recitation of a catechism. It is also, however, *not* an unwritten or unspoken law, which (as Hester imagines) "'has a consecration all its own'" (195). It is not a secret, not even in the sense of the secret workings of something like an ideology or teleology. Instead, it is a decidedly public event, much in the way that children (like Pearl, the scarlet letter incarnate) are public events. Like children, consent conveys wholly intimate, private feelings, even doubts and uncertainties, into the social arena. There, despite the fact that such expressions of consent inevitably deviate from their internal, intrinsic meanings, they are nevertheless owned. A consenting adult, like a parent, assumes personal responsibility, despite doubt. Consent, then, voices a relationship between radical doubt and the necessities of public commitment.

The coherence of American culture, in the view of this novel, its consensus within dissent (its "dissensus," in Bercovitch's word), is the consequence of the fact that dissent in America is already identified as writing/speaking, which is itself understood as already negotiating between extremes of indeterminacy and specificity and in which words themselves are the public medium of exchange between individuals (with their private subjectivities) and society. For Hawthorne, America's ideology is the negotiation that the text initiates, through its language, between a writer and a reader.

This is the negotiation that is figured forth in Hester's decision to return to New England and, from that place, to speak. It is the negotiation conducted by the novel itself, nowhere more emphatically than in its closing words:

> [O]n this simple slab of slate—as the curious investigator may still discern, and perplex himself with the purport—there appeared the semblance of an engraved escutcheon. It bore a device, a herald's wording of which might serve for a motto and brief description of our now concluded legend; so sombre is it, and relieved only by one ever-glowing point of light gloomier than the shadow:—"ON A FIELD, SABLE, THE LETTER A, GULES." (264)

Reading Hawthorne's text as itself a kind of tombstone is not inconsistent with one way of understanding Hawthorne's reading of America.[12] America, some critics have felt, represented for Hawthorne the sinister triumph of repression, symbolized from first to last by the Puritans' A. The novel's conclusion might well seem to nail shut the coffin of this repetition and redundancy. The legend on the stone repeats the legend contained in Hawthorne's story; the simple letter *a* is none other than the Puritans' A, which is also Hester's A, which is the legend on the stone, the legend that also drifts across the ocean like "a shapeless piece of driftwood . . . with the initials of a name upon it" (261), which is now the legend on Hawthorne's page ("our now concluded legend," he calls the book—[264]). The final words of Hawthorne's text, furthermore, seem to turn a picture (the tombstone) into words as earlier Hester and the Puritans had converted words into a picture (the letter A).

Thus this brief description identifies a tension felt throughout the text between the scarlet letter as reductive sign (a pictograph or hieroglyph) and as symbol or language. It seems to be both, to the mutual annihilation of word and world. To top the death blow that the words seem to serve to Hawthorne's text, the motto is represented as a quotation, a "herald's wording," set off in capital letters and quotation marks. There seem to be no words that escape the repetitiveness of language. We begin and end with the A, no more sure what the A means now than then, no more certain we can escape its tug back into the lack of articulation that the letter *a* by itself, outside the context of other letters, might signify.

By reading Hester's tombstone, as earlier Hawthorne read her letter, the author seems to reveal reading to be repetition, quotation in one form or another. Interpretation, then, seems nothing more than a substitution of one set of words for another, words for pictures and pictures for words. The way in which language calls attention to itself at the conclusion to the novel (as, through the device of the A, it calls attention to itself throughout Hawthorne's romance) further enhances our sense of being trapped in a linguistic prison. But the situation is not nearly this simple. For, despite what Hawthorne's reading of the tombstone (as of Puritan history) seems to be telling us, Hawthorne claims—and his book, in the view of most readers, affirms—that reading (Hawthorne's reading of Hester's story, our reading of Hawthorne's) does provide some kind of relief. This is what the final words say: that the gloom is "relieved" by "one ever-glowing point of light," which, however more singular and gloomy than anything else, still exists to shine its relief. This point of light is the sentence "ON A FIELD, SABLE, THE LETTER A, GULES." Is this relief just a matter of self-clarification, self-illumination? Or does the book's culminating phrase wrestle with and own a genuine insight?

In the first instance, the final words reveal how the pattern of redundancy or quotation is by no means perfect. Quite simply, the series of letter A's or legends do not fall into place as neatly as one might imagine. The phrase is as much a misquotation as a quotation, and it crosses national boundaries, going outside the American context. The quotation approximates the final line of Marvell's "The Unfortunate Lover," a poem that has several elements in common with Hawthorne's novel.[13] Insofar as Marvell's line itself quotes and hence interprets a herald's wording, the rewording in Hawthorne's text, right at its conclusion, initiates a new series of interpretive endeavors. The sentence, for all its doubling and redoubling back on the text, does achieve something, even if this something is not everything we might hope from language. It goes outside the text, outside the consensus it summarizes, to broaden the context in which we debate the issue of how words mean.

But then the text goes on to achieve even more. The quotation of a "herald's wording" is placed at the end of the book, in the context of a narrative, and not within a book of emblems. For this reason it does not remain a simple phrase designating the relative positions of objects and colors (a red letter on a black background). Rather, with the word *gules* sitting uncomfortably at the end of the phrase (not to mention the end of the book), the phrase metamorphoses, for the native English speaker, into a sentence that reads, "On a field sable, the letter A, gules." Grammatically, the word *gules* is not an intransitive verb. It is most often an adjective, occasionally a noun, and sometimes a transitive verb. But as Hawthorne places the phrase in a text governed as much by the sound of language as by a set of syntactical and grammatical rules, *gules* takes on a verbal power. In this way it becomes a "glowing point of light gloomier than the shadow," making that light happen, making it gule.[14]

In order to bring light to the text, the word *gules* must also guile and beguile, gild and gull—all of which suggest themselves as meanings of the word *gules*. Hawthorne would not have us miss any of the sham that words (including his own) play upon us. But for all the ambiguity of language, for all the shadow in which its light exists, the light of language does illuminate and relieve. By placing his words within the context of other words, Hawthorne forces a statement out of the stalemate of language. He demonstrates how we may harness language's capacity for making sense out of nonsense, how we may induce language not simply to be but to act. Hawthorne's sentence makes language enter into the meaning-making process, discovering in an adjective the possibility for action, wording the world.[15] The letter gules. It causes something to happen, something deceptive perhaps (as the meanings of *guile*, *gild*, and *gull* suggest) but something potentially active and affirmative as well.

The tombstone might well be one more figure for the silent, ideologically gagged or deconstructively evasive text. It is relieved, we are told, only by an ever glowing point of light gloomier than shadow. But this point of light, this sentence, does exist to relieve it. Hawthorne does not create this sentence out of nothing. By respectfully recording each and every different A, by quoting it and trying it on for size (as he does the A in "The Custom-House"), Hawthorne acknowledges each of these A's in such a way as not to wrest it out of the control of others but to make it his own A as well. Thus the letter A gules; it glows; it creates a point of light, much like the rose (another meaning of the word *gules*) that grows upon the threshold of the prison at the book's opening.[16]

Through the word *gules* (as rose), the book circles back on itself. It reads itself and makes good on one of its promises. The text, like language, cannot avoid certain kinds of deathly repetition. The tombstone substitutes for the prison, one kind of death for another (Chillingworth, in the opening scene, already alludes to this tombstone with its guling A). At the same time, however, the book restores to the reader the flower it plucks for him or her at the beginning of the text. It suggests that the text itself can "relieve [its own] darkening close of a tale of human frailty and sorrow" (48). The rose, which is still there at the end, guling and providing its relief, is Hawthorne's substitute for Hester's scarlet letter. It is all that he, like Hester and the Puritans before him, and like the whole of the human community who has spoken or written, has to offer. But it is enough.

Through the text's final sentence, which is no longer a quotation, either of a herald's wording or of a line from Marvell or of the A, Hawthorne expresses his consent. His text becomes the self-sentencing process of meaning-making (like Hester's glancing at her own letter), which places Hawthorne's words, his writing, in a never-ending relationship with America. For Hawthorne, letters and words are both the intractably obfuscating symbols and building blocks of language. They are at once artifacts, handed down from generation to generation, and private instruments of personal expression. One cannot separate out the functions and conditions of language, except through usage, through listening to the voice of other texts and through placing both its words and one's own in relation to each other. Can one refuse such consent?

Like the Puritans, Hawthorne knows that the prison and the cemetery are essential features of any society. Hawthorne's final words, therefore, recall these institutions. Not to speak, which is to say not to consent, is a choice. But it is a choice that carries with it heavy consequences. If there is, as Bercovitch claims, a teleological force to Hawthorne's novel, it is contained in the silence to which nonconsent (rather than consent) may deliver us. For what the prison and graveyard also represent are the deadly, stultifying alternatives to society and to life itself. In absolute defiance of its alternative, silence—which, like Hester's withdrawal from society at the beginning of the novel or like Pearl's departure at the end, the failure to speak can effect—Hawthorne speaks, both to protest and to consent.

Like Hester's letter, which is, of course, Hawthorne's as well, Hawthorne's words place him in a richly aversive relation to America. If we, as readers, take up these words, they place us in this same relation. They make us responsible to listen and to speak. We can refuse these words. But if we do so, if we refuse to voice our consent, then, the letter on the tombstone also warns us, we may render ourselves and our community as silent as a tomb. The decision—but also the responsibility—is ours.

Chapter 5

THE ROMANCE OF NATURE: HERMAN MELVILLE'S MOBY-DICK

For Nathaniel Hawthorne the world is of distinctly human manufacture—prisons, cemeteries, religion, customs, language. Unlike Poe, therefore, he is neither paralyzed nor terrified before the skeptical questions, Does the world exist? Do I exist in it? Instead, he raises the question of knowledge in order to assert human responsibility in and for a world that cannot be verified except in its human construction. In other words, rather than answer the skeptical question, either in the affirmative or the negative, Hawthorne probes and ponders it. He opts neither for denial nor a sense of open-endedness and multiplicity. He chooses instead moral, philosophical realism.

Hawthorne writes skepticist texts—romance fiction—in order to impress upon the reader that there are no transcendent, extrahuman truths in this world, of which the world is a model or imitation, and to which we can apply in our search for meanings. And yet Hawthorne will not, for that reason, conclude that the quotidian world does not, as such, exist. Rather, he constructs texts that preserve the pressure of the skeptical dilemma, so as to bequeathe to the reader not an answer to an unanswerable question but the question itself, with all of the imperatives to assuming personal responsibility that that question produces. The form of Hawthorne's fiction reproduces its theme: to live morally in the world requires that we live in doubt, for only in sustaining such doubts—concerning our own existence as well as the existence of others and of the world itself—can we come to accept responsibility for this world, the moral dimensions of which depend on nothing other than our accepting precisely this responsibility.

In his shorter romances, "Bartleby, the Scrivener," "Benito Cereno," and *Billy Budd,* and in the longer *Pierre,* Herman Melville shares Hawthorne's sense of the human construction of the world in which we exist. Like Hawthorne he raises the question of knowledge largely to launch his fictions on questions rather than on answers. For this reason, perhaps, Melville dedicates his masterpiece of romance fiction, *Moby-Dick, or the Whale,* to Hawthorne—to acknowledge their shared territory. But Melville's is a far gloomier, more anguished fiction than Hawthorne's. In all of his writings, but most particularly in his master romance, he looks back to Poe and invokes Poe's awareness of the fragility of the border separating the mind from the world. He recalls the ease with which one can slip out of contact with this world and find oneself in a solipsistic universe of one's own imaginings.

In *Moby-Dick* Melville pursues the skeptical dilemma almost to its limit, almost, although not quite, as far as Poe does, to the place where the world disappears and one is left only with the vaguest of memories of what was, at best, an insubstantial universe. In Melville's romance the journey toward the world's dissolution is more real and therefore even more powerful and painful than in Poe's fiction. *Moby-Dick* goes out of its way to ground the world in vibrant, biological detail, so that the distance traveled in Melville, and the horror thus generated by the sacrifice of the world on the altar of the mind, is far greater than in Poe.

Most of Hawthorne's tales and longer fictions (*The House of the Seven Gables, The Blithedale Romance,* and *The Marble Faun,* as well as short stories such as "Roger Malvin's Burial") focus on the mind's attempts to dominate over the unstable and/or unfathomable meanings of the physical world. They record the ways in which human institutions emerge to restrict and falsify social reality. In Poe, the physical world as such (whether biological or physical or purely cultural, institutional) disappears. The writing examines, instead, the mind itself as it gives up on the attempt to influence the external world and retreats into and destroys itself. Like Poe, Melville, whose epic expanse in many of his novels (on the ocean as opposed to the continent) recalls the fiction of Cooper as well, also positions his writing outside culture as such. And yet, even in his most sustained romance, *Moby-Dick,* Melville's is no purely verbal, mental world of words. Rather, it is a physical and biological world peeled back (like Cooper's in the Leatherstocking Tales) to a time just preceding its moment of cultural consolidation, the moment when the mind first fathoms the possibility that it might construct the world according to its own designs. If Hawthorne records the consequences of these impulses of the detached, egocentric mind, Melville recovers their origins.

The Letter of the Law

Before turning to *Moby-Dick,* let me illustrate one aspect of the relationship among the three major figures in the romance tradition—Poe, Hawthorne, and Melville—by turning to a set of interrelated works, including one of the Melville fictions closer in its orientation to Hawthorne than, perhaps, *Moby-Dick.* The three works are Poe's "Purloined Letter," Hawthorne's *Scarlet Letter,* and Melville's "Bartleby, the Scrivener; A Tale of Wall Street." In making this comparison, one must admit immediately that "The Purloined Letter" is atypical of Poe's writing. It embodies most of the salient characteristics of Poe's fiction: the doublings or duplications, the conflict between reason and the imagination, the allegorical and symbolic features, and the self-conscious concern with language. Nonetheless, unlike the tales of terror, such as

"The Fall of the House of Usher" and "Ligeia," or the tales of the perverse, it figures forth (albeit sketchily and minimalistically) a social world. In this social arena, the dynamics of mind, so central to Poe's literary concerns, do have political, institutional implications. Similarly, "Bartleby," as I have already suggested, is one of Melville's more culturally engaged romances, more like *White-Jacket* or *Billy Budd* than like *Mardi* or *Moby-Dick.* It points more in the direction of Hawthorne's usual concern with society than toward the philosophical matters of Melville's own masterwork.

But, precisely for the ways in which the Poe and Melville stories lean toward Hawthorne, they provide useful coordinates by which to plot the continuity among these three writers. Furthermore, there is good warrant (aside from considerations of genre definition) for thinking of these three works together. First of all, it is quite likely that Hawthorne had Poe's story in mind when he wrote *The Scarlet Letter.* Similarly, Melville may have been thinking of Hawthorne's story (and Poe's) when he wrote "Bartleby." Though Poe and Hawthorne were not, like Hawthorne and Melville, personal friends (Melville and Hawthorne often exchanged ideas for stories), they were more than conscious of each other's writings. Poe's "Oval Portrait" and Hawthorne's "Birth-Mark" were revised in relation to each other, after Poe published a review of Hawthorne's story in one of the literary journals for which he wrote. Furthermore, *The Scarlet Letter* contains internal hints pointing to a Hawthorne-Poe relationship. Hawthorne several times refers to Pearl as an "imp," once as "perverse," while Surveyor "Pue," in "The Custom-House" sketch that prefaces the book, is described in terms faintly reminiscent of Poe. It is Pue, of course, who gives us the first version of Hester's story, just as Poe gives us the story of "The Purloined Letter."

Most importantly, however, *The Scarlet Letter* concerns a woman, her sexual secrets, and the conflict between two men (Minister D—— and Dupin in Poe's story, Chillingworth and Dimmesdale in Hawthorne's) to expose or conceal those secrets—this battle proceeding over, and through, what is identified as a "letter." Indeed, insofar as the scarlet letter has to be recovered, in the Custom-House, from oblivion, Hester's letter, like that of the royal personage in Poe's story, is purloined (the word *purloined* means "lost," not necessarily "stolen").[1]

It is this self-consciousness concerning the relationship between society and language (the letter in its various senses in these three works) that ties the works together. In "The Purloined Letter" the letter is literal epistle. In *The Scarlet Letter* it is a letter of the alphabet, though at the end of the story, Hester and Pearl do exchange letters in the sense in which Poe uses the word. In "Bartleby" the letters are the words that the scriveners transcribe and the letter of law that they thus duplicate—though the tale invokes the more Poesque idea of letters as well, when it notes that, before coming to work as a scrivener, Bartleby was employed in the Dead Letter Office of the postal service. Furthermore, all are tales of crime and punishment. They all have to do, in other words, with laws and law enforcers, with who makes the laws, and how, and why, and how the law is resisted, repudiated, transformed.

Nor is crime in these stories just civic in its implications. Just as the detective and the criminal double each other in "The Purloined Letter" (as to some extent they do in *The Scarlet Letter*, through the coupling of Chillingworth and Dimmesdale; both Dupin and the prefect violate the law), so crime is doubled in each of the stories as sin or moral transgression. Thus, while the ostensible crime in Poe's story is blackmail, its victim, the story strongly implies, is guilty of a more private sexual indiscretion. This is the same "sin" as in Hawthorne's romance, while in "Bartleby," although the protagonist is guilty of a purely human crime (refusing to vacate his employer's premises), the narrator is guilty of a moral failing—refusing the obligation of Christian charity to Bartleby. In other words, there is a religious, as well as a legal, dimension to each of these works, which broadens the idea of law to an almost metaphysical dimension. It is as if these stories have more to do with structures of moral order than with any particular legal or religious code.

What these three works have in common, then, which defines them as part of a single tradition of romance fiction, is their concern with the transcription, in language, of laws (both civic and theological) and of the enforcement of those laws by society. The object of investigation in the stories is the way in which society fails to examine the validity and slipperiness of these laws. That is, conventional, secular society does not ask whether the laws adequately embody justice or morality or social equality, only whether someone has broken them. The stories carry on the interrogation of law per se, which society does not conduct.

There are, of course, also differences among these stories—but even the differences tend to affirm the shared concern among the works with the idea of law and institutionalized morality. Hawthorne begins with law as divine doctrine, examines secular law against this measure, and, finding it inadequate, ups the ante, exploring the inadequacy of divine law as well. "Bartleby" turns in the opposite direction. It is, as its original subtitle suggests, "a story of Wall Street." It proceeds along the principles of civil law, which it finds incapable of taking the full measure of the human situation. For this reason, the tale applies to religious law for solutions, only to find that religious law is equally flawed and difficult to implement. Poe leaves the religious dimension aside altogether, at least in any recognizably Christian form. Rather, he pits human law (the royal court and the police) against the laws of the mind, which he discovers to be far more acute, although hardly any more capable of producing moral order: at the end of "The Purloined Letter" the letter has only been repurloined by a character hardly less shady and susceptible to our suspicions than the official representative of the court whom he has outwitted. As Dupin repeats several times during the story, he and Minister D—— are brothers; the principles of order and transgression that characterize the one characterize the other as well.

Significantly, in Poe's story, the letter does not return to the woman to whom it belongs but remains in Dupin's, which is to say the man's, possession—and this detail points to another set of shared concerns in the three romances. I suggested in my reading of Hawthorne's *Scarlet Letter* that its skepticist argument has a strong antipatriarchal component. According to the logic of Hawthorne's text, doubt of genetic connection to their children prompts men to restrict female freedom, so as to make human history a matter of male-defined continuity—through institutions and traditions, which men designate and name, rather than through biological reproduction. Similar arguments might be brought to bear on Poe's "Usher" and "Ligeia," in which, as I also suggested, a male narrator tries to imagine women out of his world, with the dire consequence that these tales record. It is by no means incidental to Poe's and Hawthorne's purposes in "The Purloined Letter" and *The Scarlet Letter* that the individuals who generate the letters under dispute are women or that the participants in the struggle over their possession and meaning are men:

Dupin and Minister D—— (not to mention the narrator and the prefect of police) in the Poe story; Dimmesdale, Chillingworth, and the Puritan community (and perhaps even Hawthorne himself) in *The Scarlet Letter*.

Here "Bartleby" would seem to lose its connection with the other two stories, and yet, in the intensity of its focus on an exclusively male world, with men endlessly copying out laws made by other men, "Bartleby" realizes the patriarchal tendencies dramatized by both the Poe and Hawthorne stories. Even more strictly than Poe in his gothic tales of horror, Melville in "Bartleby" (and even more powerfully in *Moby-Dick*) imagines a world without women, a world given over to the unceasing repetition by men of masculinist law.[2] The skepticist imperative of romance fiction almost seems to necessitate the recovery of the woman as that which male culture has excommunicated in order to ensure itself a kind of certainty that is wholly within male hands.

As in so many aspects of the later romance tradition, the antipatriarchal move is already anticipated in Cooper, and, before getting to Melville's master romance, which will realize many of the issues (including the feminist issue) hinted at in "Bartleby," it is worth briefly returning to Cooper's *Prairie*. As I suggested in my discussion of that book, *The Prairie* deconstructs the essentialist difference not only between myth and history (imagination and world) but among races (Indian, white, black) and religions (Catholic, Protestant, Indian) as well. A further dualism the author deconstructs is that separating man from woman. This is not to say that Cooper's *Prairie* exhibits no gender bias or, for that matter, racial or religious bias (though the fact that Cooper took his mother's name—Fenimore—suggests something about his feelings in relation to women).[3] Cooper is a 19th-century male writer, as are Poe, Hawthorne, and Melville; and their prejudices in these matters reflect the cultural moment in which they write. But in the matter of gender, as in the matters of race and religion, Cooper (like his inheritors in the tradition) attempts to exceed the rigid dichotomies and hierarchies of his society.

Take, for example, the blurring skirts and bosom in the passage I have already examined in my reading of Cooper. The terms surely sexualize the nation, rendering it feminine and, to some degree at least, passive, like most of the women in the story (though the land in Cooper's book can hardly be said not to play a role in the drama of the story).[4] But in the logic of redefinition that governs this text, the skirts and bosom also serve to locate the importance of the feminine in this new nation. The "ever-receding borders," Cooper tells us, "mark the skirts and announce the approach of the nation" (69). The female presence is at the forefront of the national enterprise. Furthermore, the "skirts" are only the barest intimation of the importance of the female component. They precede, as we recall, the "bosom" of the nation. Only a few lines later Cooper explains that "Ishmael Bush had passed the whole of a life of more than fifty years on the skirts of society" (70). Dwelling 50 years on the skirts, the masculinist, patriarchal Bush, no matter how literally procreative he is, will never become the father of this nation. "Though some of the numerous descendants of this peculiar pair were reclaimed from their lawless and semibarbarous lives, the principals of the family themselves were never heard of more" (427). Neither, for that matter, will the unmarried and childless trapper become the literal father of this nation. "When I am gone there will be an end of my race" (450), he quite simply declares.

The hope, therefore, for the future of America lies with two couples (female and male), Inez and Middleton and Paul and Ellen, and with their children and with the children of the Indian nations—who will bring the bosom of society into the wilderness. Cooper is a "humble narrator of home-bred incidents" (69). He is concerned with nothing less than what kind of home this nation will become. As the very idea of home already suggests, this home will depend as much on its women as on its men. Not only does the book generally condemn the sexism of the Indians (which carries over to include the sexism of Bush and company), but it creates in Esther Bush a female figure even more powerful than Bush himself. It is Esther (the heroine of Jewish lore) and not Ishmael (antihero of the Old Testament) who conquers in this text (405). She is the powerful presence who conducts the search for her dead son and directs her husband in his search for justice for the murderer. In fact, in the final judgment scene, when the patriarch of the clan dispenses biblical law (the same law that will emerge so importantly in Hawthorne's *Scarlet Letter* and in Melville's "Bartleby" and *Billy Budd* as well), it is Esther who is the presiding presence.[5]

Most importantly, however, Esther provides powerful support for Ellen's desire to marry Paul. Esther conveys, through Ellen, a legacy that will not fast perish in the wilderness. Insofar as Hawthorne's Hester recalls this Esther, Esther is as much the mythic matriarch of the nation as the trapper is the mythic patriarch. The story of America, Cooper suggests, is as much her story as his, a story neither of Israelites nor of Ishmaelites but of human birth and settlement—of women as much as of men. This will be precisely Hawthorne's point in *The Scarlet Letter*. It will be a large element in the argument of Melville's *Moby-Dick* as well.

History and Stasis

In many ways, Melville's *Moby-Dick* takes up the narrative imperative of *The Prairie* to tell the story of the nation as it realizes itself both as ironic or paradoxical biblical idea and as a mythically determined historical contingency. "Call me Ishmael," Melville's story begins, recalling both the Old Testament history of the Israelites and the imitation/inversion of that story (as yet untold, perhaps unknown or unrealized) in the story of Ishmael. And it concludes by recalling another biblical story, the flood in Genesis, which is also about the undoing or redoing or duplication/repetition of history—perhaps only ironically or perversely, since with the coming of Christ (Melville's Ishmael is a Christ figure as well) it will be duplicated once again. The question that Melville's text raises and that it shares with the fiction of Poe and Hawthorne is: Is there any way out of the repetitions and redundancy of human history, in which actions repeat actions, and words and actions replicate each other, with a deadening circularity? This is the concluding passage of Melville's *Moby-Dick*:

> The drama's done. Why then here does any one step forth?—
> Because one did survive the wreck.
>   It so chanced, that after the Parsee's disappearance, I was he whom the Fates ordained to take the place of Ahab's bowsman, when the bowsman assumed the vacant post; the same, who, when on the last day the three men were tossed from out the rocking boat, was dropped astern. So, floating on the margin of the ensuing scene, and in full sight of it, when the half-spent suction of the sunk ship reached me, I was then, but slowly, drawn towards the closing vor-

tex. When I reached it, it had subsided to a creamy pool. Round and round, then, and ever contracting towards the button-like black bubble at the axis of that slowly wheeling circle, like another Ixion I did revolve. Till, gaining that vital centre, the black bubble upward burst; and now, liberated by reason of its cunning spring, and, owing to its great buoyancy, rising with great force, the coffin life-buoy shot lengthwise from the sea, fell over, and floated by my side. Buoyed up by that coffin, for almost one whole day and night, I floated on a soft and dirge-like main. The unharming sharks, they glided by as if with padlocks on their mouths; the savage sea-hawks sailed with sheathed beaks. On the second day, a sail drew near, nearer, and picked me up at last. It was the devious-cruising *Rachel,* that in her retracing search after her missing children, only found another orphan. (565–66)

Like much of Hawthorne's fiction and almost all of Poe's, and like the rest of Melville's book, the scene of Ishmael's survival takes place on the indeterminate ground that Hawthorne, in "The Custom-House," calls the "neutral territory," "between the Imaginary and the Real" (36). Ishmael's survival is neither clearly accidental nor obviously predetermined ("It so chanced . . . I was he whom the Fates ordained"). It is an event equally controlled by nature and by human intellect, exhibiting at every point contradiction and paradox ("liberated by reason of its cunning spring, and, owing to its great buoyancy . . . the coffin life-buoy shot lengthwise from the sea, fell over, and floated by my side"). Ishmael is the only survivor of this narrative and therefore the only character who can be thought to generate a narrative beyond this one. Nonetheless he is, at the end of the story, no less than throughout it, only at "the margin of the ensuing scene, and in full sight of it," an "orphan" who, without history and genealogy preceding him, of which his story might be understood as a further evolution, is unlikely to produce any history after him. Just as the "devious-cruising *Rachel*" only retraces her steps, so Ishmael's story (a vor*text*?) is only a repetition of itself, going over old ground (or, shall we say, old sea) with a consummate deviousness.

Like the majority of Poe's tales, *Moby-Dick* ends where it begins. By imagining the dissolution of the world, its return out of physical, material existence and back into an idea of God or nature (following closely the contours of Poe's neo-Platonism), the narrative consciousness in this story undoes itself, regressing back into a fetal nonexistence. At the end of the narrative, Ishmael is afloat on womblike waters, about to be birthed by the contractions of these waters and their expulsion of the matter within. But Ishmael will be spared (once again) the moment of genuine biological birth that might sustain the natural world by being yanked out of the waters ("a great shroud of sea"—[565]) by sailors on another ship.

The moment recalls two previous moments of unnatural birth in the book: the first, when Ishmael himself is breech-birthed out a chimney by his nonnatural stepmother; the other when Tashtego is brought back to life out of the whale's body by Queequeg (also almost in a breech position). What all of these moments, themselves significant repetitions of each other, suggest is the fact of repetition itself, of the stasis of Melville's world as it attempts to conform itself not to a principle of nature (with all of its uncertainties and newnesses) but to a retracing of a single, clearly defined, already articulated story, a history of known events, where the events themselves are known even prior to their historical emergence in the myths and parables that precede and determine those events.

As in Poe's short stories, the world in *Moby-Dick* is sealed within a mind that is determined never to lose control of its authority over nature and that is therefore doomed to perpetual reenactment of the one law of nature over which we have no control whatsoever: death. Though this mind-set seems most clearly to characterize the tragic hero of the romance, Ahab, it characterizes as well the narrator, who duplicates Ahab as surely as Ahab conforms himself to a pattern of mythical, philosophical, and religious thought.

The Transcendental Journey to Death—and Life

Ahab's voyage on the *Pequod* has been generally understood as a quest for transcendent meaning, though whether Ahab's pursuit of such meanings—in the form of a great white sperm whale, who has bitten off one of his legs—is heroic or deranged, spiritually motivated or purely vengeful, is hardly clear. A compromise is to see Ahab as both courageous, inspired, and intellectually profound but also egomaniacal and misguided. He exemplifies a human tendency at its most extreme, both for better and for worse. Ishmael, in such a reading, emerges as the hero of his own narrative, for it is Ishmael who, learning from Ahab's lesson, is able to strike a balance between the physical and spiritual universes and live to tell the tale. But Ishmael is not all that different from Ahab. The problem with displacing the major drama from Ahab to Ishmael is that it tidies up too many loose ends. It essentially replicates rather than revises the dominant features of Ahab's story, perhaps even exaggerating them in the process. In the Ishmael-centered reading the story emerges as even more allegorical of the search for significance in an ambiguous universe, since Ishmael's journey is a journey redoubled. It is conducted by Ishmael, through Ahab, and purely within his imagination, whereas in the narrative world created by the text it is conducted by Ahab, through the whale, within a vividly realized natural universe.

Thus understood, the structure of the book corresponds quite closely to a typical Poe story, in which a narrator witnesses or, more likely, fantasizes events that closely parallel his own destructive tendencies. These tendencies are now rendered as story, informing the narrator of his imminent peril and permitting the narrator to step back and avoid disaster—if, indeed, what happens at the end of "The Fall of the House of Usher" and "Ligeia" (or *Moby-Dick*) is to be understood as the narrator's retreat from disaster as opposed to the moment before he, like the characters within his mental drama, succumbs to it. Perhaps it is to acknowledge his predecessor Poe in the literary tradition that Melville alludes in his romance to an "Etymology / (supplied by a late consumptive Usher to a grammar school.): The pale Usher—threadbare in coat, heart, body, and brain; I see him now. He was ever dusting his old lexicons and grammars, with a queer handkerchief, mockingly embellished with all the gay flags of all the known nations of the world. He loved to dust his old grammars; it somehow mildly reminded him of his mortality" (xix). Melville expands the range of Usher's reference, so that it is international, representing the "flags of all the known nations of the world." But, like Poe's Usher, this one smells of death. He is also "queer" and "gay," revealing something about the dynamics of Poe's tale that barely skims the surface there.

What this link between Poe and Melville forces us to do is to ask whether Ishmael's survival (afloat on a life buoy that is clearly designated a coffin on a "shroud of sea") is anything more than a temporary respite from death (like the narrator's fate in "Usher"), his story more a prophecy of impending doom than a record of catastrophe avoided. For if Ahab's major error is that he transforms a phenomenal world into a transcendental idea of one, then, for all its apparent rationality and decorum, Ishmael's book reconstitutes that error, writ large. Ishmael's world, like that of Poe's narrators, is wholly verbal; he writes as words what Ahab, inside the world of the fiction, enacts as life.

Taken this way, Ishmael's narrative, like Poe's tales of terror, may be read as a very long suicide note. Or, given the sexual implications of this story—its pursuit of a sperm whale named Moby Dick—it may, as I have suggested elsewhere (1994), be understood as a sustained masturbatory fantasy, an idea that locates features of Poe's fictions as well. By preferring a verbal, autoerotic relationship to the self to physical, sexual relations between human beings, the story leads out of the world of history and procreation into the dead-endedness of endless self-replication and dying.

Although Ahab is the chief figure in this book for the transcendentalizing bent of the human imagination—in all of its power and rage—Ishmael is no less given to such tendencies than Ahab. "All visible objects . . . are but as pasteboard masks," Ahab explains in the book's most famous statement of its presumably neoplatonic metaphysics:

> [I]n each event—in the living act, the undoubted deed—there, some unknown but still reasoning thing puts forth the mouldings of its features from behind the unreasoning mask. If man will strike, strike through the mask! How can the prisoner reach outside except by thrusting through the wall? To me, the white whale is that wall, shoved near to me. Sometimes I think there's naught beyond. But 'tis enough. He tasks me; he heaps me; I see in him outrageous strength, with an inscrutable malice sinewing it. That inscrutable thing is chiefly what I hate; and be the white whale agent, or be the white whale principal, I will wreak that hate upon him. (161)

Ahab's sense of a world behind this world, to which we can, at moments, break through, accords perfectly with Ishmael's own transcendental leanings, although Ishmael is both less embattled and far less confident of success in his quest for meaning than Ahab is in his. Thus, Ishmael tells us, immediately following the book's famous opening, "Call me Ishmael":

> Some years ago . . . having little or no money in my purse, and noth-
> ing particular to interest me on shore, I thought I would sail about a
> little and see the watery part of the world. It is a way I have of dri-
> ving off the spleen and regulating the circulation. Whenever I find
> myself growing grim about the mouth; whenever it is a damp, driz-
> zly November in my soul; whenever I find myself involuntarily
> pausing before coffin warehouses, and bringing up the rear of every
> funeral I meet . . . then, I account it high time to get to sea as soon as I
> can. This is my substitute for pistol and ball. (1)

Nor is the impulse to go to sea a personal idiosyncracy of
Ishmael's (or of Ahab's): the "crowds," too, he tells us, pace
"straight for the water . . . bound for a dive. . . . Nothing will content them but the extremest limit of the land. . . . They must get
just as nigh the water as they possibly can without falling in" (2).

Ishmael will discover life on the sea to be as violent as life on
land, but until he does, the sea offers to Ishmael just what it
affords Ahab: the possibility for philosophical speculation and
discovery. Ishmael knows, however (at least after he has had his
experiences aboard the *Pequod* and become the narrator of
Ahab's story), that this quest after meaning is far more dangerous, far less susceptible to success, than Ahab imagines: "To a
dreamy meditative man," Ishmael explains, catapulting the experience of being at sea to an even higher degree of dematerialization and essentialization, standing aloft the masthead is a singularly "delightful" and yet terrifying experience:

> There you stand, a hundred feet above the silent decks, striding
> along the deep, as if the masts were gigantic stilts, while beneath you
> and between your legs, as it were, swim the hugest monsters of the
> sea. . . . There you stand, lost in the infinite series of the sea, with
> nothing ruffled but the waves. The tranced ship indolently rolls; the
> drowsy trade winds blow; everything resolves you into languor. . . .
> [L]ulled into such an opium-like listlessness of vacant, unconscious
> reverie is this absent-minded youth by the blending cadences of
> waves with thoughts, that at last he loses his identity; takes the mys-
> tic ocean at his feet for the visible image of that deep, blue, bottom-
> less soul, pervading mankind and nature; and every strange, half-
> seen, gliding, beautiful thing that eludes him; every dimly-
> discovered, uprising fin of some undiscernible form, seems to him
> the embodiment of those elusive thoughts that only people the soul
> by continually flitting through it. . . . There is no life in thee, now,
> except that rocking life imparted by a gently rolling ship; by her,

borrowed from the sea; by the sea, from the inscrutable tides of God. But while this sleep, this dream is on ye, move your foot or hand an inch; slip your hold at all; and your identity comes back in horror. Over Descartian vortices you hover. And perhaps, at mid-day, in the fairest weather, with one half-throttled shriek you drop through that transparent air into the summer sea, no more to rise for ever. Heed it well, ye Pantheists! (152–57)

As in Ahab's own formulation of his transcendentalist philosophy, Ishmael's presentation of his shipboard revery recognizes the mind's desire to pass through the physical world to a spiritual world beyond. But Ishmael also acknowledges the identity-dissolving, killing potential of the "Descartian vortices" of philosophical reflection. To doubt the existence of the physical world, to imagine the mind as of a different substance and therefore as being able to pierce through or dissolve the material world in order to recover the like-minded spiritual world behind it, may not recover lost unities but destroy the self altogether.

For this reason, *Moby-Dick* (like Poe's and Hawthorne's romances) must be understand as precisely *not* allegory, although it is also not symbolic text either. It does not tell a story, either mythically or historically conceived, that it imagines to figure real-life events; nor does it produce a purely linguistic universe in which nothing but words have verifiable existence. Rather, like Poe's and Hawthorne's romances, *Moby-Dick* is antiallegorical allegory. That is, it defeats the function of allegory, which one way or another evades the question of knowledge, by warning against the dangers of such allegorical evasion as leaves the mind in pure relation to nothing but itself.

The story does this, however, not by recourse to symbolism, which would assert the interpenetration of world and mind, meaning and language—thus answering the question of knowledge in the affirmative (for this reason the book is also antisymbolic symbolism). Rather, the book, structurally as well as thematically, constitutes an exploration of skepticism. It posits symbols in order to investigate what symbolism is and how it produces meaning. It forces mind and world (on the more philosophical plane of the novel) and self and community (on the more social plane) into patterns of mutual interrogation, thus opening up the possibility for affirmation and acknowledgment of the world and of other people, not as epistemological acts (based on knowledge) but as gestures of human responsibility and will (predicated on doubt). For this reason the book is filled with phenomenal, biological, and botanical detail, which portends no meaning outside itself and thus defies the strategies of human interpretation.

If *Moby-Dick* is the most purely philosophical and speculative of the American romances, it is also the most intensely naturalistic. Chapters on sea life and ship life, whale anatomy and hunting (such as the one entitled "Cetology") abound. Indeed, despite the story's distance from society as we normally know it, *Moby-Dick* is the most intensely sociological of the romances, providing vivid details about the communal constitution of the ship. This is a social world of sharp racial, religious, and class distinctions (not so different from the United States of America, we might feel) both on the level of government and on the level of citizenry. Furthermore, Ahab, Starbuck, Stubb, and Flask are as sharply distinguished from each other as they are separated as a group from the common mass of sailors—the mass including general sailors (like Ishmael) and the more servantlike class (Queequeg, Tashtego, and Daggoo), who are racially different from the other sailors and officers (Polynesian, Indian, and African).

Given the elaborateness of its physical and social detail, it is difficult not to think of this book as being about just the relation between the two ontologically different worlds—the one phenomenal and/or social, the other noumenal. Nowhere does the book more powerfully probe this relation, and link it to the moral purposes of the narrative, than in the sexual imagery that abounds in the text. Almost all recent critical studies of *Moby-Dick* have taken into account its pervasive, sometimes outrageous, sexual punning. If there is some serious purpose behind the text's sexual comedy, it has to do with the ways in which sexuality partakes of both the worlds of mind and body, self and other, and the way it can therefore become either (re)productive or static and killing. As I have already suggested, Ishmael's narrative may constitute nothing more than an elaborate masturbatory fantasy, which will lead to no procreative acts, no future. Melville's text, however, recording this dream of Ishmael's, may itself point the way, through its elaborate natural imagery, back to the world of nature, which is a world of racial, religious, and sexual difference.

The book's various lines of argumentation and imagery (meta-physical and physiological) come together at several points in the narrative, as, for example, in the following incident to which I have already alluded: Tashtego's birth out of the head of the whale in chapter 78, which significantly prefigures the conclud-ing scene of Ishmael's own survival from the "creamy" "vortex" of the ship's "half-spent suction." Tashtego (one of the "seamen"; semen?) is "milking" the whale for "sperm" when the "queer accident" occurs and he "drop[s] head-foremost down into this great Tun of Heidelburgh" (338–39). The scene recalls other moments of sexual gaming in the book, when the seamen are represented as squeezing sperm out of the whales in ecstatic revery. Here, however, the descent into the whale's head takes on metaphysical as well as sexual implications. "Had Tashtego perished in that head," Ishmael explains,

> it had been a very precious perishing; smothered in the very whitest and daintiest of fragrant spermaceti; coffined, hearsed, and tombed in the secret inner chamber and sanctum sanctorum of the whale. Only one sweeter end can readily be recalled—the delicious death of an Ohio honey-hunter, who seeking honey in the crotch of a hollow tree, found such exceeding store of it, that leaning too far over, it sucked him in, so that he died embalmed. How many, think ye, have likewise fallen into Plato's honey head, and sweetly perished there? (342)

Smothered in the secret inner chamber, the sanctum sancto-rum of the whale's body, or sucked into the crotch of a tree, Tashtego and the honey-hunter die in a totality of sexual ecstacy (in an effluvium of masculinist semen and female honey), which is simultaneous with their absorption (or perhaps, given the terms of human birth, reabsorption) into the female body. This fantasy may do no more than realize a fear of heterosexual rela-tions and their potentially castrating effects. In this way, it may reenforce the powerful homosexual eroticism of the text, as in the "marriage" of Ishmael and Queequeg. It may also, however, point toward the self-destructiveness of the characters' auto-erotic, masturbatory tendencies. These tendencies parallel the world-denying self-absorption of Platonic metaphysics. The "life-less head" of the whale, we are told, "throb[s] and heav[es] just below the surface of the sea, as if that moment seized with some momentous idea; whereas it was only the poor Indian uncon-sciously revealing by those struggles the perilous depth to which he had sunk" (339). Philosophical reflection, the text suggests, may constitute one more form of male masturbation; and masturbation, whether physical or mental, is neither life sustaining nor life creating.

The terms of Tashtego's rebirth from the tun of the whale are hardly reassuring for the implications of Ishmael's own rebirth later on, especially given the fact that Tashtego will not long survive this rebirth. Queequeg is a good midwife in this obstetrical "delivery." He even manages, upon seeing that "a leg was presented" first, to turn his infant around and "so haul . . . out our poor Tash by the head" (341). But Ishmael is right to note that this is not spiritual "deliverance" but bodily "delivery." Furthermore, in delivering Tashtego's "head," the "great head" of the whale is lost (341). The political implications of this statement, given the fact that Tashtego is an Indian, cannot be separated from the major political debate of the time, the deliverance from slavery. When discussing the appalling whiteness of Moby Dick, Ishmael notes that the "pre-eminence" of whiteness "applies to the human race itself, giving the white man ideal mastership over every dusky tribe" (184). Although Tashtego, in this scene, may be reborn from death, the place he comes to occupy in this world is identical to what it was before his accident. This is birth as replication, not reproduction.

The price of all-male birth is nothing less than the loss of the world itself, in all of its racial, religious gendered difference and abundance. In the divisions produced by Melville's text, the sperm whale, albeit a symbol of the masculine on the literary axis, is, within the physical dimension of the text, linked to the natural and therefore the feminine. As the two planes of reference coincide in this scene, the tendency toward the symbolic taken to its extreme ("Man overboard," Daggoo exclaims—[339]) becomes part and parcel of the disregard for the physical, so that birth itself becomes one more form of intellectual and philosophical sterility. It is murderous and suicidal both. Ahab recognizes the self-destructiveness of his self-directed sexual desire. "What is it," he asks, toward the end of the book,

> what nameless, inscrutable, unearthly thing is it, what cozening, hidden lord and master, and cruel, remorseless emperor commands me; that against all natural lovings and longings, I so keep pushing, and crowding, and jamming myself on all the time; recklessly making me

ready to do what in my own proper, natural heart, I durst not so much as dare? (534–35)

But Ahab's soul, like Starbuck's, "is more than matched; she's overmanned" (166). And when he tries to dismember his dismemberer, he more than castrates himself. He kills himself, leaving only the orphaned Ishmael, his barely viable surrogate offspring, in the vortex of his orgasmic wake.

Chapter 6

FROM ROMANCE TO REALISM: HENRY JAMES'S PORTRAIT OF A LADY

Melville's *Moby-Dick* realizes most of the major implications of romance fiction generally. It is the skepticist text stretched to its philosophical and social limit. Like Hawthorne, Melville recognizes that without sustained philosophical doubt—without, that is, asking the questions, Does the world exist? And do I exist in it?—the world (physical, social, and cultural) quickly dwindles to a monomaniacal self-conception of self, endlessly self-repeating. But, like Poe, Melville realizes as well the dangers of too great an infatuation with doubt. To answer the skeptical question, No, the world does not exist, and my existence (such as it is) depends upon my constant enactment of the world's negation, replicates the problem of not asking the question at all. Such skeptical engagement, Melville suggests, which relocates reality from the phenomenal to the noumenal world, ironically reproduces the same tendency toward egocentric self-replication that the absence of doubt (as in Hawthorne's world of religious law) also produces. The world ceases to function as a reality outside the self, filled with variety and contradiction, pain and love. Instead, it becomes a prison or cemetery, containing only the dead or dying self.

In 20th-century American fiction, William Faulkner inherits the more purely philosophical, more pessimistic line of romance fiction inaugurated by Poe and Melville. Hawthorne's direct descendant in the tradition is Henry James. James not only shares Hawthorne's skepticism but participates as well in his faith that such salvation as human beings achieve exists in a relationship (aversively defined) between the social and the private worlds.

In many literary critical histories, Henry James represents the consummate American realist. He exemplifies the break with the 19th-century tradition, discovering or recovering a continuity with the 19th-century British novel of Austen, Thackeray, and Trollope. In terms of his American origins, James would seem to have more to do with the tradition of women's fiction—with its domestic focus and its decidedly social implications—than with the gothic romances of Poe, Melville, or even the more socially modulated romances of Hawthorne.[1] In fact, in his preface to *The American* James articulates a very forceful rejection of the strategies and assumptions of romance fiction. Nonetheless, as critics have also acknowledged, and as James's own volume on *Hawthorne* more than indicates, Hawthorne is an important predecessor for James—especially in his early writings, such as *The American* and *The Portrait of a Lady*, as well as in many of his novellas (*Daisy Miller*, for example, *The Aspern Papers*, and *The Turn of the Screw*) and short stories ("The Beast in the Jungle," "The Figure in the Carpet," and "The Real Thing," among others).[2] James's writing career charts a path from romance back to realism; his *Portrait of a Lady* can be read as being about just that journey.

Traditionally James's fiction (from early to late) has been understood as an exploration of consciousness—of the mind's attempts to know a world that is baffling, contradictory, even sinister. A major difference between James and the 19th-century romancers is this direct evocation of human consciousness. Through a skepticist strategy that shies away from mimetic psychological representation, the fictions of Poe, Hawthorne, and Melville probe the social, moral, and philosophical implications of doubt for human beings and the world they create or, more often, fail to create. James's novels and stories, on the other hand, produce vivid, detailed portraits of individuals privately grappling with their experience of doubt. Like the protagonists of the major 19th-century romancers, James's heroes must come to see what Emerson in his essay *Nature* designates the "shining apparition" in which this world consists. They must become philosophically skeptical. But whereas Poe, Hawthorne, and Melville dramatize the necessity for such philosophical reflection, James traces its consequences as his heroes move back into the real world of people, places, and events.

Many of James's protagonists (especially in his romance fictions) are Americans, often women or children (sometimes, as in the case of Daisy Miller, a combination of the three). They are innocents (like the typical hero of a Hawthorne or Melville romance), with very little significant experience of the world, who must come to explore the world. The place of their exploration is typically Europe, which serves for James the same function that Puritan New England served for Hawthorne. Europe is the place of history and tradition (social convention in James's case as opposed to religious ritual or belief in Hawthorne's). It is the patriarchal place, in which certainty, rather than doubt, reigns supreme. Into this world enters the American and/or child and/or woman—Daisy Miller in the story that bears her name, Christopher Newman in *The American,* Isabel Archer in *The Portrait.* What these individuals have to learn is nothing less than what Hawthorne's protagonists must learn: how to see the world. The cost of their education is very high. Nonetheless, most of James's heroes (unlike most of Hawthorne's; Hester Prynne and Phoebe Pyncheon are notable exceptions here) will learn this lesson and come to incorporate their knowledge as part of their ongoing relationship to society.

Of these characters, Christopher Newman (perhaps because he is neither a woman nor a child, "only" an American male) fares the best. Newman will lose the lady he loves because he will never succeed in wholly penetrating the surface of Europe's self-protective coating. He will come to the end of his experience far less cheerful and far less optimistic than he was at the beginning. But Newman does survive, and he even achieves a certain moral advantage as he recognizes the depths of immorality to which he will refuse to sink. As an American businessman, Newman can go back home to a country and a livelihood that will sustain him in the new consciousness he has acquired. And his gain will be the nation's. This is crucial to James's purposes. For James's subject is not only individual consciousness; it is national consciousness as well. And for James, America, as a nation, cannot realize its own best gifts (including its skepticist consciousness) without maturing into something like (though in no way identical to) a European perspective.

In other words, James's *American* (like other of his stories and novels) concerns the maturation of America, its growing up by its moving back toward and acknowledging its origins in European culture and tradition—not so that America can become Europe or even replace Europe but so that America can come to see itself, within its historical and cultural context. Like Hawthorne, who retrieves for mid-19th-century Americans their Puritan past so that the world of the present can see the living ghost of the past when it crosses its threshold, James stages the confrontation between two nations, one of which represents the past reality of the other, so that the new nation can perceive its present by fully recognizing its past.

This process is not so different from what Hawthorne dramatizes in *The House of the Seven Gables,* which, as he tells us in the preface, "comes under the romantic definition [by] connect[ing] a by-gone time with the very Present that is flitting away from us" (1). In an early scene in *The House of the Seven Gables,* Hepzibah Pyncheon, a descendant of a powerful Puritan family, directly faces and fails to recognize the descendant of the family's 17th-century antagonist, remarking ironically that "if old Maule's ghost, or a descendant of his, could see me behind the counter to-day, he would call it the fulfilment of his worst wishes" (92). Until Hepzibah—either directly or through her surrogate, her niece, Phoebe Pyncheon—comes to identify that ghost, the Pyncheon family will remain stuck in the past, a victim (like Roderick Usher in his house, which the title of Hawthorne's romance recalls) to the terrors and mysteries of the past, powerless (again like the Ushers) to produce a future. At the end of *The House of the Seven Gables,* Phoebe will not only come to recognize the ghosts of the past but she, herself one of their descendants, will marry another of their heirs. This will release those ghosts (quite literally in Hawthorne's story: they float upward to heaven) and thus release the present from them. By making visible the invisible, through his art, Holgrave (like Hawthorne) will free the present to get on with the business of producing a future.

As we shall see in a moment, Isabel Archer, in *The Portrait,* also learns to see ghosts. So, too, do Christopher Newman (the ghosts in *The American* have to do with no less a mystery than murder) and Daisy Miller (for whom the ghost is an invisible contagion, to which she is rendered vulnerable by her inability to see beyond the surfaces of her world). Ghosts are important to James, as they are to Hawthorne (and Poe). For James, as for Hawthorne, reality is as much (if not more) what cannot be known or understood. But whereas for Hawthorne the agent of skeptical seeing is the art of romance (in *Seven Gables,* Holgrave's daguerrotype), for James only a hard, unwavering look at reality can bring the world's specters into focus. James glances back at the art of romance to acknowledge the importance of the ghosts that haunt and thus inform human perception. For him, as for his predecessors in the tradition, the world is shrouded in what we cannot know and cannot say. But James's skepticism leads him away from the romancers' art, away from the skepticist text. *The Portrait* registers this move from romance to realism as it charts Isabel's journey from certainty to doubt to commitment to an unrelentingly solid and "real" world that no amount of philo-sophical reflection will soften.

Self-Reliance and the Portrait of a Woman

As an American, *The Portrait*'s Isabel Archer (like a host of other American heroes, from Hester Prynne on) is an Emersonian indi-vidualist, confident of the powers of her own mind, resisting social conformity. What Isabel has to come to learn, according to James, is not the powerlessness of her imagination, or its irrele-vance or even its impropriety (which is what Isabel's husband, Gilbert Osmond, wants her to learn). Instead, she must come to understand its "requirements" (158), by which James means not simply what it requires in order adequately to perceive the world but what is required of it in order properly to function in it. Isabel must learn what Hester learns: to think aversively.[3]

Isabel's "theory," early in the novel, "that it was only under this provision life was worth living, that one should be one of the best, should be conscious of a fine organisation . . . , should move in a realm of light, of natural wisdom, of happy impulse, of inspi-ration gracefully chronic," is a virtual gloss on Emerson, at least as he has been popularly understood (53). It contains all of the important Emersonian categories, including "a certain nobleness of imagination," feelings of "beauty and bravery and magnanim-ity," and "infinite hope" (53).[4] But her Emersonianism is hardly sufficient to direct her growth into adult maturity. This is so because, as a kind of misreading of Emerson (Isabel is neither the first nor the last American protagonist to misread Emerson), it lacks the one major caution without which Emerson's own tran-scendentalism would degenerate into mindless optimism and egotism. This is Emerson's "noble doubt," in its two mutually skeptical directions: the self doubting the world and, equally, the world casting doubt on the self.[5]

Isabel believes "it was almost as unnecessary to cultivate doubt of one's self as to cultivate doubt of one's best friend: one should try to be one's own best friend and to give one's self, in this manner, distinguished company. . . . She had a fixed deter-mination to regard the world as a place of brightness, of free expansion, and irresistible action. . . . She was in no uncertainty about the things that were wrong" (53). Isabel has all of Emerson's criteria but none of his philosophical depth. She resists, for example, "inconsistency" (54), which is perhaps one of the hallmarks of Emerson's philosophy, one of many of Emerson's words for the mutual opposition and interdepen-dence of self and other out of which the relationship between the self and the other is established. Self-consistent, Isabel is solipsist and conformist both.

Part of what Isabel's idealism precludes is other people. In Isabel's view "her life should always be in harmony with the most pleasing impression she should produce; she would be what she appeared, and she would appear what she was" (54). Idea and reality would be one; and that oneness, in which the self is the self's own best friend, would be a self-containedness that would exclude the rest of the world. Like Madame Merle, who is the "cleverest woman" Ralph knows, "excepting" Isabel herself, Isabel is what, using Ralph's word for Merle, we might call "com-plete" (153). "She never called it a state of solitude," because, unlike Emerson's notion of solitude (or Thoreau's), it has less to do with a momentary retreat from the world than with an eclips-ing of it. Like Gilbert Osmond's "indifference" (354) later on, Isabel's "independence" (the word is used to describe Osmond as well—[354]) is not a self-confessed position in relation to the world, a point of view from which one views difference and dependence. Rather, it is an escape, a repression of relation.

As I have already suggested in my reading of Hawthorne, relationality is what Hawthorne's skepticism, like Emerson's, is all about—hence Hester's return at the end of *The Scarlet Letter,* which constructs her aversive relationship to the community. James's *Portrait* similarly ends with a return as Isabel goes back to Rome to fulfill her promise to Pansy. In many ways, Isabel's return is more courageous than Hester's and also more altruistic. Isabel returns to a suffocating and loveless marriage, Hester to her private domicile on the outskirts of the town. Isabel returns to a daughter who is not her own. Hester leaves her daughter behind in Europe. In a sense Hester's return is more theoretical than Isabel's, since it will in no way lessen her prospects for happiness. Indeed, as Hester becomes a major figure in the community, we might even feel that she maximizes her chances for happiness by returning to New England. Perhaps for this reason, Hester's return is made to seem not only literal but self-consciously literary: her return (as her existence itself) is from first to last figured in Hawthorne's book by the letter. In terms of Hawthorne's strategies of representation, Hester is less a person returning to a place than an image being restored to a culture. She figures language being renewed and brought to bear once again on the community from which it has become divorced. Hester's return figures America's return to itself, as a place of conversation and dialogue, a place of aversive thinking. For this reason, Hawthorne represents himself, in "The Custom-House," as discovering Hester's letter and taking it upon himself, in the form of the romance he writes.

Isabel's return is not theoretical in this way. Like Hester's return to the scene of her suffering, Isabel's in no way signifies her unwilling capitulation to societal norms and values. It signals her acceptance (like Hester's) of the simple fact that one's individualism cannot meaningfully express itself except in relation to others, especially those others (like one's daughter) for whom one bears special, familial responsibility. But Isabel's return is less to the *idea* of responsibility than to responsibility as such. In evolving his theory of skepticist thought, Cavell, as I have been noting, emphasizes the way in which doubt can become the condition for our affirmation of the world and our acknowledgment of the existence of other people in it. In *The Portrait of a Lady,* James follows such a course from doubt to affirmation and acknowledgment as Cavell describes. But the source of doubt for

Isabel is not, as it is for Hester or Phoebe Pyncheon or even James's own protagonists, like Daisy and Christopher Newman, the large complex of social institutions that ensnare her. Rather, it is the particular individual, her husband, to whom she must, at the end of the story, return, putting herself forever in intimate, personal relation to the source of both her suffering and her doubt.

It is as Isabel begins to mistrust or distrust Osmond, and to "doubt" and mistrust herself as well, that she starts her journey toward skeptical maturity (349, 343, 347). Isabel had "taken all the first steps in the purest confidence"—childlike and innocent, we might say, like Phoebe or even Hester, who is no more than a child-bride before she arrives in Salem. But Isabel suddenly finds "the infinite vista of a multiplied life to be a dark, narrow alley with a dead wall at the end. Instead of leading to the high places of happiness, from which the world would seem to lie below one, so that one could look down with a sense of exaltation and advantage . . . it led rather downward and earthward." As she comes to realize, "it was her deep distrust of her husband [that] darkened the world" (349). Osmond as the agent of skeptical reflection reduces Emerson's shining apparition, the natural world, to the sly malice of greed and egocentricity. As in earlier works in the tradition of romance fiction, the doubt that Osmond introduces has to do, specifically, with sexual matters. This doubt is no less effective an instrument of skepticist education than the noble doubts produced by nature itself. It does make, however, the consequences of Isabel's experience far less hopeful.

Because of this doubt, Isabel, by the end of the book, comes to see the *nothing*, which is James's figure (as it is Emerson's) for the insubstantiality of the world, the immateriality that produces the questions, Does the world exist? Do I exist? And how can I know or describe this world?

> [Ralph] had told her, the first evening she ever spent at Gardencourt, that if she should live to suffer enough she might some day see the ghost with which the old house was duly provided. She apparently had fulfilled the necessary condition; for the next morning, in the cold, faint dawn, she knew that a spirit was standing by her bed. . . . It seemed to her for an instant that he was standing there—a vague, hovering figure in the vagueness of the room. She started a moment; she saw his white face—his kind eyes; then she saw there was nothing. She was not afraid; she was only sure. (472)

These lines refer specifically to Ralph's death and Isabel's intuition of it. The ghost she sees is Ralph. Only suffering, the passage implies, enables us to contemplate the nothing that is our own mortality. But moments later the word *nothing* appears in a somewhat different context, which turns the book back to its origins in the romance tradition.

Isabel has kept her rendezvous with her previous suitor, Caspar Goodwood, who wishes to save Isabel from Osmond by taking her away with him. They have shared a moment of passionate embrace. But Isabel rejects Caspar, as much for the escape he promises her as for the desire to possess her that he also expresses. In her final encounter with Caspar, Isabel recognizes that the "ghost" that we come to see in our maturity is not the specter of death (which might be thought to frighten us into social conformity) but the "nothing" around which we construct our world and which makes our world a choice rather than an inevitability of social obligation.

> When darkness returned she was free. She never looked about her; she only darted from the spot. There were lights in the windows of the house; they shone far across the lawn. In an extraordinarily short time—for the distance was considerable—she had moved through the darkness (for she saw nothing) and reached the door. Here only she paused. She looked all about her; she listened a little; then she put her hand on the latch. She had not known where to turn; but she knew now. There was a very straight path. (482)

Seeing the nothing, Isabel comes to understand that what distinguishes this nothing from the eclipse of consciousness that we call death or unconsciousness is the choice to affirm life despite the nothing.

Putting her hand on the latch, opening the door, Isabel decides to return home, to Pansy, and to the life and love that Pansy represents. She chooses life over death, freedom over fate, and relationality over solipsism. In so doing, she chooses a world of depths and meanings (shrouded in shadow and doubt) over a universe of brightly illuminated simplicities and surfaces, which affords no place for individual will and imagination. She has chosen the world itself, the very straight path (like a cable), with all of its contingencies and conventions, demands and frustrations. By the end of the novel Isabel has done exactly what she had set out to do and what her cousin Ralph Touchett had meant to assist her in doing by leaving her a part of his father's fortune. She has met the requirements of her imagination, where such requirements, she has come to understand, are as much responsibilities and commitments in relation to others as needs and desires of her own. James's novel follows the cable of imagination back down to earth, which is where human beings reside and where they must meet the requirements of their imaginations.

The Democracy of Readership

The readings I have provided of five major American romance fictions hardly exhaust what can be said concerning either these five works or the range of romance fiction generally. Nonetheless, I hope they have pointed to salient features of the tradition; most particularly, its philosophical skepticism, both on the level of theme and structure, and its concern with the moral and social implications of such skepticism. In the final analysis, the Americanness of these fictions can be defined as the way in which they realize one of the basic premises of democracy: that society shall be governed not from above (either according to some preestablished sociopolitical hierarchy or according to some religious or social law or truth) but from below, where such government of the people, for the people, and by the people does not represent an evasion of cultural consensus (as if we could all function as independent individuals within the body politic) but a particular way of evolving such consensus.

Therefore, each one of these works not only makes the point that the universe is unknowable except through the subjectivity of our private perceptions, but it provides the equally important countermove, which requires that individuals nonetheless (and with a full consciousness of the partiality of their judgments) assume responsibility for the world that they collectively create. American romance fiction is a training ground for the interpreters of America, who are as much the citizens of the state as they are the readers of its texts.

Notes and References

1. Toward a Definition of American Romance

1. George Dekker, *The American Historical Romance* (Cambridge, England: Cambridge University Press, 1987), 15–17.

2. Richard Chase, *The American Novel and Its Tradition* (N.Y.: Doubleday, 1957), 12–13; F. O. Matthiessen, *American Renaissance: Art and Expression in the Age of Emerson and Whitman* (London: Oxford University Press, 1941); Charles Feidelson Jr., *Symbolism and American Literature* (Chicago: University of Chicago Press, 1953); R. W. B. Lewis, *The American Adam: Innocence, Tragedy, and Tradition in the Nineteenth Century* (Chicago: University of Chicago Press, 1955); Lionel Trilling, *The Liberal Imagination: Essays on Literature and Society* (N.Y.: Viking, 1950); and F. R. Leavis, *The Great Tradition: George Eliot, Henry James, Joseph Conrad* (N.Y.: Anchor, 1954).

3. Nathaniel Hawthorne, *The House of the Seven Gables, The Centenary Edition of the Works of Nathaniel Hawthorne,* ed. William Charvat et al. (Columbus: Ohio State University Press, 1965), vol. 2:1.

4. Henry James, *The American, The Novels and Tales of Henry James* (Fairfield, N.J.: August M. Kelley Publishers, 1976), vol. 2:xvii–xviii.

5. Critics who challenge the existence of the genre as such include Nina Baym, "Concepts of Romance in Hawthorne's America," *Nineteenth-Century Fiction* (1984), 38; and *Novels, Readers, and Reviewers: Responses to Fiction in Antebellum America* (Ithaca, N.Y.: Cornell University Press, 1984); George Dekker, *The American Historical Romance* (Cambridge, England: Cambridge University Press, 1987) and "The Genealogy of American Romance," *ESQ: A Journal of the American Renaissance* 35 (1989), 69–83; John McWilliams, "The Rationale for 'The American Romance'" *boundary 2 New Americanists: Revisionist Interventions into the Canon*, special issue of *boundary 2*, ed. Donald E. Pease, vol. 17 (1990), 71–82; and William C. Spengemann, "What Is American Literature?" *Centennial Review* 22 (1978), 119–38; and "American Writers and English Literature," *ELH* 52 (1985), 209–38, now collected in *A Mirror for Americanists: Reflections on the Idea of American Literature* (Hanover: University Press of New England, 1989). Also relevant in this context is David Reynolds, *Beneath the American Renaissance: The Subversive Imagination in the Age of Emerson and Melville* (N.Y.: Knopf, 1988).

6. Michael Davitt Bell, *The Development of American Romance: The Sacrifice of Relation* (Chicago: Chicago University Press, 1980).

7. Richard Poirier, *A World Elsewhere: The Place of Style in American Literature* (N.Y.: Oxford University Press, 1966).

8. Frederic Jameson, *The Prison-House of Language: A Critical Account of Structuralism and Russian Formalism* (Princeton, N.J.: Princeton University Press, 1972).

9. Writing literary history is at best a tricky business. For a study of the writing of American literary history, which still has much to teach us, see Howard Mumford Jones, *The Theory of American Literature* (Ithaca, N.Y.: Cornell University Press, 1948; reprinted 1965).

10. Edgar Allan Poe, *Collected Works of Edgar Allan Poe: Tales and Sketches: 1831–1842* and *1843–1849*, ed. Thomas Ollive Mabbott (Cambridge, Mass.: Harvard University Press, 1978); Nathaniel Hawthorne, *The Scarlet Letter, Centenary Edition*, vol. 1; Herman Melville, *Moby-Dick, or The Whale*, intro. Newton Arvin (N.Y.: Holt, Rinehart and Winston, 1961).

11. Leslie Fiedler, *Love and Death in the American Novel* (New York: Criterion Books, 1960), xxvi.

12. Benjamin T. Spencer, *The Quest for Nationality: The American Literary Campaign* (Syracuse, N.Y.: Syracuse University Press, 1957).

13. Jean de Crèvecœur (1735–1813), *Letters from an American Farmer* (1782): *The Norton Anthology of American Literature*, ed. Nina Baym et al. (New York: Norton, 1989), 263–65.

14. *Of Plymouth Plantation*, in *The Norton Anthology*, ed. Baym, 38.

15. Sacvan Bercovitch, *The Puritan Origins of the American Self* (New Haven, Conn.: Yale University Press, 1975). See also *The American Jeremiad* (Madison: Wisconsin University Press, 1978).

16. Reprinted in *The American Literary Revolution, 1783–1837*, ed. Robert E. Spiller (Garden City, N.Y.: Doubleday, 1967), 163–74.

17. Alexis de Tocqueville, *Democracy in America*, trans. Henry Reeve (Cambridge, England: Sever & Francis, 1862), vol. 2:40–42.

18. *The American Scholar*, in *The Selected Writings of Ralph Waldo Emerson*, ed. Brooks Atkinson (New York: Modern Library, 1968), 62–63.

19. Michael P. Kramer, *Imagining Language in America: From the Revolution to the Civil War* (Princeton, N.J.: Princeton University Press, 1992).

20. For contrast, see John Pickering, *Memoir on the Present State of the English Language in the United States of America* (1816), in which he argues for continuing to use British English; Spiller, 175–86.

21. Kenneth Dauber, *The Idea of Authorship in America: Democratic Poetics from Franklin to Melville* (Madison: University of Wisconsin Press, 1990). See also Edgar Dryden, *The Form of American Romance* (Baltimore, Md.: Johns Hopkins University Press, 1988), and James D. Wallace, *Early Cooper and His Audience* (New York: Columbia University Press, 1986).

22. See my discussion of Cavell's work at the end of the bibliographic essay.

2. The Romance of Storytelling

1. Poe, who is probably America's first full-fledged romancer, notoriously imitated and even plagiarized European gothic fiction. See Kenneth Silverman, *Edgar A. Poe: Mournful and Never-Ending Remembrance* (New York: HarperCollins Publishers, 1991), 70–72, 112–17. For studies of Washington Irving, see Edward Wagenknecht, *Washington Irving: Moderation Displaced* (New York: Oxford University Press, 1962); William L. Hedges, *Washington Irving: An American Study 1802–1832* (Baltimore, Md.: Johns Hopkins University Press, 1965); and Jeffrey Rubin-Dorsky, *Adrift in the Old World: The Psychological Pilgrimage of Washington Irving* (Chicago: University of Chicago Press, 1988). For studies of Brown see Donald Ringe, *Charles Brockden Brown* (New York: Twayne, 1966); Norman S. Grabo, *The Coincidental Art of Charles Brockden Brown* (Chapel Hill: University of North Carolina Press, 1981); and Alan Axelrod, *Charles Brockden Brown: An American Tale* (Austin: University of Texas Press, 1983).

2. John P. McWilliams Jr., *Political Justice in a Republic: James Fenimore Cooper's America* (Berkeley: University of California Press, 1972), 1–3.

3. Cf. Wallace, *Early Cooper*: "*The Pioneers* [constitutes] the major victory in Cooper's campaign to create an audience for American fiction. . . . [H]e courted a whole new class of readers by assimilating the substance of pioneer and travel narratives; he structured the novel in such a way that it taught his audience how to read an American novel and warned them against the danger of misreading; finally, the theme of *The Pioneers* instructed his readers in what it meant to inhabit the American landscape, to inherit American history—to be an American." The novel, concludes Wallace, was for Cooper a "democratic form . . . whose responsibility is to limit itself to 'the nature "common to man"'" (169, 121).

4. See, for example, Jane Tompkins, *Sensational Designs: The Cultural Work of American Fiction 1790–1860* (New York: Oxford University Press, 1985), and Lewis, *The American Adam.*

5. See Bercovitch, *Puritan Origins.*

6. James Fenimore Cooper, *The Prairie: A Tale* (New York: Holt, Rinehart and Winston, 1961), 39.

7. The blurring of distinctions between margins and centers goes to the heart of Cooper's concern—discussed throughout Cooper criticism—with the relationship between private authority and individual rights on the one hand and civil order and the needs of community on the other. See McWilliams, *Political Justice*; Warren Motley, *The American Abraham: James Fenimore Cooper and the Frontier Patriarch* (Cambridge, England: Cambridge University Press, 1987; especially the discussion of *The Prairie*, 105–25); and Charles Hansford Adams, *"The Guardian of the Law": Authority and Identity in James Fenimore Cooper* (University Park: Pennsylvania State University Press, 1990).

3. The Romance of the Word

1. Kenneth Dauber, "Criticism of American Literature," *Diacritics* 7 (1977), 55–65.

2. I have discussed this in "Sacvan Bercovitch, Stanley Cavell, and the Romance Theory of American Fiction," *PMLA* 107 (1992), 78–91.

3. Evan Carton, *The Rhetoric of American Romance: Dialectic and Identity in Emerson, Dickinson, Poe, and Hawthorne* (Baltimore, Md.: Johns Hopkins University Press, 1985); John Carlos Rowe, *Through the Custom-House: Nineteenth-Century American Theory and Modern Fiction* (Baltimore, Md.: Johns Hopkins University Press, 1982); and Gregory S. Jay, *America, the Scrivener: Deconstruction and the Subject of Literary History* (Ithaca, N.Y.: Cornell University Press, 1990).

4. *The Purloined Poe: Lacan, Derrida, and Psychoanalytic Reading*, eds. John P. Muller and William J. Richardson (Baltimore, Md.: Johns Hopkins University Press, 1988).

5. Michael Williams, *A World of Words: Language and Displacement in the Fiction of Edgar Allan Poe* (Durham, N.C.: Duke University Press, 1988).

6. For readings of Poe's women see Leland Person Jr., *Aesthetic Headaches: Women and a Masculine Poetics in Poe, Melville, and Hawthorne* (Athens: University of Georgia Press, 1988), and Cynthia S. Jordan, *Second Stories: The Politics of Language, Form, and Gender in Early American Fictions* (Chapel Hill: University of North Carolina Press, 1989).

7. Stanley Cavell, "Being Odd, Getting Even: Threats to Individuality," In *Quest of the Ordinary: Lines of Skepticism and Romanticism* (Chicago: University of Chicago Press, 1989), 105–49.

4. The Romance of History

1. Wolfgang Iser, *The Fictive and the Imaginary: Charting Literary Anthropology* (Baltimore, Md.: Johns Hopkins University Press, 1993).

2. Stanley Cavell, "Hope Against Hope," *Conditions Handsome and Unhandsome* (Albuquerque, N. Mex.: Living Batch Press, 1989), 138. See also "Aversive Thinking" in the same volume.

3. I discuss this in *Engendering Romance: Women Writers and the Hawthorne Tradition, 1850–1990* (New Haven, Conn.: Yale University Press, 1994).

4. I discuss this idea in *Fiction and Historical Consciousness: The American Romance Tradition* (New Haven, Conn.: Yale University Press, 1989).

5. For this history of Puritanism see especially Perry Miller, *Orthodoxy in Massachusetts, 1630–1650* (New York: Harper and Row, 1933); *The New England Mind: The Seventeenth Century* (New York: Macmillan, 1939); *The New England Mind: From Colony to Province* (Cambridge, Mass.: Harvard University Press, 1953); *Errand into the Wilderness* (Cambridge, Mass.: Harvard University Press, 1956); and *Nature's Nation* (Cambridge, Mass.: Harvard University Press, 1967); Bercovitch, *Puritan Origins* and *American Jeremiad*; and Michael J. Colacurcio, *The Province of Piety: Moral History in Hawthorne's Early Tales* (Cambridge, Mass.: Harvard University Press, 1984).

6. For a discussion of patriarchy and male skepticism, see Mary O'Brien, *The Politics of Reproduction* (Boston: Routledge & Kegan Paul, 1983); Stanley Cavell, *Disowning Knowledge in Six Plays of Shakespeare* (Cambridge, England: Cambridge University Press, 1987), 15–19, 193–221; Mieke Bal, *Death and Dissymmetry: The Politics of Coherence in the Book of Judges* (Chicago: University of Chicago Press, 1988); Lynda E. Boose, "The Father's House and the Daughter in It: The Structures

of Western Culture's Daughter-Father Relationship," in *Daughters and Fathers,* eds. Lynda E. Boose and Betty S. Flowers (Baltimore, Md.: Johns Hopkins University Press, 1989), 19–74; and my own *Engendering Romance.*

7. I explore many of the issues I discuss here in my essay "Sacvan Bercovitch, Stanley Cavell, and the Romance Theory of American Fiction," a part of which also appears in *Engendering Romance.*

8. Cf. Charles Feidelson Jr.: "[A]s a single letter, the most indeterminate of all symbols, and first letter of the alphabet, the beginning of all communication, Hawthorne's emblem represents a potential point of coherence within a manifold historical experience"—"The Scarlet Letter," *Hawthorne Centenary Essays,* ed. Roy Harvey Pearce (Columbus: Ohio State University Press, 1964), 36.

9. Stanley Cavell, *The Senses of Walden* (New York: Viking Press, 1972).

10. Sacvan Bercovitch, *The Office of the Scarlet Letter* (Baltimore, Md.: Johns Hopkins University Press, 1991), xii. For related readings see Donald Pease, *Visionary Compacts: American Renaissance Writings in Cultural Context* (Madison: University of Wisconsin Press, 1987), 81–107; Larry J. Reynolds, *European Revolutions and the American Literary Renaissance* (New Haven, Conn.: Yale University Press, 1988); Leland S. Person Jr., "Hester's Revenge: The Power of Silence in *The Scarlet Letter,*" *Nineteenth-Century Literature* 43 (1989), 465–83. For good deconstructionist readings of the book, see Millicent Bell, "The Obliquity of Signs: *The Scarlet Letter,*" *Critical Essays on Hawthorne's The Scarlet Letter,* ed. David B. Kesterton (Boston: G. K. Hall, 1988), 157–69, and Steven C. Scheer, *Pious Impostures and Unproven Words: The Romance of Deconstruction in Nineteenth-Century America* (Lanham, Ga.: University Press of Athens, 1990).

11. Compare Richard Millington, *Practicing Romance: Narrative Form and Cultural Engagement in Hawthorne's Fiction* (Princeton, N.J.: Princeton University Press, 1991).

12. For a discussion of the tombstone as a potential figure for the closing down of meaning and how Hawthorne's text resists that possibility, see James Walter, "The Letter and the Spirit

in Hawthorne's Allegory of American Experience," *ESQ: A Journal of the American Renaissance* 32 (1986), 35–54.

13. In Marvell the line reads: "In a Field, *Sable,* a Lover gules"— quoted by Hyatt Waggoner, *The Presence of Hawthorne* (Baton Rouge: Louisiana State University Press, 1979), 71. On the connection between Hawthorne's ending and Marvell's poem, see Robert L. Brant, "Hawthorne and Melville," *American Literature* 30 (1958), 366.

14. For another discussion of the dynamics of the end of the novel, see Viola Sachs, "The Gnosis of Hawthorne and Melville: An Interpretation of *The Scarlet Letter* and *Moby Dick*," *American Quarterly* 32 (1980), 123–41, and Waggoner, *Presence,* 67–75.

15. Stanley Cavell, *Senses of Walden,* 43.

16. Hyatt Waggoner is thus wrong to conclude that "[a] story in which the action has moved, metaphorically, between the points defined in the first chapter as the cemetery, the prison, and the rose, ends with one of its reference points, the rose, missing"—*The Presence of Hawthorne,* 70.

5. The Romance of Nature

1. According to the dictionary, the word *purloin* originates with a Middle English root meaning "to put away" or "to render ineffectual."

2. For feminist readings of these three writers, see David Leverenz, *Manhood and the American Renaissance* (Ithaca, N.Y.: Cornell University Press, 1989); Cynthia S. Jordan, *Second Stories*; Leland Person, *Aesthetic Headaches*; and my own *Engendering Romance.*

3. See James Grossman, *James Fenimore Cooper* (London: Methuen, 1950), 10.

4. Compare Annette Kolodny, *The Lay of the Land: Metaphor as Experience in American Life and Letters* (Chapel Hill: University of North Carolina Press, 1975), and Myra Jehlen, *American Incarnation: The Individual, the Nation, and the Continent* (Cambridge, Mass.: Harvard University Press, 1986).

5. I have argued elsewhere that Hawthorne reconstructs this scene in his short story "Roger Malvin's Burial," which is also about covenant and westward expansion—*Fiction and Historical Consciousness*, 56–58.

6. From Romance to Realism

1. Alfred Habegger, *Henry James and the "Woman Business"* (Cambridge, England: Cambridge University Press: 1989); Nina Baym, "Revision and Thematic Change in *The Portrait of a Lady*," in *Henry James Washington Square and The Portrait of a Lady: A Selection of Critical Essays*, ed. Alan Shelston (London: Macmillan, 1984), 184–201; and Habegger, *Gender, Fantasy and Realism in American Literature* (New York: Columbia University Press, 1982), 66–79.

2. See Robert Weisbuch, *Atlantic Double-Cross: American Literature and British Influence in the Age of Emerson* (Chicago: University of Chicago Press, 1986); Elissa Greenwald, *Realism and the Romance: Nathaniel Hawthorne, Henry James, and American Fiction* (Ann Arbor: University of Michigan Research Publications, 1989); John Carlos Rowe, *The Theoretical Dimension of Henry James* (Madison: University of Wisconsin Press, 1984); Laurence Holland, *The Expense of Vision* (Princeton, N.J.: Princeton University Press, 1964); Richard Chase, *The American Novel*; and Quentin Anderson, *The American Henry James* (New Brunswick, N.J.: Rutgers University Press, 1957).

3. The following discussion includes elements of my more extensive treatment of this text in *Engendering Romance*, 45–58.

4. *The Portrait of a Lady* (New York: Riverside, 1963).

5. The phrase "a noble doubt" is contained in Emerson's *Nature*, in *Selected Writings*, ed. Atkinson, 26; see also "Experience": "Dream delivers us to dream, and there is no end to illusion" (345).

Bibliographic Essay

As I suggested in chapter 1, the story of 19th-century American romance is as much a story of literary criticism as it is the definition of a genre. It is that story that I now wish to unfold. To do so I return to Richard Chase's 1957 *American Novel and Its Tradition* (New York: Doubleday) and the critical studies that both inspired and were inspired by it. Chase's theory, which builds on the definitions of the writers themselves (especially Hawthorne and James), was preceded by several important books in the 1940s and early '50s—namely, F. O. Matthiessen, *American Renaissance: Art and Expression in the Age of Emerson and Whitman* (London: Oxford University Press, 1941); Lionel Trilling, *The Liberal Imagination: Essays on Literature and Society* (New York: Viking, 1950), which reprinted essays that had appeared earlier, in particular "Reality in America," first published in *Partisan Review*, January–February 1940, and *The Nation*, April 20, 1946, as well as "Manners, Morals, and the Novel," first published in *The Kenyon Review*, 1948; Charles Feidelson Jr., *Symbolism and American Literature* (Chicago: University of Chicago Press, 1953); and R. W. B. Lewis, *The American Adam: Innocence, Tragedy, and Tradition in the Nineteenth Century* (Chicago: University of Chicago Press, 1955); also Perry Miller, *The Raven and the Whale: The War of Words and Wits in the Era of Poe and Melville* (New York: Harcourt, Brace, 1956); Harry Levin, *The Power of Blackness: Hawthorne, Poe, Melville* (London: Faber, 1958);

Leslie Fiedler, *Love and Death in the American Novel* (New York: Criterion Books, 1960); and A. N. Kaul, *The American Vision: Actual and Ideal Society in Nineteenth-Century Fiction* (New Haven, Conn.: Yale University Press, 1963). It was succeeded, in the years immediately following its publication, by a group of like-minded analyses, including Maurice Bewley, *The Eccentric Design: Form in the Classic American Novel* (New York: Columbia University Press, 1963); Richard Poirier, *A World Elsewhere: The Place of Style in American Literature* (New York: Oxford University Press, 1966); Joel Porte, *The Romance in America: Studies in Cooper, Poe, Hawthorne, Melville, and James* (Middletown, Conn.: Wesleyan University Press, 1969); and Quentin Anderson, *The Imperial Self: An Essay in American Literary and Cultural History* (New York: Knopf, 1971), which were in turn followed in the 1970s, '80s, and '90s by another wave of romance criticism, most importantly Michael Davitt Bell, *The Development of American Romance: The Sacrifice of Relation* (Chicago: Chicago University Press, 1980) and Evan Carton, *The Rhetoric of American Romance: Dialectic and Identity in Emerson, Dickinson, Poe, and Hawthorne* (Baltimore, Md.: Johns Hopkins University Press, 1985). Also in this category are John Caldwell Stubbs, *The Pursuit of Form: A Study of Hawthorne and the Romance* (Urbana: University of Illinois Press, 1970); Michael Davitt Bell, *Hawthorne and the Historical Romance of New England* (Princeton, N.J.: Princeton University Press, 1971); Richard Brodhead, *Hawthorne, Melville, and the Novel* (Chicago: University of Chicago Press, 1976); Michael T. Gilmore, *The Middle Way: Puritanism and Ideology in American Romantic Fiction* (New Brunswick, N.J.: Rutgers University Press, 1977); Edwin M. Eigner, *The Metaphysical Novel in England and America: Dickens, Bulwer, Melville, and Hawthorne* (Berkeley: University of California Press, 1978); Sam B. Girgus, *The Law of the Heart: Individualism and the Modern Self in American Literature* (Austin: University of Texas Press, 1979); John T. Irwin, *American Hieroglyphics: The Symbol of the Egyptian Hieroglyphics in the American Renaissance* (New Haven, Conn.: Yale University Press, 1980); Harold Peter Simonson, *Radical Discontinuities: American Romanticism and Christian Consciousness* (Rutherford, N.J.: Fairleigh Dickinson University Press, 1983); Samuel Chase Coale, *In Hawthorne's Shadow: American Romance from Melville to Mailer* (Lexington: University of Kentucky Press, 1985); Edgar Dryden,

The Form of American Romance (Baltimore, Md.: Johns Hopkins University Press, 1988); Emily Miller Budick, *Fiction and Historical Consciousness: The American Romance Tradition* (New Haven, Conn.: Yale University Press, 1989) and *Engendering Romance: Women Writers and the Hawthorne Tradition, 1850–1990* (New Haven, Conn.: Yale University Press, 1994); Kenneth Dauber, *The Idea of Authorship in America: Democratic Poetics from Franklin to Melville* (Madison: University of Wisconsin Press, 1990); Michael P. Kramer, *Imagining Language in America: From the Revolution to the Civil War* (Princeton, N.J.: Princeton University Press, 1992); and Richard H. Millington, *Practicing Romance: Narrative Form and Cultural Engagement in Hawthorne's Fiction* (Princeton, N.J.: Princeton University Press, 1990). I will discuss some of these studies below.

There is, of course, a danger in lumping together the works of so many different critics, all of them having their own priorities and affiliations, all producing distinctly different works of literary analysis. What these studies share, however, which makes them part of a single (albeit variegated) tradition of literary criticism, is a sense that Poe, Hawthorne, and Melville write a particular kind of fiction, that this fiction is characterized by the qualities first identified by Chase and his predecessors in the tradition (including Matthiessen and Trilling), and that it produces a certain legacy for the tradition of American fiction as such.

An important division within the romance criticism—to which I will return—is whether what distinguishes the romance from other forms of fiction is purely stylistic or formal (i.e., simply its way of representing the world, the existence of which it doubts no more than conventional fiction doubts it) or whether the romance signals a totally different relation to the subject of fiction, which becomes, in the romance tradition, not the sociopolitical or even physical world, as it is in the traditional British novel, but the mind or the imagination itself. This division within the romance school, often hard to define, would bear directly on the development of literary criticism of the 1980s and '90s, when scholars set themselves in opposition to the romance school. Nonetheless, it is possible to say that the romance theory (in its two varieties) established, in the decades of the 1960s and '70s, a dominant mode of American literary criticism—both in period studies and in single-author studies as well—which has become, in the last 20 years, the position against which American literary revisionists have defined their own critical projects.

Frederick Crews announced the appearance of this new group of literary revisionists, whom he called the New Americanists, in a review article in *The New York Review of Books* (Oct. 27, 1988), 68–81. The books that Crews reviews and that epitomize this new way of thinking about American texts are Walter Benn Michaels and Donald E. Pease, eds., *The American Renaissance Reconsidered: Selected Papers from the English Institute, 1982–83* (Baltimore, Md.: Johns Hopkins University Press, 1985); Sacvan Bercovitch and Myra Jehlen, eds., *Ideology and Classic American Literature* (Cambridge, England: Cambridge University Press, 1986); Donald Pease, *Visionary Compacts: American Renaissance Writings in Cultural Context* (Madison: University of Wisconsin Press, 1987); Jane Tompkins, *Sensational Designs: The Cultural Work of American Fiction 1790–1860* (New York: Oxford University Press, 1985); David S. Reynolds, *Beneath the American Renaissance: The Subversive Imagination in the Age of Emerson and Melville* (New York: Knopf, 1988); Philip Fisher, *Hard Facts: Setting and Form in the American Novel* (New York: Oxford University Press, 1985); and Russell J. Reising, *The Unusable Past* (New York: Methuen, 1986). Books that Crews does not cite but that might well be added to the list include Annette Kolodny, *The Lay of the Land: Metaphor as Experience in American Life and Letters* (Chapel Hill: University of North Carolina Press, 1975); Sharon Cameron, *The Corporeal Self: Allegories of the Body in Melville and Hawthorne* (Baltimore, Md.: Johns Hopkins University Press, 1981); Robert Clark, *History and Myth in American Fiction, 1823–52* (New York: St. Martin's Press, 1984); John McWilliams, *Hawthorne, Melville, and the American Character: A Looking-Glass Business* (Cambridge, England: Cambridge University Press, 1984); Michael T. Gilmore, *American Romanticism and the Marketplace* (Chicago: Chicago University Press, 1985); Richard Brodhead, *The School of Hawthorne* (New York: Oxford University Press, 1986); Myra Jehlen, *American Incarnation: The Individual, the Nation, and the Continent* (Cambridge, Mass.: Harvard University Press, 1986); Robert Weisbuch, *Atlantic Double-Cross: American Literature and British Influence in the Age of Emerson* (Chicago: Chicago University Press, 1986); Fred G. See, *Desire and the Sign: Nineteenth-Century American Fiction* (Baton Rouge: Louisiana

State University Press, 1987); George Dekker, *The American Historical Romance* (Cambridge, England: Cambridge University Press, 1987); Larry J. Reynolds, *European Revolutions and the American Literary Renaissance* (New Haven, Conn.: Yale University Press, 1988); Robert S. Levine, *Conspiracy and Romance: Studies in Brockden Brown, Cooper, Hawthorne, and Melville* (Cambridge, England: Cambridge University Press, 1989); William Ellis, *The Theory of American Romance: An Ideology in American Intellectual History* (Ann Arbor: University of Michigan Research Press, 1989); and Sacvan Bercovitch, *The Office of the Scarlet Letter* (Baltimore, Md.: Johns Hopkins University Press, 1991), *Rites of Assent: Transformations in the Symbolic Construction of America* (New York: Routledge, 1993), and (editor) *Reconstructing American Literary History* (Cambridge, Mass.: Harvard University Press, 1986). I will discuss some of these studies separately as I proceed.

According to Crews, the authors of these studies distinguish themselves as a group by setting themselves in direct opposition to the founding generation of Americanist critics. This was the generation of critics (Matthiessen, Trilling, and Chase among them) who had, in the years following the Second World War, established the field of American Studies as an academic enterprise and made American literature a part of the international literary curriculum. The New Americanism, Crews understood, was part of a larger movement in literary studies, both in America and abroad. The "questioning of absolutes is now being conducted in all branches of literary study," he notes; "it reflects an irresistible trend in the academy toward spurning unified schemes and hierarchies of every kind" (68). Still, the New Americanism distinguishes itself in important ways:

> What gives the New Americanist critique a special emotional force . . . is its connection both to our historic national shames—slavery, 'Indian removal,' aggressive expansion, imperialism, and so forth— and to current struggles for equal social opportunity. When a New Americanist shows, for example, that a canonical work such as *Huckleberry Finn* indulges in the stereotypical 'objectifying' of blacks, Native Americans, women, or others, a double effect results. First, the canon begins to look less sacrosanct and is thus readied for expansion to include works by long-dead representatives of those same groups. Second, their contemporary descendants are offered a reason

for entering into an academic dialogue that had previously slighted them. In short, the New Americanist program aims at altering the literary departments' social makeup as well as their dominant style of criticism. (68–69)

(For recent overviews of this subject, see George Dekker, "The Genealogy of American Romance," *ESQ: A Journal of the American Renaissance* 35 [1989], 69–83; Russell Reising, *The Unusable Past: Theory and the Study of American Literature* [New York: Methuen, 1986]; and Jonathan Arac, *Critical Genealogies: Historical Situations for Postmodern Literary Studies* [New York: Columbia University Press, 1989], 157–77).

The New Americanists, in other words, issued two powerful challenges to the literary criticism of the preceding decades. In the first place, they questioned the canon of American literary texts, which, they persuasively argued, systematically excluded certain kinds of writers and texts—African-American and women writers, for example, and sentimental and popular fictions. Secondly, they questioned dominant modes of literary interpretation, specifically New Critical or formalist interpretation, which prevailed in literary criticism from the 1940s through the 1970s. This kind of criticism had emphasized the autonomy, unity, and integrity of the literary work. It had called for close textual analysis (explication of the text), and it therefore had produced a canon of texts that tended to confirm the separation of the literary artifact from the real world.

The two aspects of the New Americanist attack are, of course, interrelated. Modes of critical interpretation will determine what kinds of texts will seem to us to constitute great literature. Analogously, a set canon of great works will present us with a kind of literary expression more susceptible to one rather than another kind of critical interpretation. In order to rewrite the canon, and reread it, both literary critical principles and the objects of such criticism had to be transformed.

The New Americanist criticism that Crews reviews concerns itself with a range of literary texts and issues in American studies. Nonetheless, a primary target of its rewriting of American literary history is the romance theory of American fiction and the canon that first produced and later perpetuated this theory. The essential issue separating the New Americanists and the

143

romance critics, as both Crews and the New Americanists themselves describe it, concerns the place of ideology within literary
analysis and, therefore, the way in which literary texts are understood to mediate social reality. "I am particularly concerned,"
writes Russell Reising, "with the way [the previous generation of
Americanist critics] narrow the American canon and discourage
us from viewing literature as a form of social knowledge or
behavior. . . . I am . . . interested in the ways that essentially cultural projects such as Matthiessen's *American Renaissance* . . . —all
at least implicitly political—reduce the scopes of their projects by
adhering to aesthetic assumptions that deny or highly qualify literature's ability to mediate American social reality" (6, 32).

Myra Jehlen, in her introduction to the book of essays that she
edits with Sacvan Bercovitch, shares this concern:

> F. O. Matthiessen, whose *American Renaissance* ushered in the forties
> and a new classical canon, shared the [ideological, social and Marxist,
> concerns] of many of his predecessors. But unlike them he did not
> deal directly with political issues. Instead he recast these issues as
> artistic problems within a separate literary frame of reference. . . .
> While on one hand continuing the cultural history of Brooks by
> proposing a model of American literary identity, therefore, he was
> responding on the other hand to an opposite thirties tendency codi-
> fied in the New Criticism. . . . Theoretically the New Critics were mili-
> tantly anti-ideological. They maintained that the meaning of art had
> nothing to do with its social interpretation but lay within the individ-
> ual work that constituted a world of its own. In the political world
> outside the text, however, the New Critics typically took right-wing
> stands and . . . endorsed English styles and cultural traditions. (2)

According to Jehlen and Reising and others, the canonizers
and theorists of the romance tradition (such as Matthiessen,
Trilling, and Chase) responded to the pressures of the Second
World War and the Cold War by seeking to disengage the
United States from ideology. As William Ellis points out, "[T]o
understand the theory of the American romance, we must consider the consensus interpretation of American history upon
which it was based":

> By the consensus interpretation I refer, of course, to a body of histori-
> cal writing that interpreted American history in the light of two
> assumptions. The first was that Americans had been throughout

their history remarkably successful in avoiding ideological conflict and had, as a consequence of consensus, developed a society remarkably free of significant class conflict. . . . From this followed the second assumption that because it possessed a unique historical dynamic the United States had developed a civilization radically different from that of Europe, where ideological and class conflicts had been constant factors in social life. . . . By this token American civilization could be seen as a historical fulfillment, its consensus marking an appropriate end to the historical process, contributing to the myth of a "people outside history, uniquely favored by fortune, faced with no difficulties that could not be resolved by goodwill, physical hardihood, and technological virtuosity." (19–20; Ellis quotes from Christopher Lasch)

The romance critics produced out of consensus history a vision of American exceptionalism, which realized in the American tradition the unassailable bases of democracy, individualism, and pluralism. That democracy, individualism, and pluralism were themselves ideologies the Old Americanists (according to the New) did not seem to understand.

Therefore, the "animus" informing contemporary resistance to the New Americanist reposition of American literary studies, Donald Pease suggests in his response to Crews's essay, can "be reduced to a single complaint: the New Americanists have returned ideology to a field previously organized by an end to ideology consensus" ("New Americanists: Revisionist Interventions into the Canon," *boundary* 2 17 [1990], ed. Donald Pease, 1–37; quotation on 2; see also, in the same volume, John P. McWilliams, "The Rationale for 'The American Romance,'" 71–82; Reising 13–27; and Jehlen 1–2).

There is no point in denying the differences between the literary criticism of scholars like Matthiessen, Chase, Porte, Poirier, and others, on the one hand, and, on the other, the criticism of contemporary Americanists like Pease, Jehlen, and Reising. Nonetheless, the New Americanist claim that the romance critics (at least the majority of them) ignored ideology and relocated the text outside the sociopolitical and economic world may not accurately locate the salient differences between the Old and New Americanist methods and intentions. As a result, it may miss the genuine distinctions to be drawn between the Old Americanism and the New and, for that reason, the achievement not only of the romance critics but of the texts that centrally preoccupied them—the fictions of Poe, Hawthorne, and Melville.

For the most part, the romance theorists of American fiction did not eliminate from their textual analyses the social, political, and economic determinants of the romance texts. They did not ignore issues like sexism, racism, and classism, concealing the ideological assumptions either of their authors or of themselves. They did, however, turn their interpretive tools as much to structural as to thematic issues, focusing on the ways in which the form of American fiction expressed 19th-century American beliefs and commitments (note that the subtitle of Poirier's book is "The Place of Style in American Fiction" while the subtitle of Bewley's study is "Form in the Classic American Novel"). It is this form (symbolic, allegorical, self-conscious, and self-reflexive, according to most of the romance critics) that the majority of romance theorists understood to distinguish the 19th-century American romance from other forms of prose fiction, both in the United States and Europe.

Although for some exponents of the romance theory of American fiction, style or form will become a subject largely unto itself, most romance critics are less concerned with purely philosophical or linguistic matters than with the relationship between literary structures and the world that such structures intend to represent. For Chase, Porte, Lewis, and Poirier, as for Hawthorne and James, the difference between the romance and the novel had to do not with whether a social or political world exists but with how experience and ideology in that world are represented in a fictional text. Indeed, that sociopolitical conditions pertain to the formation of 19th-century American romance fiction—that such conditions determine the very form of this fiction—is made very clear in the writings of the first generation of romance critics. Such conditions are not, as Jehlen, for example, claims, merely used as "'background' or 'context' rather than as an integral part of the literary language" (3). Rather, they function for the romance critics as vital elements—albeit in specially defined ways—in the generation and disposition of the text.

Thus in Chase's view, ideology is actually what romance fiction is all about, the "events" of the narrative having "a symbolic or *ideological,* rather than a realistic, plausibility" (13; italics added). Joel Porte in *The Romance in America* makes a similar claim while simultaneously pointing the direction for the linguistic/philosophical focus of some later romance criticism:

> All these writers [i.e., Cooper, Poe, Hawthorne, Melville, and James] created, partially or completely, according to a theory of stylized art—heavily dependent on the use of conventional, or archetypical, figures and on symbol, parable, dream, and fantasy—*in order to explore large questions (and this list is not exhaustive) about race, history, nature, human motivation, and art.* Particularly from Poe to James, I have tried to suggest that the American romance is characterized by a need self-consciously to define its own aims, so that 'romance' becomes frequently . . . the theme as well as the form of these authors' works. (x; italics added)

For Porte, American romance fiction in no way ignores human issues, such as history and race. It is not ideology-free. Rather, the romance constitutes a specific "form" of engagement with social and political issues. Porte emphasizes two elements of this form that become important in later romance criticism as well: the generation of certain political (i.e., ideological) myths concerning America, and the self-consciousness and self-reflexivity of romance fiction as a way of using language.

In proceeding this way, Porte follows quite closely the line of thinking developed earlier by critics like Lewis and Chase. "This book has to do with the beginnings and the first tentative outlines of a native American mythology," begins Lewis in his 1955 *American Adam.* "A century ago, the image contrived to embody the most fruitful contemporary ideas was that of the authentic American as a figure of heroic innocence and vast potentialities, poised at the start of a new history" (1). Lewis is aware that this "image" is "crowded with illusion" and that "the moral posture it seemed to indorse was vulnerable in the extreme." He also realizes that the myth he is describing is itself a product of historical circumstance and of what he calls the "dialogue" or "conversation" of culture (1–2). "Myth," suggests Richard Chase, is "a way of sanctioning and giving significance to those crises of human experience which are cultural as well as personal" (53).

Therefore, when Jane Tompkins, in her discussion of Cooper in *Sensational Designs,* locates her position as in opposition to the romance theories of critics like Chase, we have to ask whether such opposition is more apparent than real. In her view, Chase and others misunderstand myth or romance as providing a universal view of human nature. They erroneously divorce Cooper's fiction from the cultural context of its composition. Cooper's Leatherstocking Tales, Tompkins claims, are neither "ahistorical romance" nor "inartistic social commentary." Rather, they are "social criticism written in an allegorical mode."

"Cooper's interest," Tompkins suggests, is "in the phenomena of cultural difference," i.e., Native American vs. white; African American vs. white, female vs. male, and so on. This interest Tompkins shows to be pervasive throughout early 19th-century America, not only in the fiction of the period's novelists but within other American writings as well (Tompkins notes that between the years 1812 and the Civil War 73 novels concerning Native Americans were written). The Leatherstocking series, Tompkins concludes, in an argument that has much in common with Philip Fisher's treatment of some of the same texts in *Hard Facts*, laments the passing of the Indians while simultaneously affirming the necessity of civilization over savagery, Christianity over paganism. It attempts to come to terms with the passing of the dream of universal brotherhood.

Both Tompkins and Fisher provide fresh, new readings of Cooper's Leatherstocking books. They go about the work of literary criticism in ways that are different from the methodologies of Lewis, Chase, and Porte. In particular they, along with critics such as Larry Reynolds, David Reynolds, Donald Pease, Jonathan Arac, and others, explore in vivid detail the cultural contexts (including works of popular fiction and journalism) that seem to impinge upon the texts they are interpreting. The issue, however, concerning these new critical voices and the older ones that they oppose is not whether contemporary literary critics might not find new things to say about old texts (or new things to say about new texts). Literary criticism as a profession could not proceed in the absence of the belief that interpretation will never exhaust the canon. The question, rather, is whether the newness of their saying is as radical and theoretical a break from an old way of saying as the New Americanists claim and whether New Americanist interpretation disqualifies earlier interpretation.

The issue, in other words, is whether the assumptions of the New Americanists and the romance theorists concerning the relationship between cultural/historical context and the literary work are in fact radically different and whether the romance theorists in any way deny the relationship (upon which the New Americanists insist) both between ideology and literature and between ideology and literary criticism. Another way of putting this is: Granted that ideology is an indispensible component of any literary composition, what, exactly, is the ideological component of a particular text, say a work of romance fiction? How might a critic go about specifying it? And what other concerns, aside from ideology, might the critic have to bring to bear in order adequately to address the text as a whole?

Answers to these questions depend first and foremost on our definition of the word *ideology*. Is ideology a particular political or social or economic philosophy—democracy or Marxism or racial superiority or sexism or so on? Or is ideology, as Sacvan Bercovitch has employed the term, something more general, more cultural, more inevitable? Ideology, writes Bercovitch (Crews quotes this in his review), is "the system of interlinked ideas, symbols, and beliefs by which a culture . . . seeks to justify and perpetuate itself; the web of rhetoric, ritual, and assumption through which a society coerces, persuades, and coheres."

What Bercovitch goes on to say, which Crews does not quote, is equally important:

> So considered, ideology is basically conservative; but it is not therefore static or simply repressive. As Raymond Williams points out, ideology evolves through conflict, and even when a certain ideology achieves dominance it still finds itself contending to one degree or another with the ideologies of residual and emergent cultures within the society—contending, that is, with alternative and oppositional forms that reflect the course of historical development. In this process, ideology functions best through voluntary acquiescence, when the network of ideas through which the culture justifies itself is internalized rather than imposed, and embraced by society at large as a system of belief. Under these conditions, which Antonio Gramsci described as "hegemony," the very terms of cultural restriction become the source of creative release: they serve to incite the imagination, to unleash the energies of reform, to encourage diversity and accommodate change—all this, while directing the rights of diversity into a rite of cultural assent—"The Problem of Ideology in American Literary History," *Critical Inquiry* 12 (1986), 635; reprinted in revised form in *Rites of Assent*, 353–76.

I suggest that if there is a difference between the romance critics and the New Americanists it has primarily to do with their definitions of ideology. The first generation of romance critics (Chase, Porte, et al.) were just as sensitive to ideology in the Bercovitchian sense as are Bercovitch and the group of contemporary culture critics who have followed his lead. This means that the romance critics were interested both in the particular social and political contexts of the literary text and (equally) in the context of ideas that (as Bercovitch explains it) coexists with (determines and is determined by) the more purely political and economic considerations of any particular place and time. This context of ideas Lionel Trilling calls manners, "a culture's hum and buzz of implication . . . the whole evanescent context in which its explicit statements are made" ("Manners, Morals, and the Novel," *The Liberal Imagination,* 201).

Thus, R. W. B. Lewis suggests in *The American Adam,*

> If there was a fictional Adamic hero unambiguously treated—celebrated in his very Adamism—it was the hero of Cooper's *The Deerslayer:* a self-reliant young man who does seem to have sprung from nowhere and whose characteristic pose, to employ Tocqueville's words, was the solitary stance in the presence of Nature and God. But after *Deerslayer,* there begins the march of those more complex and sometimes tragic Adams of Hawthorne and Melville and Henry James. (91)

Lewis's "if" is important here, as is his "does seem." What Lewis is describing is not a fact about America, which he imagines American fiction to verify. Nor is it a claim as to the truth value of Cooper's text. Even *if* the American Adam *seems* once to have existed, Lewis admits, his life span was very limited. It does not even span all five of Cooper's Leatherstocking novels but perhaps only one of them.

Lewis is concerned here with myth, the myth of America that Cooper's novels recorded and that they themselves may have come (over time) to have constituted (cf. D. H. Lawrence in *Studies in Classic American Literature:* "The Leatherstocking novels . . . go backwards from old age to golden youth. That is the true myth of America. She starts old, old, wrinkled and writhing in an old skin. And there is a gradual sloughing off of the old skin, towards a new youth. It is the myth of America" [New York:

Viking, 1954; orig. printed 1923]). It is not a myth that the writers necessarily endorsed or that they attempted to pass off as truth. Nor did such a myth avoid reality; it stated reality in a particular way. As Chase puts it,

> In his departures from realism, Cooper is strictly a mythic writer. [He] banks on the powers of myth to make his narratives vivid and to reaffirm and transmit the values he cherishes. . . . [A]re these values really 'cultural'? Can we transpose them into any imaginable social form? Do the mythicized life and opinions of Natty Bumppo affect in any way our idea of culture? The answer to these questions must be radically equivocal, because the significance of the myth of Cooper's hero is itself equivocal, and in fact self-contradictory. In its more conscious and constructive meanings, it is a myth of culture, since the critical episodes in the life of the hero are those which universally involve the life of society, no matter what that society may be. Also Cooper's own ideal social order is imaginatively recaptured and enhanced by the myth—that shared and harmonious social order in which the hereditary artistocracy dwells in its country mansions while on the borders of its lands Natty Bumppo stalks the forests. Such a culture was momentarily possible in eighteenth-century America. But since it had become all but impossible in the time of Cooper, the myth that enhances and justifies it has perforce to be nostalgic, ironic, and self-contradictory. Out of this dilemma come Cooper's most powerful feelings, and the myth of the Leather-Stocking tales, cultural in intent and in its ideology becomes distorted under the pressures of history in such a way that its ultimate meaning is anti-cultural. If, Cooper seems to say, we cannot have the aristocratic agrarian society, in which Cornelius Littlepage and Natty Bumppo are the intuitive coadjutors and twin ideals, then let us have no society at all. Let us depend on the purely solitary and personal virtues of the isolated and the doomed. (53–54)

For Lewis, as for Chase and Porte, Cooper's fiction is no less anxious and self-contradictory, no less an attempt to come to terms with historical realities, which is to say culture in its largest sense (including issues such as sexism and racism), than it is for critics like Tompkins and Fisher. For Porte, for example, as for Leslie Fiedler (*Love and Death in the American Novel*), sexism and racism are paramount subjects (in many ways Fiedler, whose book treats both popular and canonical writers and who places the American literary tradition within the larger tradition of

European writing, anticipates the direction of much contemporary criticism).

The critic who most powerfully renders the ideological component of American literature in the 1970s is not accidently the same critic who, in the '80s and '90s, provides the definition of *ideology* that I have quoted above. Sacvan Bercovitch's two studies—*The Puritan Origins of the American Self* (New Haven, Conn.: Yale University Press, 1975) and *The American Jeremiad* (Madison: University of Wisconsin Press, 1978)—recover the ideological assumptions that (as much as themes or methodology) give 19th-century American fiction its special texture. Already anticipating the direction of literary criticism in the 1980s and '90s (the course of which has largely been directed by his writings), Bercovitch's two-volume investigation of the Puritan origins of the American self sets the terms for many studies of romance criticism.

By concentrating on early American Puritan texts (in the tradition of analysis most definitively established in American criticism by Perry Miller), Bercovitch describes an American symbology of self that extended from the 17th century into the 19th and that profoundly determined the American literary tradition. (The most relevant Miller texts in this context are *Orthodoxy in Massachusetts, 1630–1650* [New York: Harper and Row, 1933]; *The New England Mind: The Seventeenth Century* [New York: Macmillan, 1939]; *The New England Mind: From Colony to Province* [Cambridge, Mass.: Harvard University Press, 1953]; *Errand into the Wilderness* [Cambridge, Mass.: Harvard University Press, 1956]; and *Nature's Nation* [Cambridge, Mass.: Harvard University Press, 1967]). Bercovitch then seeks to understand American writing in terms of the ways in which it was determined, not only by immediate social or political events but by a continuing conception of the American self.

Bercovitch's idea of a profound continuity in 19th-century American literary culture (often based on shared myths of biblical promises and fears of divine retribution) and his particular claim that this American myth of self originated with the Puritan founders of New England were definitive for more than a generation of Americanist scholars, who increasingly read American literary texts as self-consciously and self-reflexively about "America," which is to say about the nation's imaginings of itself. Though Bercovitch's way of thinking about American fiction produced his own brand of culture criticism, it can nonetheless be

seen as providing a link between the criticism of the first generation of romance critics (who saw the formal devices of romance
writing as ways of embodying social and political ideas) and the
criticism of the next group of such critics (for whom the formal
features themselves constituted the Americanness of romance fiction, its way of embodying and producing American ideology).

Before I trace the development of this other, more philosophically and linguistically oriented strand within romance criticism,
let me stay for a moment longer with the first generation of
romance critics (Chase, Trilling, Matthiessen, Lewis, Porte, et al.).
The New Americanists and the first generation of romance critics
(and many of the second generation as well) do *not*, I have been
suggesting, differ so much as they concur in their views of the
19th-century romance tradition, vis-à-vis the major social and
political issues of the time. However, the romance critics, I have
argued, were also interested in what most New Americanists
(Bercovitch excluded) by and large ignore: the ideological context in which particular American ideologies proceeded. That is,
they were also interested in the formal features of the text
whereby this "system of interlinked ideas, symbols, and beliefs"
is put into play.

The romance position represented a generational revolt. It
constituted a response to the expressly nonaesthetic concerns
and methodologies of the generation of critics who preceded
them—such figures as Granville Hicks and V. L. Parrington, for
whom (as Myra Jehlen points out in her introductory essay in
Ideology and Classic American Literature) ideology, whether as an
affirmation of democracy or as an invocation of Marxist ideals or
as an attempt to put American culture on a footing equal to that
of England and Europe, was a primary concern, a very reason for
the existence of both a literary and a literary-critical tradition. To
a large degree, the New Americanist revision of the romance critics represents a similar revolt, in this case moving back toward,
as opposed to away from, ideology as the defining condition of
literary production.

In the preface to his *Cycle of American Literature: An Essay in
Historical Criticism* (New York: Macmillan, 1955), Robert E. Spiller
reminisces about literary criticism in the early part of the 20th-
century, when he and other noted critics were putting together
their comprehensive history of American literature:

> There seems now to be little doubt in the minds of critics at home and abroad that the United States has produced, during the twentieth century, a distinctive literature, worthy to take its place with the great literatures of other times and other peoples. There is no similar agreement on the reasons for this, or for the apparently sudden cultural maturity of a people which, throughout nearly two centuries of political independence, has thought of itself as heterogeneous and derivative in its racial and cultural make-up. American writings of the past quarter-century give evidence of a literary renaissance which could only come from a long tradition and unified culture. This literary renaissance, the second to occur in the United States, must have both a history and a pattern of relationships within itself. And yet it has not been clearly defined or understood, because literary historians have failed to comprehend it as an organic whole. (ix)

(For a useful history of the development of American literary studies in the 20th century, see Kermit Vanderbilt, *American Literature and the Academy: The Roots, Growth, and Maturity of a Profession* [Philadelphia: University of Pennsylvania Press, 1986].)

Spiller's concern with the national implications of American literature was not unique to him. Nor was the direction of his investigation, which was more toward identifying the ideological conditions of the Americanness of American writing rather than its formal differences from other literatures. "In what sense is our literature distinctively American?" Norman Foerster had asked in 1928, in his introduction to *The Reinterpretation of American Literature* (New York: Russell and Russell, 1959; orig. published 1950). "In what ways does it resemble the literatures of Europe? and . . . What are the local conditions of life and thought in America that produce these results?" (xxiv–xxv).

His words could easily be taken for a contemporary new historicist statement, as could the rest of his argument as well as the following sentiments expressed (respectively) by Spiller and by Van Wyck Brooks (*The Writer in America* [New York: Avon, 1953]), who specifically resists the criteria of formalist criticism, which were fast gaining ascendency mid-century:

> There is current today a desire not only to reinterpret but also to revaluate American literature. We are increasingly aware of the inadequacy of some of the traditional estimates. . . . Yet the new estimates tend to be capricious, indicative of a provincialism of time (the measurement of past literature by the ideas and moods of a narrow pre-

sent) far more insidious than the provincialism [of the past].
(Foerster, xxv)

The writer of this new history must first recognize that the major
author, even though he becomes major by rising above his times or
otherwise alienating himself from his society, is nevertheless the specific product of his times and of his society, and probably their most
profound expression. Literature, therefore, has a relationship to
social and intellectual history, not as documentation, but as symbolic
illumination. (Spiller, xii)

In reality books are bred by men, men by life and life by books
through a constant interrelation and cross-fertilization, so that an element of social history can scarely be dispensed with in any account
of literary phenomena and forces. . . . I would ask the new critics . . .
whether they have not ignored the larger bearings even of their own
professions, for they seem never to have asked themselves how far
their obsession with form is ultimately good for the writers who produce their texts. (Brooks, 13–19)

This is the direct academic background out of which the
romance critics wrote. The early part of the 20th century was
characterized by an intensely nationalistic focus. It witnessed a
flurry of interest in the Americanness of American literature. The
romance critics of the '50s and '60s did nothing more (though
nothing less) than take up the challenge handed them by the
previous generation of critics. They would discover and define
the Americanness of American literature, although—and this
was the important difference from their predecessors—they
would do this by discovering in American literature new structural and aesthetic as well as political or thematic interests.

Thus F. O. Matthiessen, the figure who stands directly behind
Chase and represents, perhaps, an even more formidable influ-
ence on subsequent Americanist studies, conceived his *American
Renaissance* as more than a response to certain publishing facts,
namely the appearance in "the half decade of 1850–55 . . . of
Representative Men (1850), *The Scarlet Letter* (1850), *The House of the
Seven Gables* (1851), *Moby-Dick* (1851), *Pierre* (1852), *Walden* (1854),
and *Leaves of Grass* (1855)" (vii). Rather, he imagined it as also a
reaction to a kind of criticism embodied in Vernon Louis
Parrington's eclectic and highly intellectual *Main Currents in
American Thought,* vol. 1, *The Colonial Mind (1620–1800),* and vol.

2, *The Romantic Revolution in America (1800–1860)* (New York: Harcourt, Brace & World, 1927; a third volume, *The Beginnings of Critical Realism [1860–1920]*, appeared posthumously in 1930). Parrington was willing to make certain, limited kinds of literary statements (Hawthorne, for example, is only "in a narrow and very special sense" in Parrington's view, a "romantic. With the romance of love and adventure he was never concerned; what interested him was the romance of ethics"—[436]). Nonetheless, he defines his project as intellectual history rather than literary criticism. Matthiessen quotes Parrington: "'With aesthetic judgments I have not been greatly concerned. I have not wished to evaluate reputations or weigh literary merits, but rather to understand what our fathers thought.' My concern," Matthiessen continues, "has been the opposite" (ix).

This is, of course, not to say that Matthiessen is unconcerned with the history of ideas, with *why* the writers of the American Renaissance wrote what they wrote. It is only to note that, to the intellectual, historical interests that preoccupied Parrington (and, before Parrington, Hicks) he will add aesthetic judgment. In so doing, Matthiessen is in many ways repeating the move of the 19th-century romancers as they attempted to create a literary form commensurate with the undertakings of the new nation. Like them and like Matthiessen, the 20th-century romance critics turned their attention to isolating the aesthetic (literary, cultural, *ideological*) features—the system of beliefs as opposed to the subjects or themes—that had made American literature exceptional and unique among world literatures. For critics like Chase, Porte, and Bewley this meant describing what Richard Poirier calls a "world elsewhere," just as for Poe, Hawthorne, and Melville it meant creating this world. The New Americanist revision of the romance position in many ways returns to the views of Hicks and Parrington, though within the contemporary moment there remain critics who continue to pursue the romance line.

During the 1950s, '60s, and '70s many single-author studies appear that apply elements of the romance theory of American fiction to individual authors or works (see the list at the end of this chapter). The period studies that continue to carry forward the salient features of the theory as introduced by Chase, et al., include Richard Brodhead, *Hawthorne, Melville, and the Novel;*

Michael T. Gilmore, *The Middle Way;* Edwin M. Eigner, *The Metaphysical Novel in England and America;* Sam B. Girgus, *The Law of the Heart;* Eric J. Sundquist, *Home as Found;* Harold Peter Simonson, *Radical Discontinuities;* John T. Irwin, *American Hieroglyphics;* Samuel Chase Coale, *In Hawthorne's Shadow;* and Michael Davitt Bell, *The Development of American Romance.* *American Hieroglyphics* pushes forward Feidelson's original insights in *Symbolism and American Literature,* introducing a more Lacanian (as opposed to Freudian) view of the psycholinguistic dynamics of literature. Eric Sundquist's more Freudian *Home as Found,* which focuses on Cooper, Thoreau, Hawthorne, and Melville, proposes that

> for each of four nineteenth-century American writers the source of satisfaction found wanting is tied in an urgent way to his family or genealogy, which by virtue of either their instability or their unwanted pressure act as surrogates for a more abstractly envisioned 'past,' and to this extent stimulate the writer's *desire* to find in the family a model for the social and political constructs still so much in question for a recently conceived nation. (xii)

Bell's *Development of American Romance* is the most important of this group of studies because it crystallizes a previously implicit notion in romance criticism: that romance fiction may not be, simply, a methodology, a way of representing reality, but an evasion or even denial of reality altogether. Bell provides a rich theoretical basis (in terms of contemporary 19th-century philosophy) for the definition of the genre, which goes to the heart of romance fiction's concern with the imagination itself:

> The fundamental property of romance . . . was conceived to be its departure from "truth," from "fact," its cutting of the Jamesian cable tying imagination to "reality." To describe romance in this way was not, finally, to distinguish it from realism or mimesis, for the general run of nineteenth-century comments on romance distinguish it not from *realism* but from *reality*—and this point is crucial. Romance was not an abstract or symbolic representation of objective reality. . . . What matters most . . . in nineteenth-century discussions of romance, is neither content nor form but psychological motive and effect. (10)

In many ways Bell's study consolidates and brings to a close a certain phase of romance criticism, even as it opens out onto the

criticism of the 1980s and '90s, with its emphasis on the self-conscious, self-reflexive qualities of romance fiction, its concern with
language in some disrelation to reality.

The critics who write in the 1980s and '90s can roughly be
divided into at least three groups vis-à-vis the issue of romance
fiction, if we put aside those critics of 19th-century literature for
whom the romance tradition holds no interest at all. There are
first those critics who are less interested in defining or redefining
what kind of fiction Poe, Hawthorne, and Melville write than in
reading them within the context of 19th-century literary production generally. These critics are concerned with opening the
canon to other, heretofore unread writers, very often women and
African-American writers. They also aim to lessen the claim of
American exceptionalism that adheres to Poe, Hawthorne, and
Melville. Second, there are those critics who are inclined to view
Poe, Hawthorne, and Melville as the crystallization of 19th-cen-
tury American culture as such but who want to dispute the idea
that the fiction they write is apolitical, symbolical or allegorical, as
opposed to sociopolitically and economically engaged. These
scholars recover the sociopolitical and economic context in which
the romancers write, and they attempt to see their fictions as
engagements with concrete contemporary issues. Both of these
two groups of critics can be labeled New Americanist or new historicist, with varying degrees of neomarxist, African-Americanist,
and feminist concerns characterizing their work. And finally there
is the group of critics who continue to view the 19th-century texts
as formally, stylistically unique but who attempt to discover new
terms in which to describe this uniqueness.

A good review both of the development of romance criticism
and of its revision in contemporary literary criticism is contained
in Russell J. Reising's *The Unusable Past* and William Ellis's *Theory
of the American Romance,* both of which take a New Americanist
stance. Both Reising and Ellis, furthermore, are more interested
in romance theorists than in romance texts. Indeed, Ellis's objective in his book is to prevent the reemergence of romance theory
in the new guise of ideological criticism (171–88). Four collections
that bring together a sampling of such new contemporary critical
approaches are Michaels and Pease, eds., *The American
Renaissance Reconsidered;* Bercovitch and Jehlen, eds., *Ideology and
Classic American Literature; The New Americanists;* a special issue of
Pease, ed., *boundary 2;* and Philip Fisher, ed., *The New American*

Studies: Essays from Representations (Berkeley: University of California Press, 1991).

Perhaps the most encompassing attempt to reconstitute the romance writers as part of a larger moment of cultural production in the United States is David S. Reynolds's *Beneath the American Renaissance,* while George Dekker casts the net even wider and views the 19th-century American authors in the context of a European tradition of romance fiction in *The American Historical Romance.* The canon, Reynolds maintains, reflects popular culture; the canonical writers, he suggests, are not estranged from their culture but are a reflection of it. Also relevant here is Robert Weisbuch's *Atlantic Double-Cross,* which sees in American literary texts an attempt to define the relationship between the United States and England.

David Leverenz, *Manhood and the American Renaissance* (Ithaca, N.Y.: Cornell University Press, 1989), is a good example of a study that bridges several contemporary agendas. Leverenz deals with canonical figures, such as Emerson, Melville, and, in particular, Hawthorne, in relation to a popular contemporary issue: gender identity and the status of women within society. He does this within the context of a much larger circle of similarly engaged authors, of fiction and nonfiction both, including Frederick Douglass, Sarah Hale, Caroline Kirkland, Susan Ann Warner, Harriet Beecher Stowe, Richard Henry Dana Jr., and Francis Parkman Jr. Leverenz's focus is not on what distinguishes the romance writers as unique but on what they share with other 19th-century authors confronting the same set of social problems. Leverenz's study is related to several new feminist readings of the 19th-century male writers, which I will get to in a moment.

The idea that the 19th-century romancers wrote within the general realm of 19th-century literary production is supplemented by a second critical position, in which what are sought are not so much continuities between Poe, Hawthorne, Melville, and James, and other 19th-century American writers, but the ways in which the romancers expressed dominant social, economic, and intellectual issues of the time. Leverenz's study, as I have suggested, and Reynolds's as well, represents aspects of this concern, which is now the major preoccupation of what has been labeled New Americanist criticism. A more sustained New Americanist study of the romance writers (in this case Emerson,

Thoreau, Hawthorne, and Melville), which focuses on the field of economics, is Michael T. Gilmore's *American Romanticism and the Marketplace* (Chicago: University of Chicago Press, 1985):

> [T]he four authors in this study shared their culture's ambivalent reaction to the extension of the market. While they were harshly critical of the new economic order, they were also strongly drawn to what they saw as the positive effects of commerce, and they were all willing, at least for a time, to accommodate themselves to the imperatives of writing for the mass public. They fought out in their careers and art the question of the market's merits and liabilities. (8)

This idea is complemented by Richard Brodhead's more culturally tilted *School of Hawthorne* (N.Y.: Oxford University Press, 1986), in which Brodhead analyzes the romance tradition in terms of its later canonization:

> I understand the literary history of Hawthorne's tradition to be inseparable from the history of how literature itself has been organized as a cultural system in America. Accordingly, my readings of relations between writers and between texts keep moving in from, then leading back out toward, questions about the history of literary establishments; about how the literary past has been selected and enforced within such establishments; and about the changing organization, within such establishments, of the American authorial career. (vii–viii)

Tradition, Brodhead argues, is something more than a literary transaction. "It also bears . . . on the way writers accept and remake literature's place in the human world at large" (ix).

In the field of international relations, Larry J. Reynolds, *European Revolutions and the American Literary Renaissance* (New Haven, Conn.: Yale University Press, 1988), shows how "historic international developments, especially the European revolutions of 1848–49, helped effect [the flowering identified by F. O. Matthiessen as the American Renaissance]" (xii; Reynolds discusses Emerson, Hawthorne, Melville, Whitman, and Thoreau alongside Margaret Fuller and Harriet Beecher Stowe; see also Bercovitch's *Office of the Scarlet Letter*). Similarly, in *Cross-Examinations of Law and Literature: Cooper, Hawthorne, Stowe, and Melville* (Cambridge, England: Cambridge University Press, 1987), Brook Thomas brings various 19th-century legal controversies to bear upon the fiction of the time.

Still other studies pursue the relationship between 19th-century works and more domestic and political 19th-century issues, such as racism, the relocation and extermination of Native Americans, and, of course, sexism: Robert Clark, *History and Myth in American Fiction, 1823–52* (New York: St. Martin's Press, 1984), which deals primarily with Cooper, Hawthorne, and Melville; Philip Fisher, *Hard Facts,* which focuses on Cooper, Stowe, and Dreiser; and Jane Tompkins, *Sensational Designs,* which deals with Brockden Brown, Cooper, and Stowe. All three of these books attempt to recoup 19th-century cultural backgrounds so as to make texts written in this period accessible to the modern reader. They also locate the social issues to which the writers, they argue, are responding, specifically rebutting the notion of fictional texts that take place in a "world elsewhere." Writes Robert Clark,

> When Cooper and Hawthorne described their works as romances they were reluctantly conceding to critical demands that their works be mere entertainments and therefore politically irrelevant. Behind these concessions their works were so acutely addressed to the political life of the nation that a failure to understand their politics becomes a failure to understand their central literary significance. . . . [W]hen writers are banished to what might seem like a world elsewhere they discover nothing less than the contradictions they were banished to repress. . . . The most significant fictions of the period are those which articulate the ambiguities of land conquest. (ix, 3, 60)

For Clark, Fisher, and Tompkins, literary texts do what these critics think of as "cultural work." That is, in the view of these studies, texts exorcise and consolidate cultural anxieties and tensions in order to permit society to function. The "simple argument" of Fisher's book is that,

> within the 19th-century American novel, cultural work of this fundamental kind was often done by exactly those popular forms that from a later perspective, that of 20th-century modernism, have seemed the weakest features of 19th-century cultural life. . . . I am writing . . . about three cultural acts that by their very success made themselves obsolete, and perhaps even a hindrance, once their cultural work was complete. One of my goals is to recover and name the work that they did, and to understand the capacity of popular forms to accomplish just this self-terminating work of the imagination. The historical

> novel [Cooper's Leatherstocking tales], the sentimental novel [*Uncle Tom's Cabin*] and the naturalist novel [*Sister Carrie*] are three of the forms with which the weakness of 19th-century culture is, when seen from the perspective of 20th-century modernism, most often identified. It is my claim that these forms were not forms for the future, but forms for the active transformation of the present. (5–7)

Of primary importance to Fisher and Tompkins is the idea of sentimentalism as a literary form that the culture invited but that Hawthorne and others resisted. Fred G. See, in *Desire and the Sign*, attempts to explain why, in the eyes of 20th-century readers, romance fiction supplanted sentimentalism as the dominant 19th-century literary tradition by "scandalizing" it.

These studies by Clark, Fisher, Tompkins, and See are anticipated earlier in American literary criticism by Leslie Fiedler's *Love and Death in the American Novel*. Staunchly Marxist and Freudian, Fiedler's study reads the major texts (and many popular texts as well) in terms of their repressions, both psychological and cultural, thus anticipating many of the themes of the new historicists while maintaining the differences between American and European fiction. "Our fiction," argues Fiedler, "is not merely in flight from the physical data of the actual world . . . it is . . . nonrealistic and negative, sadistic, and melodramatic" (29).

The difference between sentimentalism as a literary strategy and the romance fiction of Poe, Hawthorne, and Melville returns us to the issue of sexism in the 19th century and in the literary criticism purporting to explicate 19th-century literature. Already in 1975 Annette Kolodny had set the foundations for the feminist revision of American literary theory. In *The Lay of the Land*, she analyzed the sexist language in which the male tradition of texts described the American continent. Tompkins's and Fisher's studies may be thought of as continuing this feminist direction, as can Myra Jehlen's *American Incarnation*, though Jehlen broadens her focus beyond feminist concerns to deal with the whole tendency within American writing to subordinate the other to the self. This idea is central to Carolyn Porter's *Seeing and Being: The Plight of the Participant Observer in Emerson, James, Adams, and Faulkner* (Middletown, Conn.: Wesleyan University Press, 1981) as well. I will return to Jehlen's book in a moment.

Also positioning the 19th-century writers against their cultural moment, but permitting them more self-intentioned resistance, and also carrying forward the feminist concerns of contemporary scholarship are Leland S. Person Jr.'s *Aesthetic Headaches: Women and a Masculine Poetics in Poe, Melville, and Hawthorne* (Athens: University of Georgia Press, 1988) and Cynthia S. Jordan's *Second Stories: The Politics of Language, Form, and Gender in Early American Fictions* (Chapel Hill: University of North Carolina Press, 1989). Person's and Jordan's books share a sense that, for writers like Poe, Hawthorne, and Melville, women constitute an unknowable "otherness" that the male writer must come to accept and acknowledge as a part of what defines his own consciousness of the world. But whereas for Jordan the romance writers' purposes are political (positioning Jordan's study more firmly within the New Americanist school), for Person, recurring to an older model of literary studies, they are more psychological.

Writes Jordan, describing what she calls "the patriarchal politics of language in America,"

> Franklin, Brackenridge, and Brown . . . believed with varying degrees of optimism that language could be used to maintain a patriarchal social order in the new nation. The narrative fictions they wrote to promote such a belief, however, are curiously doubled: their promotional surface narratives are constantly threatened by evidence of opposing views, and that evidence constitutes a rival second story which the authors try to suppress or defuse but which they find increasingly difficult to hold in check. In the romantic period that followed, Cooper, Poe, Hawthorne, and Melville repeatedly criticized the patriarchal linguistic politics that tried to silence other views—"otherness" itself—in American culture, and their own experiments with narrative form reflect their attempts to unmask the fraud perpetrated by their cultural fathers and to recover the lost second story. (x)

For Person, however, the poetics of Poe, Hawthorne, and Melville "reflect a tension between identification with women whose creative energy resists easy formalization and the containment of such women in artistic forms that subject creative energy to the artist's control—often to the detriment of the work as a whole." Person continues that "none of these three writers was very interested in examining the social and political status of women. Each writer was interested in gender and gender-related issues, but more from a psychological than from a social or political point of view" (2–5). Nonetheless, for both Person and Jordan, the romancers were not, as in David Leverenz's view, simply struggling with issues of gender conflict. They were inscribing significant personal positions on these issues. My own study, *Engendering Romance,* participates in this effort to read the antipatriarchal argument of romance fiction.

A more neomarxist work of revisionary scholarship is Donald E. Pease's *Visionary Compacts.* Unlike David Reynolds, Fisher, Tompkins, and Leverenz, Pease more or less maintains the traditional canon (Hawthorne, Whitman, Poe, Emerson, and Melville). He also (like Bercovitch) attempts to discover shared, common ideologies and philosophical assumptions among the writers. But like the other New Americanist critics, he attempts to overturn the idea that these writers were not politically engaged. In particular, he attacks the idea that the 19th-century writers advocated a radical, antisocial individualism. Like Clark, Pease specifically critiques the position of an earlier generation of critics. What Richard Poirier and others see as the canon's "oppositional model," Pease claims, "did not sustain but threatened the nation's identity" (9).

For Pease, as for Clark, Fisher, Tompkins, and See, literary texts perform important cultural work:

> During this period the writers comprising what we refer to as our American Renaissance did not adhere to the Revolutionary mythos but devised in their writing what I call visionary compacts. The Revolutionary mythos sanctioned a notion of negative freedom keeping the nation's individuals separate from one another. Visionary compacts sanctioned terms of agreement from the nation's past—capable of bringing together the nation's citizens in the present. Instead of corroborating the Revolutionary mythos which would have justified a civil war, they restored the terms constitutive of the nation's civil covenant, terms of agreement every American citizen could acknowledge as binding. . . . American Renaissance writers . . . wished to avoid a civil war by returning America to agreed-upon relations, thereby restoring to America a common life all Americans could share. (x)

In a related study, John P. McWilliams Jr. (*Hawthorne, Melville, and the American Character*) sees these two canonical writers in terms of their development of an idea of national character and their search for a usable past for the nation.

Reflecting large social concerns but paying deft attention to more psychological and rhetorical elements of the texts is

Jehlen's *American Incarnation*. A more purely philosophical investigation (strongly inspired by the work of philosopher Stanley Cavell), which heads toward some of the same conclusions, is Sharon Cameron's *Corporeal Self: Allegories of the Body in Melville and Hawthorne* (Baltimore, Md.: Johns Hopkins University Press, 1981). Cameron maintains that the fiction of Hawthorne and Melville is "preoccupied with questions of identity conceived in corporeal terms, and that they make use of, while transcending, the philosophic dualism [body versus soul] available to them" (3).

These studies constitute a bridge to the third group of contemporary critics: those that reinstate the theory of romance fiction, but on differently defined, more contemporary, theoretical grounds. Thus Cameron, for example, citing Quentin Anderson's *Imperial Self,* Chase's *American Novel,* Poirier's *World Elsewhere,* and Lawrence's *Classic American Literature,* takes as her point of departure the traditional Americanist view that "distinguish[ed] the American novel from its British counterpart by suggesting that the American novel depicts the self outside the confines of a social context." She then states her own purpose as "particulariz[ing] this observation, suggesting that in at least one strain of American literature the distinction is cruder and more palpable than the critical commentary has yet acknowledged, that American fiction is concerned not simply with definitions of the self but also, more specifically, with problems of human identity predicated in terms of the body" (6).

Of this group of studies the most far ranging and definitive is Evan Carton's *Rhetoric of American Romance,* which brings a decided deconstructive aspect to the analysis of romance fiction:

> The term "romance" has long been an enticing one for students of American literature seeking to characterize one of the most distinctive, prominent, and complex strains of our literary tradition. Its formalistic application to a species of extended prose narrative, however, has limited both its usefulness and its interest and squandered its potential force, even with regard to a writer like Hawthorne, who seems explicitly to authorize the term's conventional sense. This book seeks to vitalize our understanding of American romance by reconceiving it as a specific and urgent kind of rhetorical performance, a self-consciously dialectical enactment of critical and philosophical concerns about the relation of words to things and the nature of the self. Through juxtaposed readings of texts by Emerson,

Dickinson, Poe, and Hawthorne, I develop this conception of romance and illustrate: its transgression of formal generic boundaries; its exploration of the divide—and its fabrication of connections—between phenomena and noumena; and its fusion of extravagant claims to linguistic and imaginative power with self-critical analyses of the bases, nature, and extent of such power. (1)

(Part one of Carton's study deals with Emerson, Dickinson, and Poe; part two with Hawthorne.)

Edgar Dryden, in *The Form of American Romance,* pursues a similar direction, also employing insights provided by Derridean Deconstruction. For him romance fiction enacts as well as thematizes the problem of writing. Romance, he says, recurring to Frederic Jameson and others, is not just a name but a content "which reaches fulfillment in the process of its expansion or manifestation." But for American writers "there is an incompatibility between the shaping power and that which is shaped, and this problem of form enters into their works as an essential theme" (x). Dryden's emphasis is on the instability of the romance texts. For James, for example, there is, in Dryden's view, "'an intimate connection' between his hero or heroine and the 'story of [his] story itself' . . . romance for James is a sign for a certain form of interpretation or understanding that occurs when the writer through the process of revision becomes the reader of his own work" (114).

Gregory S. Jay's *America, the Scrivener: Deconstruction and the Subject of Literary History* (Ithaca, N.Y.: Cornell University Press, 1990), which contains a very useful discussion of the limitations of the New Americanism (236–74), is similarly deconstructive, as are Jonathan Auerbach's *Romance of Failure: First-Person Fictions of Poe, Hawthorne, and James* (New York: Oxford University Press, 1989) and Steven C. Scheer's *Pious Impostures and Unproven Words: The Romance of Deconstruction in Nineteenth-Century America* (Lanham, Ga.: University Press of Athens, 1990). Jay's book concerns the "triple-play among language, subjectivity, and history" (2): "The 'I' that speaks 'Civil Disobedience,'" he writes,

> obeys the grammar of ["a rhetorical and ideological tradition"] even as it describes the historical effects (imperialism and slavery) of patriarchy. This ambivalence, in which the male speaker identifies both with the position of emasculation (often figured as feminine) *and* with a renewed power of male virtue, occurs through this period in

texts by Poe, Emerson, Melville, and especially Hawthorne, who figures this ambivalence by suggesting that Hester, Dimmesdale, and Chillingworth can be read allegorically as the contradictory impulses of a single mind or culture. (19)

In a related vein, Auerbach argues that the fictions of Poe, Hawthorne, and James enforce the idea that the "I" exists only in its self-articulation, so that the text, both thematically and formally, becomes about the "difficulty of plotting a self" (5).

Kenneth Dauber, in *The Idea of Authorship in America: Democratic Poetics from Franklin to Melville* (Madison: University of Wisconsin Press, 1990), shares Carton's and Dryden's sense of the romance text as an interpretive field, but he casts this field in terms of the relationship between the writer and the literal reader of his text. Dauber argues that a major concern of the romance writers was to create a readership and, by so doing, to develop literature as a mechanism for perpetuating and securing political democracy.

Two books that develop the idea that romance fiction concerns subjectivity and perspective are Judith L. Sutherland, *The Problematic Fictions of Poe, James, and Hawthorne* (Columbia: University of Missouri Press, 1984) and Pamela Schirmeister, *The Consolations of Space: The Place of Romance in Hawthorne, Melville, and James* (Stanford, Calif.: Stanford University Press, 1990). Sutherland argues that such works as Poe's *Pym*, James's *Sacred Fount*, and Hawthorne's *Marble Faun* "educate the reader to the dangers of subjectivity that are inherent in the reader-response approach. . . . [T]hey teach us a healthy respect of their 'otherness,' for their own integrity" (11). Argues Schirmeister, the "landscape" of romance fiction is, "by nature, visionary, so that its details necessarily constitute a trope of perspective" (3). A study that reads a range of American romances through the optics of several different theoretical perspectives is John Carlos Rowe's *Through the Custom-House: Nineteenth-Century American Fiction and Modern Theory* (Baltimore, Md.: Johns Hopkins University Press, 1982).

My own two studies of the romance, *Fiction and Historical Consciousness* and *Engendering Romance,* share with the aforementioned analyses a sense of the self-conscious self-reflexivity of the romance tradition, the ways in which the tradition directly engages questions of language. My own argument (much of it implicit in the readings presented in the present book) tries to find a position between the New Americanism and deconstruction that preserves, as well, something of the formalist understandings of romance fiction. In *Fiction and Historical Consciousness* I argue that romance fiction is inherently skepticist, and in *Engendering Romance* I extend that interpretation to discover the implications of philosophical skepticism for the gender concerns both in the 19th-century romancers and in their female inheritors in the 20th century.

Fiction and Historical Consciousness and *Engendering Romance* develop what one might call, following the work of Stanley Cavell, an aversive mode of literary interpretation, and, therefore, even though Americanist philosopher Stanley Cavell does not write extensively on any of the romance writers (though he does write on the romance philosophers, Emerson and Thoreau), it is relevant to the purposes of this critical review to note several of his books. These include: *The Senses of Walden* (New York: Viking Press, 1972); *In Quest of the Ordinary: Lines of Skepticism and Romanticism* (Chicago: University of Chicago Press, 1989), especially the essay entitled "Being Odd, Getting Even: Threats to Individuality" (105–49), which deals with Poe and Hawthorne; *This New Yet Unapproachable America: Lectures after Emerson after Wittgenstein* (Albuquerque, N.Mex.: Living Batch Press, 1989); and *Conditions Handsome and Unhandsome* (Chicago: University of Chicago Press, 1990), especially the opening essay, "Aversive Thinking," from which I adapt my term *aversive,* and the essay reprinted in the appendix, "Hope Against Hope." Cavell's most definitive statement of his skepticist philosophy is contained in *The Claim of Reason: Wittgenstein, Skepticism, Morality and Tragedy* (Oxford, England: Clarendon Press, 1979).

Informing Cavell's work throughout is his concern to keep "philosophy," hence thinking and writing, "open to the threat or temptation to skepticism" ("Aversive Thinking," 35). For Cavell the "pivot on which skepticism turns" is not in the potential answers that such skepticism may seem to invite but in the fact that an answer "is not up for decision" ("Being Odd," 135). For Cavell language has to do with accepting that "there is such a thing as language" and

(1) that every mark of a language means something in the language, one thing rather than another; that a language is totally, systematically meaningful; (2) that words and their orderings are meant by

human beings, that they contain (or conceal) their beliefs, express (or deny) their convictions; and (3) that the saying of something when and as it is said is as significant as the meaning and ordering of the words said. . . . Words come to us from a distance; they were there before we were; we are born into them. Meaning them is accepting that fact of their condition. To discover what is being said to us, as to discover what we are saying, is to discover the precise location from which it is said; to understand why it is said from just there, and at that time. (*Senses of Walden*, 34, 64)

Therefore, a key concept in Cavell's philosophy of language is assuming "responsibility" for words ("Being Odd," 135, and *Senses*, 33). Such responsibility does not represent one's emplacement within a status quo to which one cannot help consenting. Rather, responsibility is the consequence of a choice and a decision made available to us by language's indeterminacies and imprecisions. Responsibility is the powerful response human beings can make to the "ineluctable fact that we cannot know." This responsibility extends to words as well as to deeds; and it results in a relationship to the world defined not by knowing but, rather, by what Cavell calls acknowledgment.

In Cavell's view, reading, writing, and meaning-making are defined by the relationship that readers and writers choose to establish, through their words, with each other:

The reader's position [is] that of the stranger. To write to him is to acknowledge that he is outside the words, at a bent arm's length, and alone with the book; that his presence to these words is perfectly contingent, and the choice to stay with them continuously his own; that they are his points of departure and origin. The conditions of meeting upon the word are that we—writer and reader—learn how to depart from them, leave them where they are; and then return to them, finding ourselves there again. We have to learn to admit the successiveness of words, their occurrence one after the other; and their permanence in the face of our successions. . . . The art of fiction is to teach us distance. . . . Speaking together face to face can seem to deny that distance, to deny that facing one another requires acknowledging the presence of the other . . . But to deny such things is to deny our separateness. And that makes us fictions of one another. (*Senses*, 61–65)

The decision of one individual to acknowledge the existence of another does not depend on the assumption of their intimacy with each other (what we might, on the public level, call a consensus or a shared national identity). On the contrary, it realizes the possibility, through a mutual recognition of strangeness, of establishing such a relationship, and of reestablishing it again and again. Estrangement or distance, which is the consequence of doubt, forces something to happen, the something we call writing and speaking. Writing and speaking are thus forms of acknowledgment. They do not attempt to state the unstatable. Instead, they endeavor to fulfill responsibilities of relatedness. Fiction, therefore, teaches us distance. It reminds us of a strangeness we are likely to forget so that we can remember to acknowledge what we may also forget or take for granted—the existence of other people. Romance fiction, I suggest, in its insistently antimimetic style, develops estrangement to new depths. It locates as one of its primary goals the establishing and reestablishing of communal intimacy.

A Final Note

In reviewing the salient criticism on the romance tradition, I have not cited the numerous essays that have appeared on this subject. I have referred to some of the important ones in chapter 1 of this study. I have also not explored other kinds of 19th-century romance: the African-American romance, as discussed, for example, by Bernard W. Bell in *The Afro-American Novel and Its Tradition* (Amherst: University of Massachusetts Press, 1987), xvi–xvii, or the woman's romance—the historical romances of Catherine Sedgewick, for example, or the melodramas of Maria Cummins or E. D. E. N. Southworth. I have not discussed these rich and interesting fields of literary production because, although one might refer to them by the same designation, they do not conform to the particular kind of romance fiction I am discussing.

Major Single-Author Studies on Poe, Hawthorne, and Melville, Listed Chronologically

Poe

Davidson, Edward. *Poe: A Critical Study* (Cambridge, Mass.: Harvard University Press, 1957).

Tate, Allen. "Our Cousin, Mr. Poe," *Collected Essays* (Denver, Colo.: Alan Swallow, 1959; orig. printed 1949).

Wilbur, Richard. "The House of Poe," *The Recognition of Edgar Allan Poe: Selected Criticism Since 1829* (Ann Arbor: University of Michigan Press, 1966; orig. printed 1959), 255–77.

Wagenknecht, Edward. *Edgar Allan Poe: The Man Behind the Legend* (New York: Oxford University Press, 1963).

Hoffman, Daniel. *Poe, Poe, Poe, Poe, Poe, Poe, Poe* (Garden City, N.Y.: Doubleday, 1972).

Thompson, G. R. *Poe's Fiction: Romantic Irony in the Gothic Tales* (Madison: University of Wisconsin Press, 1973).

Kennedy, J. Gerald. *Poe, Death, and the Life of Writing* (New Haven, Conn.: Yale University Press, 1987).

Williams, Michael. *A World of Words: Language and Displacement in the Fiction of Edgar Allan Poe* (Durham, N.C.: Duke University Press, 1988).

Silverman, Kenneth. *Edgar A. Poe: Mournful and Never-Ending Remembrance* (New York: HarperCollins Publishers, 1991).

Meyers, Jeffrey. *Edgar Allan Poe: His Life and Legacy* (New York: Charles Scribner's Sons, 1992).

Hawthorne

Davidson, Edward. *Hawthorne's Last Phase* (New Haven, Conn.: Yale University Press, 1949).

Fogle, Richard Harter. *Hawthorne's Fiction: The Light and the Dark* (Norman: University of Oklahoma Press, 1952).

Waggoner, Hyatt. *Hawthorne: A Critical Study* (Cambridge, Mass.: Harvard University Press, 1955).

Male, Roy. *Hawthorne's Tragic Vision* (Austin: University of Texas Press, 1957).

Turner, Arlin. *Nathaniel Hawthorne: An Introduction and Interpretation* (New York: Barnes and Noble, 1961).

Wagenknecht, Edward. *Nathaniel Hathorne, Man and Writer* (New York: Oxford University Press, 1961).

Bell, Millicent. *Hawthorne's View of the Artist* (Albany: State University of New York, 1962).

Crews, Frederick. *The Sins of the Fathers: Hawthorne's Psychological Themes* (New York: Oxford University Press, 1966).

Baym, Nina. *The Shape of Hawthorne's Career* (Ithaca, N.Y.: Cornell University Press, 1976).

Dauber, Kenneth. *Rediscovering Hawthorne* (Princeton, N.J.: Princeton University Press, 1977).

Waggoner, Hyatt. *The Presence of Hawthorne* (Baton Rouge: Louisiana State University Press, 1979).

Colacurcio, Michael. *The Province of Piety: Moral History in Hawthorne's Early Tales* (Cambridge, Mass.: Harvard University Press, 1984).

Hutner, Gordon. *Secrets and Sympathy: Forms of Disclosure in Hawthorne's Novels* (Athens: University of Georgia Press, 1988).

Mellow, James. *Nathaniel Hawthorne in His Times* (Boston: Houghton Mifflin, 1980).

Bercovitch, Sacvan. *The Office of the Scarlet Letter* (Baltimore, Md.: Johns Hopkins University Press, 1991).

Miller, J. Hillis. *Hawthorne and History: Defacing It* (Cambridge, Mass.: Basil Blackwell, 1991).

Pfister, Joel. *The Production of Personal Life: Class, Gender, and the Psychological in Hawthorne's Fiction* (Stanford, Calif.: Stanford University Press, 1991).

Millington, Richard. *Practicing Romance: Narrative Form and Cultural Engagement in Hawthorne's Fiction* (Princeton, N.J.: Princeton University Press, 1991).

Berlant, Lauren. *The Anatomy of a National Fantasy: Hawthorne, Utopia, and Everyday Life* (Chicago: University of Chicago Press, 1991).

Melville

Sedgwick, William Ellery. *Herman Melville: The Tragedy of Mind* (Cambridge, Mass.: Harvard University Press, 1944).

Olson, Charles. *Call Me Ishmael* (San Francisco: City Lights, 1947).

Chase, Richard. *Herman Melville: A Critical Study* (New York: Macmillan, 1949).

Arvin, Newton. *Herman Melville* (New York: William Sloane, 1950).

Howard, Leon. *Herman Melville: A Biography* (Berkeley: University of California Press, 1951).

Thompson, Lawrance. *Melville's Quarrel with God* (Princeton, N.J.: Princeton University Press, 1952).

Metcalf, Eleanor Melville. *Herman Melville: Cycle and Epicycle* (Cambridge, Mass.: Harvard University Press, 1953).

Franklin, H. Bruce. *The Wake of the Gods: Melville's Mythology* (Stanford, Calif.: Stanford University Press, 1963).

Dryden, Edgar. *Melville's Thematics of Form* (Baltimore, Md.: Johns Hopkins University Press, 1968).

Zoellner, Robert. *The Salt Sea Mastodon: A Reading of Moby-Dick* (Berkeley: University of California Press, 1973).

Herbert, T. Walter. *Moby-Dick and Calvinism: A World Dismantled* (New Brunswick, N.J.: Rutgers University Press, 1977).

Sherrill, Rowland. *The Prophetic Melville: Experience, Transcendence, and Tragedy* (Athens: University of Georgia Press, 1978).

Karcher, Carolyn. *Shadow over the Promised Land: Slavery, Race, and Violence in Melville's America* (Baton Rouge: Louisiana State University Press, 1980).

Cowan, Bainard. *Exiled Waters: Moby-Dick and the Crisis of Allegory* (Baton Rouge: Louisiana State University Press, 1982).

Rogin, Michael P. *Subversive Genealogy: The Politics and Art of Herman Melville* (New York: Knopf, 1983).

Duban, James. *Melville's Major Fiction: Politics, Theology, and Imagination* (Dekalb: Northern Illinois University Press, 1983).

Tolchin, Neal L. *Mourning, Gender, and Creativity in the Art of Herman Melville* (New Haven, Conn.: Yale University Press, 1988).

Dimock, Wai-Chee. *Empire for Liberty: Melville and the Poetics of Individualism* (Princeton, N.J.: Princeton University Press, 1989).

Recommended Titles

Charles Brockden Brown

The following of Brown's works are available in *The Novels and Related Works of Charles Brockden Brown* (Kent, Ohio: Kent State University Press, 1977–82). Original publication dates in parentheses:

Wieland: or, The Transformation: An American Tale (1798)
Arthur Mervyn; or, Memoirs of the Year 1793 (1799–1800)
Ormond; or, The Secret Witness (1799)
Edgar Huntley; or, Memoirs of a Sleep-Walker (1799)

Washington Irving

The Sketch Book of Geoffrey Crayon, Gent., ed. Haskell Springer (Boston: Twayne, 1978; orig. published 1819–20), esp. "Rip Van Winkle" and "The Legend of Sleepy Hollow"

Bracebridge Hall or The Humourists. A Medley by Geoffrey Crayon, Gent., ed. Herbert F. Smith (Boston: Twayne, 1977; orig. published 1822)

Tales of a Traveller, by Geoffrey Crayon, Gent., Author's Revised Edition (New York: Putnams', 1865; orig. published 1824)

Edgar Allan Poe

All stories and tales can be found in *Collected Works of Edgar Allan Poe*, ed. Thomas Ollive Mabbott (Cambridge, Mass.: Harvard

University Press, 1978), 2 vols.; original publication dates can be found in parentheses following each title.

Tales of Terror
  "MS. Found in a Bottle" (1833)
  "The Assignation" (1834)
  "Berenice" (1835)
  "Morella" (1835)
  "Ligeia" (1838)
  "The Fall of the House of Usher" (1839)
  "A Descent into the Maelström" (1841)
  "Eleonora" (1841)
  "The Oval Portrait" (1842)
  "The Masque of the Red Death" (1842)
  "The Pit and the Pendulum" (1842)
  "The Premature Burial" (1844)

Detective Stories
  "The Murders in the Rue Morgue" (1841)
  "The Mystery of Marie Roget" (1842–43)
  "The Gold-Bug" (1843)
  "The Purloined Letter" (1844)

Tales of the Perverse
  "The Black Cat" (1842)
  "The Imp of the Perverse" (1845)

Angelic Colloquies, Parables, and Landscape Pieces
  "Shadow—A Parable" (1835)
  "Silence—A Fable" (1838)
  "The Conversation of Eiros and Charmion" (1839)
  "The Man of the Crowd" (1840)
  "The Island of the Fay" (1841)
  "The Colloquy of Monos and Una" (1841)
  "The Landscape Garden" (1842)
  "The Power of Words" (1845)
  "The Domain of Arnheim" (1847)

Tales of Conscience
  "William Wilson" (1839)
  "The Cask of Amontillado" (1846)

Nathaniel Hawthorne

All of the following titles can be found in *The Centenary Edition of the Works of Nathaniel Hawthorne*, ed. William Charvat et al.

(Columbus: Ohio State University Press, 1962–88). I have listed short stories in terms of the original volumes in which they appeared; original publication dates—both of volumes and of independently published short stories—are in parentheses. I have starred (*) the most important of the shorter romances.

Twice-Told Tales (1837, 1851)

Volume 1

"The Gray Champion" (1835)*

"Sunday at Home" (1837)

"The Wedding-Knell" (1836)

"The Minister's Black Veil" (1836)*

"The May-Pole of Merry Mount" (1836)*

"The Gentle Boy" (1832)*

"Mr. Higginbotham's Catastrophe" (1834)

"Little Annie's Ramble" (1835)

"Wakefield" (1835)*

"A Rill from the Town-Pump" (1835)

"The Great Carbuncle" (1837)

"The Prophetic Pictures" (1837)

"David Swan" (1837)

"Sights from a Steeple" (1831)

"The Hollow of the Three Hills" (1830)*

"The Toll-Gatherer's Day" (1837)

"The Vision of the Fountain" (1835)

"Fancy's Show Box" (1837)

"Dr. Heidegger's Experiment" (1837)

Volume 2

"Legends of the Province House"*

I. "Howe's Masquerade" (1838)

II. "Edward Randolph's Portrait" (1838)

III. "Lady Eleanore's Mantle" (1838)

IV. "Old Esther Dudley" (1839)

"The Haunted Mind" (1835)

"The Village Uncle" (1835)

"The Ambitious Guest" (1835)

"The Sister Years" (1839)

"Snow-flakes" (1838)

"The Seven Vagabonds" (1833)

"The White Old Main" (1835)

"Peter Goldthwaite's Treasure" (1838)
"Chippings with a Chisel" (1838)
"The Shaker Bridal" (1838)
"Night Sketches" (1838)
"Endicott and the Red Cross" (1838)*
"The Lily's Quest" (1839)
"Foot-prints on the Sea-shore" (1838)
"Edward Fane's Rosebud" (1837)
"The Threefold Destiny" (1838)

Mosses from an Old Manse (1846, 1854)
"The Old Manse" (1846)
"The Birth-mark" (1843)*
"A Select Party" (1844)
"Young Goodman Brown" (1835)*
"Rappaccini's Daughter" (1844)*
"Mrs. Bullfrog" (1837)
"Fire-Worship" (1843)
"Buds and Bird-Voices" (1843)
"Monsieur du Miroir" (1837)*
"The Fall of Fantasy" (1843)
"The Celestial Rail-road" (1843)*
"The Procession of Life" (1843)
"Feathertop" (1852)
"The New Adam and Eve" (1843)
"Egotism; or, The Bosom-Serpent" (1843)*
"The Christmas Banquet" (1844)
"Drowne's Wooden Image" (1844)
"The Intelligence Office" (1844)
"Roger Malvin's Burial" (1832)*
"P.'s Correspondence" (1845)
"Earth's Holocaust" (1844)
"Passages from a Relinquished Work" (1834)
"Sketches from Memory" (1835)
"The Old Apple-Dealer" (1843)
"The Artist of the Beautiful" (1844)*
"A Virtuoso's Collection" (1842)

The Snow-Image, and Other Twice-Told Tales (1852)
"The Snow-Image" (1850)
"The Great Stone Face" (1850)
"Main-street" (1849)*

"A Bell's Biography" (1837)
"Sylph Etherege" (1832)
"The Canterbury Pilgrims" (1833)
"Old News" (1835)*
"The Man of Adamant" (1837)
"The Devil in Manuscript" (1835)
"John Inglefield's Thanksgiving" (1840)
"Old Ticonderoga" (1836)
"The Wives of the Dead" (1832)*
"Little Daffydowndilly" (1843)
"My Kinsman, Major Molineux" (1832)*
Other Tales (not collected in original volumes)
"Sir William Phips" (1830)
"Mrs. Hutchinson" (1830)
"An Old Woman's Tale" (1830)
"Dr. Bullivant" (1831)
"The Haunted Quack" (1831)
"Sir William Pepperell" (1833)
"Alice Doane's Appeal" (1835)*
"My Visit to Niagara" (1835)
"A Visit to the Clerk of the Weather" (1836)
"Fragments from the Journal of a Solitary Man" (1837)
"Thomas Green Fessenden" (1838)
"Jonathan Cilley" (1838)
"The Antique Ring" (1843)
"A Good Man's Miracle" (1844)*
"A Book of Autographs" (1844)
The Scarlet Letter (1850)
The House of the Seven Gables (1851)
The Blithedale Romance (1852)
The Marble Faun (1860)

Herman Melville

Melville's writings can be found in *The Works of Herman Melville, Standard Edition* (New York: Russell & Russell, Inc., 1963), 16 volumes. Original publication dates appear in parentheses.

Mardi (1849)
Moby-Dick (1851)
Pierre, or the Ambiguities (1852)

The Piazza Tales (1856)
  "The Piazza"
  "Bartleby, the Scrivener"
  "Benito Cereno"
  "The Lightning-Rod Man"
  "The Encantadas, or Enchanted Islands"
  "The Bell-Tower"

Also (published posthumously)

Billy Budd, Sailor (An Inside Narrative) (1924)—ed. Harrison Hayford and Merton M. Sealts Jr. (Chicago: University of Chicago Press, 1962)

Henry James

For James's novels see *The New York Edition: The Novels and Tales of Henry James* (New York: Charles Scribner's Sons, 1909); since not all of the tales were printed in the New Edition, for the tales see *The Complete Tales of Henry James*, ed. Leon Edel (London: Repert Hart-David, 1962–64).

The American (1877)
The Portrait of a Lady (1881)
"The Last of the Valerii" (1874)
"Daisy Miller: A Study" (1878)
"The Aspern Papers" (1888)
"The Liar" (1888)
"The Lesson of the Master" (1888)
"The Pupil" (1891)
"The Real Thing" (1892)
"The Figure in the Carpet" (1896)
"Glasses" (1896)
"The Turn of the Screw" (1898)
"The Beast in the Jungle" (1903)
"The Jolly Corner" (1908)

Index

About the Author

Emily Miller Budick is professor of American Studies, and department chair, at the Hebrew University of Jerusalem. She received her Ph.D. in 1972 from Cornell University, where she wrote her thesis on Edgar Allan Poe. Her publications include *Emily Dickinson and the Life of Language: A Study in Symbolic Poetics* (Baton Rouge: Louisiana State University Press, 1985), *Fiction and Historical Consciousness: The American Romance Tradition* (New Haven, Conn.: Yale University Press, 1989), and *Engendering Romance: Women Writers and the Hawthorne Tradition, 1850–1990* (New Haven, Conn.: Yale University Press, 1994). At present she is working on studies of the mutual textual constructions of African-American and Jewish-American literary identity and the Holocaust in American culture.